D1645692

Syrian Coffee

Angela M Formby

Tales from Aleppo coffee mornings
- and afterwards

First published in 2015 by A.M.Hilal

ISBN 978.0.9932031.0.7

Printed and bound in Great Britain by:
Book Printing UK, Remus House, Coltsfoot Drive, Woodston, Peterborough PE2 9BF

angelamformby@yahoo.co.uk

Thanks to all the family and friends who have helped me. These include the members of the Elgin Writers Group for encouragement, Lara Alsayed and Paul Kendall for formatting the work and explaining my errors to me, Alaa Alsayed for the cover photo, and Verena Phillip who designed the cover. Finally, thanks to my children who financed the printing and pushed me into finishing the job.

Scotland 2015

Contents

NOTE

Most of the terms in the book are easy to understand, but names can be a problem. This is how it works:

Colonel Bassam Haddad (Smith in English) has several children, but he is called Abu (father of) Ahad, his eldest son, who is by tradition named after Col. Bassam's father. His wife is usually called Im (mother of) Ahad. They may call each other by their given names in private, but will usually refer to each other as Abu Ahad and Im Ahad when speaking to other people.

Anyone speaking to the colonel at work will call him Sidi (sir) or Colonel Bassam. This means that any one person may be referred to in more than one way (excluding 'uncle', 'aunt', etc.), and it can be quite confusing.

'Sit' is a polite title for a woman, often used before her given name.

I have used the term 'maid' for all the different types of domestic help commonly found in middle-class homes in Aleppo. Usually they are cleaners coming in for the day, but others live in and some come from as far away as Sri Lanka.

These stories are neither biographical nor auto-biographical. I took situations I have seen or imagined over the years, and asked, "What if..." The headings are the names of districts in Aleppo.

1

PROLOGUE 1995

Aleppo in September. Cool nights and hot days. Washed-out blue sky with occasional white clouds - a child's painting. The hot, dusty city centred, more or less, on the ancient citadel where Abraham is said to have milked his cow. The old market next to the citadel, covered and cool. Then the city spreading out to its suburbs of high-rise apartment blocks. To the North, East and South are large blocks of small to medium dwellings, plain and utilitarian in style but with balconies sprouting geraniums and jasmine amongst the washing and the drums of heating oil; the extreme borders of these areas are edged with constantly expanding areas of concrete shacks which the local council desperately tries to supply with utilities. On the West side the blocks a little further apart and of larger apartments mixed, in a few places, with individual villas. This side of the city is also still spreading, and has overflowed even the newest, uncompleted ring road designed to be outside the city.

Everywhere there are lots and lots of people. In the morning they are hurrying to work, the men in shirts and trousers, or gellabyas like white or khaki nightshirts, the women in summer dresses, or coats and scarves, or just showing their faces behind black scarves and long black robes. Schoolchildren are hurrying past in various uniforms, carrying enormous backpacks of books. Everywhere the traffic is swirling and honking from seven in the morning until late at night. Each driver is an egomaniac determined to get ahead of all comers, and those held up protest long and loudly with their horns. There are frequent minor bumps, when the combatants leap out of their cars shouting and occasionally even fighting before being separated by the crowds of men drawn immediately to the sound of an interesting occasion to offer opinions and advice.

On almost every street and corner there are trees, lemon trees in the old city courtyards, dusty pines and exuberant acacias and eucalyptus in the newer streets, small parks full of trees all over the city. There are trees to walk under, trees to gossip under or to wait for the bus, trees for little boys to play football or marbles under. Trees full of noisy roosting birds at dusk, and even noisier waking birds at dawn. During the day the little bats that swoop round the street lamps at night must be in the trees as well. Behind everything is the call of the muezzin from each mosque. Daybreak, mid-morning, midday, mid-afternoon and nightfall, the calls come from all over the city until they are no more noticeable then the sound of the sea to a seaside dweller.

The foreigners are mostly clustered on the west side of the city, families basking round the swimming pools or 'doing' the soukhs with visitors. Amongst the transient foreigners, but largely separate from them, are the foreign wives of Syrians who are making their permanent home there.

They are carefully washing the fruit, teaching their children nursery rhymes, being diplomatic with in-laws (or sometimes not) and cursing Arabic music played until the early hours of the morning. They often get together to gossip with and about each other, and to support each other when occasionally life gets tough. With coffee mornings, afternoon visits and telephone calls they get to know all about each others' lives – perhaps. These stories are about a few sides of their lives in 1995, when their world seemed a stable place.

'Afterwards', the last story, is set in 2013, when the life which had been slowly evolving over the centuries suddenly changed for everyone in the country.

DJAMILIA

Alibis aren't very hard to arrange, if you are determined enough and if your reputation is good enough. In this case it was Janet, who was extremely determined this time, and whose life was generally so settled and respectable that she could be sure that whatever she chose to say would be believed. She chose the day of the September coffee morning at Elizabeth's house partly because it was at least ten minutes walk from her own. The two older children were in school until half past one, and she asked her mother-in-law to have little Zaki for the morning, which the doting grandmother thought a privilege. The chatter of the women and the clatter of the coffee cups stopped briefly as she made her excuses and goodbyes, but the noise swirled back to fill the room again before she reached the front door. She shut the heavy, polished door carefully behind her and walked quietly down the gleaming staircase and into the tree-lined street of this affluent part of town.

An empty taxi appeared almost immediately, which she took as a lucky omen, and she directed it to a raw new district of large blocks of small flats. During the ride she got out her compact and checked her face and hair. Nothing could make her thirty-five year old face anything except round, freckled and healthy, but she was glad that she had listened to the hairdresser and let her wavy, auburn hair grow a bit longer. She smiled to herself as she dabbed at it with her fingers, partly at her reflection and also at the surprise there would be on her friends' faces if they had any idea what she was doing. Snapping the compact shut, she put it back in her bag and took out the taxi fare, then she settled back into her seat, trying to feel beautiful and wicked but wishing the sun were not so hot. She had put on a new yellow linen dress for the coffee morning, and she smoothed down the skirt with hands damp from a mixture of heat and nervousness.

When the taxi pulled up she was ready to pay the driver, the money in her hand. She got out quickly, automatically looking round to see if anyone was watching – the trouble with Aleppo was that no-one ever seemed to have anything more important to do than to watch the neighbours. However there wasn't anybody obviously looking at her in the street or from the balconies, and she could see a familiar black car parked near the building she wanted, so she took a deep breath and walked through the main door as casually as she could manage.

The glare of sunshine on the pale stone apartment blocks in the raw new street, still largely treeless, left her almost blind when she stepped into the gloom of the entrance to building number nine, so she stood for a moment with eyes shut to adjust to the dim light. When she opened them she saw that the second door on the left, the one she had been instructed to knock on quietly, was ajar. She could feel her heart beating as she walked up to it and tapped, but it was pulled wider open before she could finish. A slim, dark haired man, tall for an Arab and very well-groomed, took her arm and said, very quietly, in Arabic,

"Welcome. Come in quickly before anyone sees you."

Three quarters of an hour later, lying on a cotton mattress inside the extremely small flat, what surprised Janet most was simply the fact of finding herself an unfaithful wife. Like a drowning man seeing his life roll before his eyes, she was aware quite suddenly and clearly of the tiny steps which had culminated here, this morning, with Radwan. She saw how each step had moved her almost imperceptibly away from her straightforward life as the standard model of contented wife and mother.

Now she could hear him moving about in the tiny kitchen, and she knew he was making Turkish coffee, both the smell and the small sounds were calmingly familiar. She stretched her arms above her head luxuriously, then relaxed and considered whether to get up and dress. She decided not to bother and lay instead with thoughts drifting inconsequentially through her head. She giggled to herself at the thought of going home and cooking macaroni cheese as if nothing had happened, and she hoped he would have some cigarettes with him.

He walked in, a towel tied around his trim waist, carefully balancing one cup of coffee and a glass of water on a small tray with his precise, old-maidish movements, and it occurred to her that the most surprising thing about him was his sheer strength. They had been standing in what should have been the sitting room, if the place had been properly furnished, and when she had said that she had only come to talk to him he had simply lifted her up as if she were as heavy as a book or two and carried her, protesting, but not much, into here. On the whole she thought she couldn't blame him. For all that she had said no at first (she had changed it to yes at the second time of asking), her being here at all meant yes, and she was too fair-minded to deny it. She also knew, as he did not, that she had taken a lot more care than usual with her appearance, right down to the skin.

They sat facing each other on the mattress, cross-legged like children, and took alternate sips from the same cup. His gentleness had also been a revelation to her, it wasn't a characteristic one would have associated with him at first sight but she was not now surprised that he insisted on sharing a cup, and on holding it to her lips for each sip. In between sips she tried to tell him in her rudimentary French that yes, she loved him and yes, she had been happy this morning, but she couldn't come any more and he mustn't ask her. Naturally enough he either did not, or did not choose to, believe her so he took refuge in incomprehension. This was not difficult as he had no English and her limited Arabic was matched by his poor French.

As a matter of fact she did not believe herself, and when he looked at her with a loving smile, obviously not listening to a word she was trying to say, and gently stroked her cheek with the back of his index finger, she stopped and leaned forward to kiss him instead. However, when he responded by putting his arm over her shoulder she caught sight of his watch and got a shock.

"Gracious! The children! They'll be home from school in no time." In a mixture of Arabic and French she made him understand, so he just kissed her once again before they both dressed quickly.

When they were ready to leave she did not want to go, and kept turning back to his arms for just one last kiss until in the end he gently steered her to the door, telling her to turn to the right, not the left, then walk on for just a few minutes and he would catch her up. She thought it was an exaggerated precaution, but she was prepared to believe that he knew what he was talking about so she did as she was told. Leaving the building she turned right, and seemed to have been walking for more than a few minutes in the grinding heat of the one o'clock September sun when she came to the road junction, and he still had not caught up with her. She had already been feeling sleepy with reaction before she left the building, and now the heat and glare were making her dizzy and headachy, and to make her even more uncomfortable she walked into a spiky sapling, as desiccated as she felt herself, and scratched her leg. She started down the left fork, decided that she was wrong and turned back to try the right fork, all the time feeling that the eyes of the entire population of the district were boring into her back from behind the acres of shutters .

He caught up with her after she had reached a patch of scrubby new trees, and she slumped into the passenger seat, relieved to be out of the sun. Radwan looked at her once, with the quick smile that had got her into all this, and squeezed her hand briefly before driving on. Janet thought he must be the quietest driver in Syria, she had never seen him use his horn at all (most people wore out the horns on their cars long before the indicators), and she sat back to admire his hands on the steering wheel. They were regular shaped, well manicured and squared off at the tips, she wished she could touch them but that was impossible in public. He dropped her discreetly away from home, managing in English: "I am very happy. Thank you." As he drove away she could see from the set of his shoulders that he was.

When she was cooking, she simply let waves of delight wash over her, occasionally smiling reminiscently, and after lunch she 'went native' and slept for two hours, a most unusual thing for her to do. There had been a few bad moments when her husband, Mohammed, came in to eat and she realised what she had done, but as the day wore on the events of the morning seemed more and more like a dream, and she slipped back into her official role as wife, housewife and mother as if she had never left it.

By the time the Indian summer finally drew to a close her life was going on at several different levels. The every-day layer was the same old Janet, getting on with house, husband and children, and 'being there' for friends who felt the urge to drop in for coffee, sympathy or both. At the second level she was living with her husband as she had always done, when he was present she consciously put him first, shying away from the cataclysm that would overtake them all if he found out about the secret part of her life.

The deepest level was where she kept Radwan, and here she felt as if fireworks were going off inside her, just under her ribs. When they were in the same social group she lived for the occasional smile, though she was very good about not looking for it. The 'accidental' touch of his hand sent

11

electric sparks up her arm as if she were fifteen again, and he told her that it had the same effect on him. It surprised her how little people seemed to notice, as if her years of solid respectability had put her in such a settled position that no-one could imagine her doing any wrong.

The first four or five weeks after they became lovers it was almost impossible for them to remain apart. Fortunately Mohammed was very busy at the farm because October came and it was time to get on with the olive harvest. Once the children had gone to school, it was quite easy for her to get out on Zaki's kindergarten days, either at the little flat he had rented for them, or just to go for a car-ride out of town. When she asked him how he had so much time to spare, he took his hand off the steering wheel and waved it airily and dismissively. He told her, in carefully simple Arabic, that he always put the most important work first, and she was pleased to be the most important work so she didn't ask any more.

Occasional remarks from friends about their own lives, and odd comments noted only in passing, had convinced her a long time ago that she was lucky in Mohammed as a lover. He was both skilled and considerate – asked when they were first married, he had admitted to learning a lot from a book, which she believed from the seriousness of his tone, and found endearing. Sex with him always left her satisfied, sleepy and contented.

Sex with Radwan was another thing altogether. In bed he was demanding and almost aggressive, hungrily exploring but not wishing to be explored. Janet left him each time technically satisfied but longing for more. He was like a drug to her, the more she had the more she wanted. He in his turn often told her how marvellous she was, and when she was shy and said she wasn't sure of the local rules of bedroom behaviour, he laughed and said that that was what was special about her. At all events, he was as anxious as she for their meetings, and once they were together his energy was inexhaustible.

The wet weather of late November was inconvenient for them, car drives lost their appeal and the little flat was damp. It was a pity he couldn't understand her joke about 'putting a damper on things', but he almost choked laughing at her careful translation of 'mutton dressed as lamb' to describe a mutual friend.

He had to be in Damascus for the last three weeks in December, so she was able to give all her attention to the other parts of her life, and it was then that the magic began to wear thin. The carol-singing parties, arranged officially for the children, made her nostalgic for her old way of life, which now seemed happily innocent. Christmas shopping and visiting with Mohammed reminded her that even though he wasn't one for flowery compliments, he was very kind, and he did understand her jokes.

It was in this extremely muddled frame of mind that Janet went to the Christmas service, when the English vicar came from Damascus for the thirty or so English-speaking people who bothered to attend. She was standing in the tiny chapel among the other housewives, all her friends, and the few couples where the husband was also Christian. There were one or two Sudanese students, and a very well turned-out businessman who was returning to England the next day.

There had been a Christmas sermon on keeping promises, and now they were singing the old carol 'We Three Kings'. Suddenly she saw the whole affair as a sordid breaking of trust, an irrelevance to the important parts of her life. Involuntarily she thought of Mohammed and the boys out choosing her Christmas present this very minute. Everybody else seemed to be living straight, honest lives, while her own was not secret and glamorous but furtive and grubby. It was like turning over a beautiful potted plant and finding the underside covered in slugs. There and then she decided that she had somehow to find her way back to a way of life she could live with.

When Radwan returned in the New Year she tried hard to be distant, and simply not to visit people she knew he visited. It wasn't difficult to arrange as Mohammed didn't like going out in the winter anyway, but it was extremely difficult to keep to. Radwan often phoned her when he knew she would be alone, and the sound of his voice made her muscles go limp so she had to sit down quickly. She went out in the car with him once or twice, but only went back to the flat once. Even that, good while it lasted, left her feeling disgusted with herself by the time she got home.

The problem was that he couldn't see what had changed, and even if her Arabic or French (or his) had been good enough, she didn't think he could have understood what she meant. He firmly believed in falling in love then living together, preferably married, whatever the cost. It was the first time she had come across the idea of 'take what you want and pay for it' in practice. However she was full of ideals about loyalty and commitment coming before personal feelings. She could understand his point of view but didn't agree, and he just thought she was crazy. Finally, at the end of February, he told her that he had been promoted (he worked in one of the Ministries) and was moving back to Damascus. He wanted her to leave everyone and go with him, and was so angry when she refused even to find excuses to visit him there that he got into his car and drove off, leaving her to walk home.

For days afterwards she hardly left the house in case he should phone, she would have given almost anything just to hear his voice; part of her was ready to agree to any terms to avoid losing him like this. But he didn't, and slowly the routine of life with a house, three children and a husband to look after took over. She heard from mutual friends that he had left, and after a few weeks she could get from morning till night without thinking of him more than once or twice.

It was late spring when she and Mohammed were out visiting one of his old school friends and Radwan's name came up.

"Yes, said one man, "He's doing very well, especially now that his wife's back from Egypt. Didn't you hear? She took the children and went to stay there because her mother was ill. Anyway, she's back now."

"Not before time," said another. "You know what a man he is for chasing girls. He needs a wife to keep him in order, and one who's in the house, too."

Janet's hand jumped and her cigarette dropped onto the carpet. She reached down to get it before it caused any damage, and settled back in her chair hoping that her exertions would excuse the blush she felt all over her face. She drew hard on the cigarette, and had a coughing fit, drawing everyone's attention. By the time she had recovered, had a drink of water and sat down again, the subject of Radwan had been forgotten, except by the man who had started talking about him in the first place. He nudged his neighbour and continued,

"Everyone said he had someone here, but no-one seems to know who. She can't have been much to look at though, or he'd have been showing her off. Oh well, we're all getting older. I expect he has to take what he can get these days."

One or two people laughed and the conversation moved on, but Mohammed came over to her and bent down anxiously.

"Are you all right, Jan," he asked, "You look a bit strange."

"It's that cigarette. It's made me feel sick. Can we go home?" They made their goodbyes and left.

At home, Janet loaded up the dishwasher and switched it on before she went to bed. It seemed the only thing to do.

COFFEE MORNING – October

The weather was ideal for the October coffee morning. Much of the heat had gone from the early mornings, and Chris' big, shady, first-floor balcony in the expensive new suburb of Shahbaa Jedid was quiet and cool. She wandered along the balcony, touching her beloved plants and telling the pots of Busy Lizzies how clever they were to be so pretty. She, Naafa and the three children had moved into this newly-built flat only 18 months ago, but already a line of yuccas in pots was beginning to screen one end of the balcony from the neighbours, and the jasmine was doing its best to block off the other end.

She stopped to pick a heavily perfumed handful of the fresh jasmine flowers, and pondered the possibility of growing a grapevine in a pot, then training it across the front. Apart from being the nearest to the garden her green fingers itched for, it would solve permanently the privacy problem. However curious the neighbours were about their foreign neighbour, there would be no angle of the balcony where she could be seen.

By 10.15 the two balcony tables had been pushed together, covered with the biggest tablecloth, and filled with the paraphernalia of a coffee morning – cups and saucers, plates, spoons and cake forks, fruitjuice and glasses, coffee, tea, milk, sugar, cakes, and her own special Mississippi Mud Pie.

At 10.30 precisely the security doorbell from downstairs rang, and she pressed the button to let in her closest friend, Ross, who came upstairs talking to a newly-arrived young woman, and introduced her as Jane. Entering the house, Ross peered round and asked,

"Isn't your mother-in-law staying with you?"

"No. When she knew you were all coming this morning she cut short her visit and went to one of her daughters – Maisa, I think."

"You mean she ran away?"

"I don't think so." laughed Chris, "She just didn't want to sit in the middle of all of us and not know what's going on. It's a bit frustrating for her."

"Don't I know it," from Ross, "It's so boring when I have to go visiting with Rustum's mother. I'm struggling to understand what's going on, and I don't know most of the people they're gossiping about. It's a good job really, because you wouldn't believe the scandal I hear."

Jane had not spoken while they went through the living room to the balcony, but as they passed through the French doors she exclaimed,

"How lovely and green it is! It's so nice. It's almost like being in a garden."

"Where are you living?" asked Chris, "Do you have your own place yet?"

"No, not yet. We're looking for somewhere, but we're living with my husband's family until we find what we want. We decided to wait until the right place turns up. Their house is in Syriana Jedid ".

"I picked Jane up from there," broke in Ross, "Rustum met her husband somewhere and they got talking. It's extraordinary how people get found."

The doorbell rang again and Chris went to let the next visitors in while Ross and Jane settled into wicker balcony chairs .

Before eleven o'clock the coffee morning was in full swing. As it was on the balcony and at least technically visible from the street, the women who had become Muslims kept on their scarves, but that had no effect on the conversation.

Janet was relaxed and chatty, telling a funny story involving the family farm. She had already told them that she would have to leave early to get to the shops before the children finished school. Beside her, Susan was sitting as quiet and composed as usual, with her little boy cuddled up beside her. He looked too pale for Elizabeth's liking, and she was advising Susan on different types of multi-vitamins to pick him up.

"My children always found this end of the summer very hard when they were small. It has gone on so long, and now everything is so dry. One of the children's vitamin medicines used to make a big difference, but it takes a bit of time to work. Is he eating well? What about his sleeping?"

"I don't think there's anything wrong with him," answered Sue, pulling him nearer as she spoke, "I expect he'll be fine as soon as it rains."

Chris had little time for chatting between checking that everyone had helped themselves, and that the coffee and tea had not run out. The noise of the voices could be heard in the street, and occasional passers-by looked up in surprise.

Janet excused herself at midday and left quickly, to comments that she was always in a hurry these days, and she should slow down. After that, between twelve thirty and one o'clock people began to drift away home and Chris was left with the debris. She breathed a sigh of relief as she shut the door on the last woman, and went back to the balcony to clear up. From there she could hear their voices receding as they walked towards the main road and passing taxis. She loved them dearly, but your own coffee morning was always exhausting.

She called to her daughters who had been busy with friends and their little brother in their bedroom, but at eight and ten were delighted to find so much cake left over and helped her to get the balcony back to its usual order before Naafa arrived home for lunch.

SHAHBAA JEDID

Six years after arriving in Aleppo, Chris usually felt quite settled. Her two girls were in primary school and happy, her small son went cheerfully to nursery school, and her husband's practice was growing nicely. Many of his first patients had been classed as 'family', that is everything from sisters to third cousins twice removed, and their cousins as well, and of course they could not be asked for money! Chris had thought that she would go crazy trying to remember them all, until Elizabeth had kindly pointed out that when a family was big enough to fill four villages outside the Euphrates town of Raqqa, it was usually called a tribe. Naafa, who aimed at sophistication, was horrified at this, but Chris was pretty sure that Elizabeth was right. Over time his name had become known, partly through recommendations from his family, so eventually all the hassle had paid off.

They had arrived in Aleppo with two little girls and a car packed with their belongings, and had stayed at first with Naafa's eldest sister and her family. That was a desperate shock. They had left their rented semi in a pleasant part of Wolverhampton and come to a hot, untidy flat with five unruly boys aged eleven down to two. His sister, Bana, sailed serenely through the chaos, cooking or supervising a maid who spent most of the time splashing water about. Bana occasionally shouted at her boys, or reached out and hit one on whatever portion of his anatomy presented, but mostly her reaction to the noise was to raise her eyes to heaven and her hands palms up, sigh, and say, 'Boys will be boys".

Within a week their two polite little girls had started joining in the fun, and Chris had issued an ultimatum. Either they got their own house, or she took the girls and left. Naafa knew she could not take them out of the country without his permission, but in fact he secretly agreed with her. Although he always defended his sister to his wife, he was appalled at the disorder and lack of routine for the children. Ten years in England and two children who were in bed by 7.30, bathed and sweet-smelling, had changed him a lot from the village boy who thought it natural for children to run wild.

He found a house on a quiet street in the Sebil area near the park, and moved his wife and children in a few days later, as soon as the contract was complete. His mother, brothers and sisters were horrified that he was throwing money away on rent, and continued to be horrified by a lot of the things they saw. To put the two little girls – aged four and two – into a bedroom on their own, separated by the width of a small corridor from their parents, seemed little short of barbaric, and laying the thickest carpet in the sitting room instead of the front room (for visitors) was so strange that they could not live with it.

One day, soon after they moved in, Chris was making coffee for the three brothers and when she returned to the sitting room with it she found them manhandling her favourite carpet into the front room. She was wildly angry, but managed to control herself until she reached their bedroom and locked the door. There she stamped around until her hairbrush rattled itself off the dressing table, so she kicked it across the room and under the wardrobe. Feeling foolish, she had to scrabble around to retrieve it, which, if anything, made her angrier.

Naafa, caught between his wife and his family, didn't know what to do, so he inadvertently fanned the flames by saying,

"But Chris, they only want the best for us. They want people to see how well I'm doing."

"Fine. So next time they come are they going to bring you a new wife?"

"Why do you have to get it all out of proportion? They like you, they just work that way. Family is really important here, you have to understand. that." At this point Chris realized that she was going to get the 'family doesn't mean anything in England' lecture. She knew it wasn't true, but by now she was too angry to be coherent, so she stamped into the kitchen and shoved the plates and coffee cups into the sink, where a cup handle snapped off.

She thought about her brother, a little younger than her and living with a girlfriend and two cats. He was attached to her and discussed his life with her, he even asked for advice occasionally – usually on such deeply practical matters such as what to do when one of the cats was sick on the carpet. She tried to imagine his face if she came to visit and started to rearrange his furniture. She couldn't, nor that of his girlfriend, but the thought made her grin, and she finished the washing-up in a better temper.

Naafa must have said something to his mother or his brothers, because that was the only time they indulged in furniture removals in her home, but the sighs and meaningful looks at the reinstated carpet became a routine irritation.

However she was beginning to sense a much more serious problem. When they first arrived everybody cooed over the little girls and she was told how sweet they were, just like little brides. These compliments did not please her overmuch, but she accepted them as well-meant, and she assumed that the rubbing of their own stomachs, with sympathetic and enquiring smiles referred to the bad stomachs she had suffered from occasionally. It took her some time before light dawned and she understood them to be asking if she was pregnant, and even then she was not concerned, but simply said and gestured, "No" and left it at that. Slowly the appreciation of what was really happening seeped into her mind. The family was upset because she had not given Naafa a son, and totally uncomprehending that she believed that they had a complete family already.

Yet again, Naafa was caught in the middle. His mother thought his wife was disgracefully selfish not to go on having children until she produced a boy, and he was not spared comments about the lack of interest in children in foreign wives, and the folly of marrying one of them when he could have taken his pick from the village. She was too old, too tall (almost as tall as he), and 'her nose was high', which meant too stuck up, for the wife of one of their family. How would he manage in his old age without a son to care for him? The comments got sharper and sharper,

24

and increasingly frequent, so that in the end, some months after they moved into the flat, one Tuesday evening when he came from the clinic to find the children in bed and his wife quietly reading a book, he felt forced to raise the issue with her.

"They want *what*?" She said, trying to keep her voice under control. "I thought you were happy with the girls. Didn't we agree that two children is best, so we can give them everything they need?"

He nodded unhappily, in fact he had been perfectly satisfied with his beautiful daughters until his mother and the rest of the family had complained.

"It's just that....."

"Just that what? That we don't have children crawling over everywhere and screaming and shouting like your sisters' kids?" This was a wrong move, and she knew she had gone too far.

"Don't bring my sisters into it if you want me to listen to anything else." Saying which, he turned away from her, picked up his jacket and left the house. They were both furious, he because he knew that she was right on her terms, but had been brought up on different terms, she because she had adjusted to so much already and this was several steps too far. It was impossible for her to accept that his family should decide how many children they had, and if that was the wife he needed, he had married the wrong person. She raged away silently to herself that she would just take the girls and go back home. Then she remembered that she could only take the children with his permission, and fury gave place to tears of frustration. It

25

had been around 8.30 when Naafa had stamped out, now it was 10.30 and she was exhausted and still alone. Wearily, and running on automatic, she tidied a few toys and books away and took herself sadly to bed.

Next morning she woke with a headache, and the two girls climbing on the bed .

"Mummy, Sara's nappy is wet. Why is Daddy sleeping in the sitting room?"

"He came in late last night. He didn't want to wake me. Come on, Sara, let's get you clean again."

The two adults walked carefully round each other for the next few days. When they spoke, it was to snap or to make a household request with cold politeness. It was the children who eventually broke the log-jam after lunch on the following Saturday.

The meal had been conducted in silence from the adults, and in quiet voices from the children, who had disappeared to their room immediately afterwards. When Chris had made Naafa his coffee, placing the cup very firmly on the table beside his armchair so a little coffee slopped over into the saucer, the dishes had been washed and put away and Naafa was watching the news before going back to work, she went to see where the children had got to.

She found them sitting together on Sara's bed, with Lubna's arm round her small sister.

"What's the matter, cherubs?" she asked, "Why are you sitting here all alone?"

"We want to go to Granny and Grandad in England. We don't want to stay here any more." From Lubna.

"Why is that? Can you tell me what's the matter?"

"We don't like being here any more. We don't like you and Daddy. We want to be with Granny and Grandad because they don't shout."

"But Daddy and I don't shout." They had both been careful to keep their voices down, especially in front of the girls.

"You talk like you're shouting and we don't like it," very firmly from Lubna.

Chris was close to tears. She knelt down and put her arms round both of them.

"I'm sorry, girls. Daddy and I have been cross with each other, but we won't be any more. Sometimes you two quarrel, don't you?" They looked at her and both nodded. "Well, Daddy and I had a quarrel too, but we will be friends again, just like you." She went quickly out of the room before she started crying, but by the time she reached Naafa in the sitting room the tears were pouring down her face. He looked up from the television, then jumped up and came to her.

"What on earth is the matter? Why are you crying?"

Between snuffles she managed to explain about their daughters, it was easier as she went on, because he put his arms round her so she could rest her head on his shoulder.

"This has to stop. When I get back this evening we can talk. Or would it be better talk away from the house? I can ask Mama to send Almaz over to babysit for an hour or so."

"No," responded Chris quickly. She didn't want anything from his family just now, "Just come home as

27

quickly as you can. We can't have the girls upset like that, it breaks me up."

Before leaving for work, Naafa took the trouble to find his daughters and hike them onto his shoulders. He told them, much as Chris had, that Mummy and Daddy had been cross, but weren't going to be cross any more, and they waved him off much more cheerfully before getting out their dress-up dolls to play together.

That evening, after the children were in bed, Chris tidied round the sitting room and then did something she had not done for some time. She went and changed out of her jeans and sweater and into a dress, and brushed her hair. She didn't want to be obvious, so she stopped there and left the make-up alone, but she had made an effort and hoped it would be noticed.

Naafa did notice it, but wasn't sure how to respond, so he thought it better just to say,

"You look nice. I like that dress," as he took off his jacket, which, for a change, he hung up carefully in the hall. Then he came back, "It's time to talk. What do you want to say?" He stood away from her across the room, with his hands in his pockets, waiting for her to start. This was more than daunting, but Chris screwed up all her courage and started to speak.

"It doesn't seem right that we can't do anything without your family poking their noses in. Sorry, I mean helping you to make a decision. I feel as if you aren't married to me any more." It was well that she had not put on make-up because she started crying again, much to her annoyance .

"I'm sorry, dear, I know it is strange for you, but really they mean well, especially about this baby thing." Chris looked up quickly.

"I thought we decided that in England."

"Yes, but we've both moved on since then. Do you really not want to think about another one? Never at all?"

"I don't know. I thought it was decided and that was that. I'm happy with these two, but I suppose one more would be not too many. What do you want? You, not your Mother? Why do you want another?"

"It's hard to explain. When my dad died I felt that it wouldn't be too long before his name 'came back' with my son. Everyone always calls me Abu Khalil after him, and I just supposed that I would be one day."

They moved closer together and both tried to smile. Soon the smiles came of their own accord, and they were hugging each other as if they were saving each other from drowning.

"There's one thing I want from you," said Chris.

"Oh yes?" he replied, waggling his eyebrows at her in comic lechery.

"No. I'm serious. I want you to stop making decisions with your family before you make them with me. O.K? It's that or no deal."

He was serious again at once.

"You're right. That isn't working. We'll have to try better to work together. Will that be enough, Madam?" He returned to comedy, not being comfortable with too much sentiment. She knew there was no chance of prolonging the moment, so she stepped back away from him, curtseyed, and said,

"Yes, kind sir. And now would the great doctor like his supper?"

The girls were delighted to have their parents, both naturally cheerful people, back to normal. Chris took care not to ask Naafa if he had passed on their decision to his family and he avoided telling her. They had managed to negotiate an extremely difficult moment and neither one wanted to risk another fight .

Life moved on. Lubna started Nursery School in the spring and settled there quickly – Chris had to admit that spending time with their cousins had helped the girls to learn Arabic and to get on with children of a very different background. Then summer was approaching and a trip to England was mooted, and Chris discovered she was pregnant. She was prepared for this, but sad to have her trip put in doubt as her doctor wasn't too happy about her travelling in the first three months. Naafa was delighted, but managed to keep the promise she had extracted from him, not to say anything to his family for the moment, at least until the first few weeks were past.

She did not expect he would be able to keep quiet, and when she had got to the tenth week she gave him permission to tell anyone he liked. His family was delighted, and his mother made a great fuss of her, now she was a good daughter-in-law, doing her duty by her husband. His sisters added their joy, though one sister indiscreetly let it slip that her mother had been putting out feelers with her friends to find him a better wife. At first

30

she was angry again, but Naafa's obvious horror when she passed on this tidbit made her laugh. It became a private joke between them that helped them through other minor skirmishes .

Eventually the new baby was due, and she got Janet to promise to come to the hospital with her instead of Naafa's mother and sisters. It was born very easily, as the others had been, and brought joy to everyone. Chris was glad to be finished and to have a healthy baby, and both Naafa and his family were overjoyed that this time it was a boy. The baby's sisters loved having a little brother, and her friends were pleased that all had gone well.

With another girl, Chris might have been able to go home from the hospital at once, but a boy at last was too much of an occasion for Naafa's family to resist. The second day they brought in a hairdresser, a highly frilled, cream satin bedspread, and a representative of a 'baby welcoming' company. Chris was shampooed without getting out of bed, and her hair arranged 'becomingly'. The bed was changed, and covered with the new bedspread, and the room was decorated with blue teddy bears, blue balloons, and enough sweets, chocolates and cakes, all with blue packaging, to start a shop. All seemed ready, but at the last moment, before the first visitors arrived at eleven o'clock, Naafa looked in on her, bringing a diamond bracelet, which she had to wear at once .

Twenty-four hours after having a baby it was all a bit too much for Chris, but Naafa stayed a few minutes until the first women visitors arrived, and that steadicd her. His advice was just to let it flow over her, which seemed good, as she really couldn't do much else.

The visitors came, presented gifts, drank coffee, cooed over the baby being paraded around by the proud grandmother, collected their sweetmeats and departed. It went on until two o'clock, when the ward maid brought her lunch and the nurse announced she had to have a rest. At six o'clock it all started again, but this time the English wives came as well, so it was a little less fearsome. When the final visitor left at nine o'clock she was exhausted and the baby was crying to be fed. However her mother-in-law had had a wonderful time, and the sisters all told her how happy she had made Im Naafa. Naafa came in when the only women were his own family, and he saw how tired she was so he sent his family home at once and stayed with her until the baby was settled and she was ready to sleep, then the next morning she was up and dressed before the doctor came to tell her she could go home.

By the time Khalil was two years old their lives were improving a lot. The interest Im Naafa had shown in baby Khalil, explaining exactly how to feed, clothe and change him, had faded a little as her two younger sons married and provided her with other occupations. Naafa's practice was growing and the piece of farmland which he had inherited from his father was beginning to show a profit again after some years of drought so dry that there had been no point even in planting. At last they were able to consider buying their own flat, and at a suitable moment a friend met him and told him of an apartment block, built but not finished inside, which was for sale quickly for cash. It was in a smart new district where there were only three floors to each building, so they would have only two neighbours. It was what he wanted as a symbol of success and for her it was a pleasant flat in a good area, reasonably far from his family so they would have to make an effort to get there and would probably phone first to make sure someone was at home. This would be a considerable advance on their present flat, only a stroll from the family building and vulnerable to the impromptu visits of anybody who couldn't find anything worth watching on TV for an hour or two .

Raising the cash involved a lot of calculating of savings and borrowing from the family, who were torn between pride in Naafa's success and horror at the cost of the flat, and it completed Chris' education about the reality of life, at least in some families. There were endless meetings of the menfolk, smoking, drinking very strong sweet black tea and shouting. The women sometimes joined them, but were usually too busy to spend the time. The voices were so loud that Chris was expecting them at any moment to come to blows, but when she asked Naafa what they were quarrelling about, he was astonished.

"What quarrel? We were just discussing something – about the farm, I think." He gave her a puzzled look and returned to his family. She gave up and, once she had put the children to bed, sat in the kitchen reading a book from the collection going the rounds of her English friends.

Finally the deal was done, leaving them with the first floor flat, including basic drains, concrete walls and floors, holes for windows and a large sheet of metal for a door.

The two of them spent several evenings deciding how to make it into their dream home – exactly how the enormous front area would be divided with folding wooden screens into visitors' sitting room, formal dining room and general sitting room, how to arrange the kitchen, and all the other details of the basic work.

Then the family moved in on the discussion and offered helpful advice. One person knew the best plasterers in town while another could take Naafa to the suppliers who gave the absolute rock bottom deals on bathrooms and kitchen fittings, "and that colour you've chosen for the bathroom – nobody has a bathroom that like that, white marble would be much better." Of course, other relations had quite different ideas on everything related to the new flat, and no one was shy of expressing an opinion, so the arguments raged, fuelled by gallons of strong, sweet black tea and occasional cups of coffee.

Finally Chris cracked, and told her husband that he would have to take their plans and ideas to his mother's flat to let the 'design crew' work there. She was being sarcastic, but he was relieved to take her at her word, and disappeared evening after evening to his parents, the floor plan tucked under his arm. Meanwhile she was busy enough with daily life with three children together with the work involved in the approach of summer to be quite pleased to have the house to herself for a while.

Over the eighteen months that it took to finish the flat, jobs being completed when there was money available, Chris developed a 'one for you and one for me' technique which allowed her to get a lot of what she wanted. She traded green shutters for her oldest sister-in-law's choice of brown, but insisted on pale grey tiles for the kitchen walls. She gave in and accepted green tiles in the cloakroom, but stuck out for a proper toilet there, instead of a local 'hole in the floor' job. This last was a triumph as the whole family was united in disgust at the thought of strangers – even the cleaner – sitting on the same toilet seat as the family. They tried to explain that for what was, in essence, a public toilet it was much more hygienic to have the Arabic toilet, but when Chris insisted they retired, complaining to each other about foreign habits.

All good things proverbially come to an end, and this is true of bad, or even just tiring, ones as well. Despite all the delays over final decisions, money, workmen who thought 'tomorrow' was an indefinite date in the future and suppliers who failed to supply, the flat was eventually finished and they were ready to move in.

Moving house is an interesting, even exciting, experience in Aleppo. There are no companies whose staff will pack your goods and deliver them magically undamaged to the new house. The usual way is to pack everything yourself, except what you need for the final days, and move it to the new house, car-load by car-load. This disposes of clothing and everything else small and portable, so the actual removal day is reserved for the furniture. Then if it is summer there is no problem. An open truck arrives and the householder, with male friends and relations, supervises the workmen, whom he may have hired or who may come with the truck, as they move the pieces of furniture out of the old flat, down the (usually narrow) stairs and out onto the truck. Then he rushes ahead to the new flat to supervise the reverse process. The women spend their time clearing up, putting things away and keeping out of sight of the workmen, while the children are farmed out if possible – in this case they spent the day with their grandmother.

Winter moves are much more trouble. The system is the same until moving day, but then everything rests on the weather. If the weather is fine, all goes ahead, but if there is a possibility of rain everything stops until the fine weather comes back, as furniture will not improve from a soaking, or even from the amount of rain that will get to it under a tarpaulin hastily dragged over the full truck.

Suffice it to say that Naafa and Chris slept in their new flat one warm September night, with the girls delighted at their new room, and little Khalil too excited to go quickly to sleep.

Chris woke up first the next morning. She was still tired, but stretched luxuriously, pushing her toes as far down the bed as they would go. The bright white walls reflected the sunlight through the half-open shutters, and it must have been this that woke her. From the comfort of her bed she looked round the room with pleasure. The pictures and curtains were still missing, and two suitcases of clothes accused her from near the wardrobe, but at last they were in their own home .

BAD LUCK

Friday

"I thought he might have come down that extra five thousand."

"But I believed you when you said you didn't want it, and I expect he did too. And it was still an awful lot of money."

Two women in their early fifties sitting in a busy café in the smarter end of Aleppo, facing each other over a table for two. The table was against a solid column on one side, and the nearest table on the other side held a well-dressed young man and girl who were only interested in each other. A little before lunch on Friday the café was full of girls and young men, in groups or intense pairs, and middle-aged women like these, some covering their hair with scarves like the one, and some carefully coiffed like the other .

All the women of whatever age were meticulously manicured and made up, and most, like these two, had put over the backs of their chairs the coats they had needed on a cold February day. Muna, the bare-headed one went on,

"I couldn't not have bought them, not after waiting for them. Emeralds have something special about them, don't you think? And you don't often see them so nice here, you really have to go to Europe for good ones, don't you?"

"It's really a lovely set", agreed Selwa, and began to retie her scarf. "I'll have to hurry now, though, or Mahmoud's lunch will be late." She looked timidly at her friend as she spoke, and then reached over the back of her chair for her coat.

"You spoil that boy. It isn't good for him. Just like you spoiled his father." Muna's voice was severe. Nevertheless she signalled to the waiter, drawing her right index finger across her left palm to tell him to bring the bill, and starting to put on her coat as he sauntered across.

They both shivered as the wind caught them outside on the street, and Muna suddenly turned to her friend and smiled benignly,

"Look, there's a lottery ticket man. I'm going to buy one, I feel lucky today. You get one, too, and it will be like old times. We haven't done that for such a long time."

Selwa hadn't spent any money so far that morning, so she followed Muna to the old man leaning against the wall nearby and happily parted with the price of the ticket after her friend's. Then they got into separate taxis. Selwa went home to lunch with her son, Muna with her husband, both feeling that it had been a pleasant morning.

Saturday Morning

The cold wind from the open window blew the long dining room curtains wide until one of them caught on a chair and was trapped, but the shutters were pulled to so nothing showed from the outside. A fat ginger cat slunk uneasily about the flat, keeping under chairs and near walls, and occasionally mewing anxiously. In the tall, dark bedroom it looked as if someone was asleep, there was a hump on one of the pair of single beds, but there was no sound of breathing. Only the quiet tick of a little gilt clock.

It was a bright, cold winter morning. The bitter north wind chilled the people queuing for fresh bread at the baker's, stamping their feet and arguing in the untidy line. A few horses and donkeys pulling carts were frisky or irritable among the crowds of motor vehicles. Men riding heavy, Chinese-made bicycles to work wrapped either long knitted woolly scarves or the traditional red and white cotton ones round their heads and faces, and charwomen going to work looked like animated balloons with their long black cloaks covering layers of jerseys. The wind, straight from Siberia, bit through thicknesses of clothing, crept under doors and ruffled carpets.

The front door of the first floor flat in Exhibition Street was locked, and nobody answered when the rubbish collector rang the bell at seven fortyfive, so he shrugged his shoulders and trod heavily away. He had been calling at the same time every day except Fridays for the last twenty years. Sometimes the bucket of rubbish was waiting for him on the stairs and sometimes not. If it wasn't there he rang the bell and sometimes it was answered and sometimes not. He really didn't care either way, except for the first of the month when he got his money.

The cleaner arrived at eight thirty. She thought Madame Muna should have her living in, but however much she hinted, Madame Muna just said that she liked being alone with her family at night. Now she rang the bell, and inside the cat froze, one paw lifted, and turned its head towards the door, ears pricked. The fat, elderly woman was on time today, after what Madame Muna had said to her on Thursday, and what good did it do to anyone? She wrapped her rusty black cloak and shawl more tightly round her and sat down heavily on the doorstep for a minute or two, then heaved herself up breathily and pressed the doorbell again.

There was still no answer so she turned to go down the stairs, full of righteous indignation against people who didn't get up, and who even shut the inside doors so they didn't hear the doorbell. Well, it wasn't her fault, and she got paid monthly too, so she wasn't worried. She went off quite happily, thinking how she would take the chance to visit her eldest daughter, the one with the useless husband, and have a nice chat and a hot glass of tea with her – that would cheer them both up. She was out of the house and walking along the road by a quarter to nine

.

Half-past ten. Selwa's son, Mahmoud, finished his training session and he quickly changed out of his sweaty football clothes to hurry from the stale-smelling changing rooms. He didn't want to face the super-religious team members who would go to endless lengths to avoid being seen naked, nor the ultra-'liberated' ones who rushed in and out of the showers, flicking each other with wet towels. It wasn't that he objected to either set, who accepted each other cheerfully as team mates on the football field. It was that he saw them as protected children while he felt he had been pushed out into the cold, adult world; if anything, he was jealous of them.

His father's death when he was fifteen, leaving him with a loving but persuadable mother and older sisters who were either married or thinking of marriage, had left him to make his own way in the world with no firm guidance. He was deeply frightened at being alone, and so angry with his father for abandoning him that he virtually gave up bothering with school work and concentrated instead on the football club. His mother had always hoped that her beloved only son would be a doctor, or at least an engineer, but the more she begged him to study the angrier he got and the less he listened to her. He loved football and excelled at it, making the under-eighteen team when barely sixteen, so when his Baccalaureate results were, predictably, poor he naturally drifted into Education College to train as a sports teacher. By this time his mother was just relieved that he had a place in a college, whatever it was, while his sisters contented themselves with telling him at length that it was his own fault.

He enjoyed Education College, and then was happy teaching sport to High School boys – he worked at two schools, because sport is not considered a serious subject in the Syrian education system. The salary was low, but his mother asked for no housekeeping money from him, so until he was twenty four he was able to dress well, play plenty of football, and enjoy the limited possibilitics of entertainment available to an unattached young man in Aleppo.

All that had changed last summer. He had met Yasmin, three years younger than he and a star of the girls' basketball team at the same sports club. She wasn't very tall, but so active and agile, and so positive, that she energized the whole team. When he occasionally took over one of their training sessions she listened to everything he said with big brown eyes gazing at him seriously, but

41

afterwards she joined in the general chatting over orange juice in the club cafeteria where she laughed with the others, and flicked her long, wavy brown hair over her shoulder. The others realized that something special was happening for both of them, and soon it was accepted that, whether or not he had coached them that day, he would always have juice waiting for her in the cafeteria when the session finished. By the end of the summer, when he was going back to school and she to university, they were head over heels in love, and she was urging him to speak to her parents.

He tried, but as soon as they heard of his low-paid job and the insecurity, as they saw it, of his financial future, both her father and her mother refused to hear any more about him. Near-poverty, scraping by from month to month, was not what they wanted for their daughter, so they politely but firmly ushered him from their house, then completed their protection of their precious child by insisting that she withdrew from the sports club and did not meet Mahmoud again. Families are important in Syria, and when parents put their foot down about suitors the suitor in question almost always has no hope.

This morning he was too depressed to go straight home. He knew his mother would have the front room full of women and cigarette smoke – he couldn't face their kind enquiries about his job, or hearing about their successful sons. He knew, too, that the local 'jungle drums' meant that they all knew about Yasmin and were sorry for him, but that surely wouldn't stop them discussing his love life when his mother was out of the room. He wandered home past

Yasmin's house, but she wasn't visible so the only option left this morning was to stop at a friend's shop, where at least he could have a glass of tea and talk football before facing his mother's fussing at home.

At eleven o'clock visitors began to arrive at Selwa's flat, about a mile away from her son's club. She was bustling about, checking that the maid was getting out the right cups for coffee and that the cakes were elegantly placed on the trays, before opening the door to greet each woman with an enthusiastic kiss on the air near each cheek and a gushing comment on how they were welcome a thousand times. Soon eight of them were seated in the reception room that she was always happy to show off to them. She was very proud of this room – the gold of the carved and painted wooden chairs, which had been part of the furniture she and her husband had chosen before they were married, set off by the white and gold brocaded satin upholstery, the knots of flowers on the pale pink, Chinese-style carpet, the wink of the gold and crystal ashtrays (you couldn't really see the settings were only gold coloured where Muna's were silver-gilt).

The maid brought in the small cups of Turkish coffee on the silver-plated tray with the pretty handles that looked like filigree – she had chosen it after Muna had inherited a solid silver one – while Selwa followed her with a matching tray holding boxes of different brands of cigarettes. Within a few minutes nine carefully manicured right hands were holding coffee cups, showing nail polish that ranged in colour from pale pink on Luma, resolutely blonde, who was proud of her fair skin, to dark red on Randa, equally determinedly black-haired, who was as proud of her classically Arabic dark good looks. Eight of the left hands were holding cigarettes (Miriam had given up on doctor's orders), and smoke was being inhaled between sips of coffee by artistically lipsticked mouths.

"Selwa, where's Muna? She isn't usually late," asked Leila. "She rang me last night and told me to be sure to come because she had something special to show us."

"Yes," answered Selwa, "I know. I know what she wants to show you. We were out shopping together yesterday. You did hear about the land she sold, didn't you?" Randa had but the others hadn't and they begged her to explain. She continued, "Do you remember her father dying last year? Well you know he had quite a lot of land and some blocks of flats as well. When it was all sorted out between Muna and her brother, she got a big block of flats near the Soukh and three or four pieces of land in New Aleppo."

"My goodness," exclaimed Leila, putting her empty cup down on the pink marble of the coffee table top, "That must be worth a lot now. My father-in-law had to pay an enormous price per metre for a piece of land for his new building project. Is she going to sell yet? Surely she doesn't need the cash. She can wait till the price goes up again."

Selwa reached forward to put down her own empty cup, and from that position she looked up at her friends and said,

"That's what I was going to tell you. She did. She got the money in liras for one piece on Sunday, and yesterday we went out to spend some of it." The other women all sat up straighter, the combined subjects of money and spending it

44

were guaranteed an audience, and Selwa enjoyed feeling herself the centre of attention. She flicked an imaginary speck of ash from her ample green silk clad bosom and continued:

"Do you remember when she chose a ring for her daughter-in-law after little Omar was born? She's been really good to that girl, you know. It was a turquoise, about so big," she measured it out on her finger. "Diamonds all round. Very nice, but plain. She always says the girl doesn't like fancy work. Well, that same day, it was in that little jeweller just near the old church in the Azizieh," they all nodded, knowing the shop well. "He had a set there that was really nice. The necklace was like a gold rope, quite thick," demonstrated between finger and thumb. "At the front it had quite a big design of diamonds with three emeralds in the middle." She sketched it out with her hands round her own plump neck, her rings flashing in the sunlight. "Then there was a bracelet and a ring, and a long pair of earrings. It was very good, the emeralds were much better than you usually see, and most of the diamonds were pretty big, too. Anyway, we both liked it and Muna said she would buy it if she had the chance, but he wanted three million lires for it and she didn't have the cash at the time. Then she got the money for the land so we went and got it yesterday. He came down a bit, of course, but not much. She promised to bring it today to show you all."

"So where is she?"

"It's nearly twelve, it's getting late."

"Perhaps her husband's home today and she can't come."

45

"Have you phoned her this morning?" This last question was from Luma, who put down her coffee cup and stubbed out her cigarette. "Could you phone her now?" Selwa looked flustered at all the comments and replied,

"Phone her now? Oh, yes of course." She went through to the everyday living room and they heard the number being dialled, and a few minutes later she returned, saying "There's no reply, she must be on her way."

Their conversation went on to other matters – what Lamia's hairdresser had said, whether Kinda's daughter would pass her exams, and the relative merits of local maids against those from Sri Lanka or the Philippines. Whilst Randa was regaling them with the story of a neighbour of hers who could tell exactly what you were thinking even if he couldn't see you, and whose neighbours wanted to get rid of him but were too scared to make a move, Selwa took the opportunity to chivvy Assia, her maid, along in serving the cakes, and to check that the dinner was cooking.

The last of the women had gone by two o'clock, still exclaiming over Muna's absence. Wearily, Selwa piled the dirty ashtrays onto a tray and carried them into the kitchen to be washed before Assia went home. Mahmoud was there, his back against the fridge door and his hands in his pockets. When she saw him her heart went out to him, he was her only boy and she knew he was having a hard time at the moment. He had told her about Yasmin before making a formal visit to the family, and being rejected as a suitor had left him bitter and blaming her for his fate.

Just now he looked particularly dejected, in fact when his mother looked closer at him he looked positively ill, with his usually healthy colour turned yellowish, dark shadows under his eyes. She was really worried, as she had heard from the others only that morning of a new outbreak of hepatitis. However when she asked him if he was feeling ill, all she could get out of him was:

"I'm all right. I just haven't been sleeping too well. Don't fuss all the time, please. I'll be fine tomorrow, I'll think of something soon." She saw there was no use asking him any more. If he was really sick it would be obvious in a day or two, and if he was just worried about the future she couldn't do much and knew he didn't like talking about it, so she changed the subject.

"Have you put out your clothes for the cleaner? I'm expecting the boy today."

"Yes, they're all on the chair in my bedroom," he said, before pulling himself away from the fridge and drifting dejectedly away in the direction of the living room.

Selwa went to check that the maid had straightened up the front room, and slipped out of her high heels in her bedroom before going back to the kitchen to dish up lunch .

Later in the afternoon the cleaner's boy called with a skirt of hers, so she told him to wait, and went to see what Mahmoud had left out, as he had gone for athletics training. In his bedroom she found the heap of dirty trousers and jackets on the chair, and noticed his thick, dark, zip-up jacket looking rather grubby on the bed as well, so, tutting to herself, she added it to the pile after patting the pockets to make sure they were empty. She bundled all the clothes together and took them to the front door, where the boy was leaning patiently against the doorpost, sucking his teeth. Sending him off, she returned to the sitting room, turned up the oil fire, kicked off her slippers and thankfully put her feet up on the blue velvet settee for a few minutes rest. The maid had gone home, Mahmoud was out for the rest of the afternoon and she would try to phone Muna again later, but just for now everything could wait.

Saturday Afternoon

3.00pm. Muna's son, Rustum, needed to talk to his mother about money. Being a father and a husband was a surprisingly expensive business, and his mother had helped him out on more than one occasion - there were advantages to being an only child. This time he was hoping for a generous amount, as his car was just about beyond repair, even in Syria, which still occasionally looked like a mobile motor museum, and where car mechanics could do things undreamed of in Dagenham. Also his wife had been a bit put out, to put it politely, when he had suggested that they didn't really need a car as there were plenty of taxis (he didn't dare suggest buses).

What a good job his mother had sold that land – he wondered how long it would take to wheedle out of her the couple of million liras to buy a really nice new car, preferably a bit bigger than his present one. Oh well, the sooner he started the sooner he would finish. He leaned over the back of the armchair where he had been thinking and dialled his parents' number.

There was no reply, which puzzled him. He knew that his father had gone to Damascus the day before on one of his usual business trips, and he always phoned his mother at about this time when she was alone. He dialled again carefully, thinking he might have got the wrong number, and let it ring for a full minute. At the other end the bell rang shrilly through the quiet, shuttered house, and the cat watched it from her hiding place under the chair, eyes like bright beads in the darkness.

Rustum had a sudden idea. Perhaps his mother's closest friend, Selwa, would know where she had got to. He rang her, and had to wait while she heaved herself off the settee to answer the phone. She couldn't help, could only tell him that his mother hadn't arrived at her house, and wasn't at the house of any of her usual friends as they had all been waiting for her.

By now he was getting worried because he couldn't remember the last time that his mother had stepped out of routine without telling him. He called to his wife that he was going out for a minute (she already thought he spent too much time with his mother, so he didn't tell her where), and checked that he had his parent's door key with him. Then he went to his car and spent ten infuriating minutes trying to start it. By this time his imagination had his mother lying helpless on the floor after a stroke or a heart attack. He got out, slamming the door shut as hard as he could, and was lucky enough to find a cruising yellow taxi immediately, which he directed to the shady suburb where his parents lived, and into Exhibition Street.

Arriving at the front door of the flat, he thought at first that he had left his keys in his own car, and was cursing his stupidity and patting his pockets desperately when he was pulled up short by the sound of the cat mewing from inside the flat. She had been 'his' cat until he married, and she still recognized his footsteps on the stairs. It was with the certainty of something wrong that he found the key in his inside pocket and quickly shoved it into the lock. He turned the key but though it turned freely in the lock, the door wouldn't open. He tried it again before realizing that the door must be bolted on the inside, as it always was at night.

For a moment he stood looking blankly at the brown front door, then he tried once more, leaning against the door to try to lever it open though he knew this wasn't much use, and once more there was no result. He began to panic and wondered where to go for help. The woman in the top flat was a frail old lady who could do nothing, even if she wasn't having her siesta. He turned instead and hurried downstairs. His mother considered these neighbours not at all the 'right sort of people', but at least there was a man there who might be able to help.

When he rang the doorbell it was answered by a boy aged about ten in a thick brown jersey and corduroy trousers, and there were more children shouting, and a television booming away somewhere inside the house. While he was asking if anyone had seen his mother, the boy's mother came to the door behind her son, still tying the scarf she had pulled hurriedly over her hair.

"No, we haven't seen Madame Muna today. Although we don't actually see her, not to speak to, as you might say,

50

but I often hear her walking about upstairs in the mornings when the boys have gone to school. Now you mention it, I don't remember hearing her today." She paused a moment, her eyes widening, then went on, "There's something else too, I hadn't thought of it before, but she usually washes the shutters on a Saturday – at least that old woman does - but she can't have done today. It makes an awful mess in my garden, the water running down onto the tiles, but there hasn't been a drop today. It is strange, isn't it? With you not being able to get in and everything, and you do hear such terrible tales these days, don't you?"

At this point Rustum managed to interrupt her to ask if her husband might help him to force the door, but she looked doubtful and shook her head.

"Oh no, I couldn't ask him" she answered, "he's asleep and he wouldn't be pleased if we woke him. He doesn't like to have his rest disturbed." She glanced apprehensively towards the interior of the house. Despite his concern for his mother, Rustum had time to wonder how anyone could sleep in the noise which was, if anything, greater than when he had arrived.

"You wouldn't have a long ladder, then, would you?" he asked tentatively. "I might be able to get in from your garden, if I could try, over the balcony." The boy answered him.

"Yes, that's a good idea, we have a really long one. I'll bring it to the garden. Khaled!" he called over his shoulder to a smaller boy, "Show Mr Rustum through to the garden while I get the ladder." Khaled took him through the living room and out onto the patio, where they were soon joined

51

by the older boy, his mother (now in a tidy scarf and wrapped in her dressing gown against the cold wind) and the ladder.

It was useless. The ladder was quite long as household ladders go, but far too short for this job.

"That's the trouble with these old houses," observed the woman, "the ceilings are so high. You wouldn't believe the times I've nearly broken my neck while I was doing the spring cleaning."

"Thank you very much for letting me try," answered Rustum, struggling to hide how panicky he was beginning to feel as he got out his mobile, "I suppose I'll have to phone the police. There doesn't seem to be any other way to get in."

The policeman on duty wasn't particularly interested, and was inclined to put him off, until Rustum remembered that the Colonel at that particular station was a friend of his father's. As soon as he asked directly for Abu Ahad the policeman transferred his call straight through, and a non-committal

"Yes, what is it?" came down the line.

"Abu Ahad, this is Rustum. How are you? And how is Im Ahad? How are the children?"

"Hello Rustum. We're fine, thank God. And how are you and little Omar? Such a long time since we saw you. How is Abu Rustum? And Im Rustum? Your father was here yesterday."

"Everyone's very well, thank you. My wife sends her regards." With the necessary formalities over, Rustum rushed to the point. "Something must have happened to my mother. The door is bolted on the inside and nobody has seen her today and my father is in Damascus."

"Slow down, Rustum," said Abu Ahad, "and tell me what has happened, slowly now." He listened to the story again, this time in a slightly more coherent form, and said "Don't worry, I expect it's all right, but I'll send a man round to check for you, just in case." He paused a moment, then changed his mind: "No, wait a minute and I'll come myself. We can't have Im Rustum going astray, can we?"

Abu Ahad put the phone down, sighed and stood up. Then he pulled his jacket down over his generous stomach, straightened his tie and put on his hat and scarf before leaving his office. He decided to take only his driver with him, it was sure to be nothing – a key stuck in the door or something of that order – Rustum had always had too much imagination, ever since he was a little boy.

Rustum was on the pavement to meet them when the police car reached the building. They both looked up at the flat, where all the green shutters were closed as if it were empty. The four children from the downstairs flat were in the garden watching them, the littlest one with her thumb in her mouth, and Abu Ahad smiled briefly at them before ordering his driver to follow as he and Rustum turned into the entrance of the building.

Rustum was a shortish, stockily built young man with dark wavy hair, which at the moment was flopping over his forehead. The jacket of his suit was open and his tie was not straight. He looked very worried.

"Here, give me the key, let me try," said Abu Ahad, and Rustum thrust the key into his hand, hoping against hope that this time it would work. "What can be the matter?" Abu Ahad too began to look concerned. "The lock is definitely turning, but the door won't budge. I think you may be right, it certainly feels as if it's bolted. Now that really is strange." He stood back from the door and looked hard at it for a moment, as if he expected the answer to be written there. "I think we'll have to force it open. Where is your father? Is there another way in?"

The young man explained that there was no other way in, and his father was in Damascus on business. Then his control broke and he burst out, "We can't wait. Even if we can contact him he can't be home before dark. My mother must be ill in there. We'll have to break down the door."

"I think we could do with a bit of muscle on the job," said Abu Ahad, deliberately speaking calmly although he was beginning to get worried himself. "Come here, Abu Ahmed," he called to the driver, who was watching from a few steps down. The Police Corporal came up, a solid, youngish man, not tall but very heavy-shouldered. He was beginning to go bald but compensated with a luxuriant black moustache.

They all three looked at the offending door, then the driver turned to Abu Ahad and suggested,

"If you turn the key to keep the lock open, sir, I can give it a shove with my shoulder. It might loosen the hinges up a bit."

"Good idea, let's try it," answered Abu Ahad, and replaced the key in the lock, turning it to hold the mechanism open. The corporal put his hefty shoulder under one of the carved ridges on the door, muttered,

"In the name of God, the Almighty, the Merciful," to himself to keep away the devil, and heaved. The door creaked and strained, but held. He tried again, and again the door creaked and he thought he felt the hinges giving a little. For the third try he was joined by Rustum, and they both heaved with their combined and quite considerable weight, but although they could feel some slight movement, the door held.

"That's one thing about these older buildings," remarked Abu Ahad, "They're solidly built. We aren't going to just push it open." Rustum and Abu Ahmed were sitting on the stairs, panting, and one of Rustum's shirt buttons had come off. He, for one, obviously had no more energy left for another try.

Unexpectedly, Rustum sat up straight,

"I've got an idea. When I was a boy I once managed to climb up onto the dining room balcony. We'd still have to break open the shutters but it wouldn't be like this door, or we might even be able to force them open with a knife. What do you think?"

Abu Ahad handed him back the door keys,

"It's worth a try. Come on, Abu Ahmed, let's have a look at it."

They set off down the stairs with renewed energy now there was something positive to do. As they walked down the street and round the corner to the other side of the building they were watched intently by the children still standing in the garden of the downstairs flat, now accompanied by their mother, and by someone with a grey scarf sliding off her head, who looked like a maid. At the side of the building was the garage, and they stepped back to get a proper look as Rustum pointed out a way over the concrete garage roof, up about eight foot of drainpipe and on to the balcony.

"From there it's child's play to get in," commented Abu Ahad, "but only a monkey could climb the drainpipe, so we'll need a ladder." The job was beginning to take hold of him, and rather than send for help, he sent Abu Ahmed back round to the downstairs neighbours to borrow their ladder. They not only lent him the ladder, but helped him carry it as well. The maid took the back end, and the four children followed like ducks on a pond, the littlest one still with her thumb in her mouth. In this way they were conforming to the strong local tradition of never 'passing by on the other side', but always stopping to see what the other person is doing and to tell him how to do it better.

With Abu Ahmed and the maid pushing from below, over the railings and onto the garage, then setting the ladder on the garage with the head leaning against the railing of the balcony, there was soon a clear way to access the house. At this point Abu Ahad sent the children and the maid home, as he didn't want them to see what he was sure would be his undignified scramble over the railing and onto the balcony. He also suggested to their mother, who had come outside to see the fun, that she perhaps had work to do inside the house, but she ignored him and just stood there, hitching her scarf tighter to make sure her hair was covered.

From the garage roof all three men could see that one of the shutters above them was not quite shut, and Rustum became frantic with worry. He tried to push Abu Ahmed out of the way so he could go the ladder first, but Abu Ahad put him firmly to one side and motioned to his corporal to climb up to the balcony. Once there, Abu Ahmed put his fingers between the slats of the shutters and pulled gently. They swung out and open silently at the pressure. Abu Ahad called up sharply,

"Be careful, Abu Ahmed. There's something wrong here. What does it look like from there?"

"The window's not shut. It's broken and I can get inside," came the reply. "What do you want me to do?"

"Go in carefully, then go to the front door and let us in. Don't touch anything. We'll be right round".

He and Rustum scrambled heavily back down, to the delight of the downstairs children who had joined their mother in the garden, and ran round the building and up the stairs to the front door. Rustum got there first as Abu Ahmed was opening it from the inside, and was almost tipped backwards down the stairs as the terrified orange cat dashed between his legs on its way out.

Abu Ahmed wouldn't let him in until the Colonel, puffing and red in the face, caught up with them. The corporal was happiest as a driver, and didn't mind dealing with crowds or even street fights, but here he certainly wasn't going to be the one blamed for letting in members of the public to what looked like a burglary. He stood back and saluted very correctly as Abu Ahad reached the doorway.

"I didn't notice anything in the dining room or the hall, sir, except a bit of glass from the window. There was a cat, but it ran off when I opened the door."

Abu Ahad thanked him somewhat breathlessly, and took Rustum's arm above the elbow in a grip that was friendly but quite firm. Together they went in and Abu Ahmed shut the door on the four children, their mother, the maid and a man who must have been their father and who appeared to have rolled out of bed to see what was going on. They stood in a family group half way down the stairs, and Abu Ahmed noticed that the small one still had its thumb in its mouth.

Inside the house, the living room was dark because the shutters were shut, but it looked quite normal and there was no one there, just a magazine and an empty Turkish coffee cup on the table. Abu Ahad leaned down to look at the cup without touching it and could see that it must have been there for some hours as the grounds had congealed at the bottom. He left it and put on all the lights to check the front room, dining room and kitchen. By now there was hardly enough light left in the winter afternoon to make it worthwhile opening the shutters, and as they walked through the rooms they heard the muezzin at the nearby mosque calling people to the early evening prayers. The only sign of disturbance they could see was in the dining room, where there were some broken pieces of glass from the hole in the French windows where they had been opened from the balcony. Even there, the Colonel saw that the pieces had fallen on the carpet and would have made very little noise.

Then came the back of the house. The bathroom was in order, so were Rustum's old bedroom and his father's office. The only room left was the master bedroom, which Abu

58

Ahad had never seen, although the front of the house was quite familiar to him.

Rustum had only been restrained from rushing from room to room by the firm grip Abu Ahad had maintained on his arm. When they reached the bedroom Abu Ahmed was sent in first, followed by his boss and Rustum. Their eyes were all drawn to the hump under the quilt on the far bed. The shock made Abu Ahad relax his grip for a second, and Rustum pulled away from him and rushed around the foot of the twin beds crying:

"Oh, no! Oh, my God! Mama!" He dropped to his knees and touched the slim, white hand with the long, carefully painted scarlet nails. "She's dead. Oh my God. And I didn't know," he wailed, tears pouring down his cheeks and dripping onto her cold hand. Abu Ahad had come up behind him, and he now lifted the quilt and found Im Rustum's face. He quickly replaced the quilt, but not before Rustum had caught a glimpse of the protruding tongue, the purple cheeks and the bulging eyes.

The young man stood up quickly and rushed to the bathroom where they could hear him being violently sick, again and again. Abu Ahad felt queasy himself, but stood back and took a few deep breaths. Then he motioned his driver out of the room, followed him and locked the door behind him, before waiting for Rustum in the living room.

The taps in the bathroom were turned on, unnaturally loud in the silent house, when the door bell rang. Abu Ahmed answered it and found one of the downstairs children outside.

"Mama says can we have our ladder back before someone takes it?" he said, while he tried his best to see round the solid policeman who almost filled the doorway. Abu Ahmed looked over his shoulder into the living room where Abu Ahad nodded to him.

"Yes, you can. Say thank you to your mother for me, and run along downstairs now, boy," responded Abu Ahmed kindly, then he shut the door firmly again. Both policemen sat down on the elegant grey settee to wait for Rustum.

Abu Ahad had seen other dead bodies, even murdered ones, but never one that he recognized. This was different. He and Abu Rustum had been friends since being schoolboys together, and then when he was posted back to Aleppo in the police force they had renewed their friendship. Abu Rustum often dropped into his office for a cup of coffee or a glass of tea, and had several times advised him on investing his savings profitably. They had also visited as married couples, though this had not been quite so successful, as the rich Muslim wife with one son had almost nothing in common with his own wife, who was the barely comfortably off Christian mother of five. (He had noticed many times that the men of the different religious groups got on together without any problems, it was the women who were likely to be suspicious and reserved with one another). For a few moments he sat still, absorbing the street noises but doing nothing, until Rustum came from the bathroom, flushed and damp but more composed, and Abu Ahad stood up, ready to take charge.

"Abu Ahmed, get Doctor Abdul, his number is here in my book. Let's see, 54323, but I don't have his home number, so I hope he's in his clinic. Ask him to come at once. Then I want to speak to Sergeant Nihad at the station." He turned to Rustum and motioned to him to sit down, saying "Do you have a phone number for your father?" Rustum nodded and got out his diary from his inside pocket.

"Here's the number of the hotel he always stays at. Oh, and here are the numbers of two customers he is going to see." Abu Ahad wrote the numbers carefully in his notebook, while Abu Ahmed spoke to the doctor and then to the police station. When the numbers were safely written down he put the book away and took the receiver to instruct Sergeant Nihad about what had happened and to tell him to come with two men to give a hand.

As soon as he finished, Rustum asked him about phoning the Sheikh of the nearest mosque to have the death announced from the minaret, the usual custom. Abu Ahad hated having to tell him that they couldn't do anything until 'the formalities have been completed', and did not point out that 'the formalities' would include an autopsy.

They left messages at the hotel and at the other two numbers that he was to call Rustum as soon as possible, about Im Rustum. By this time Rustum looked a lot more composed so Abu Ahad thought it was time to ask him some questions. He cleared his throat and considered where to start.

"Do you have any idea why someone would want to kill your mother?" he asked, aware in saying it how banal it sounded.

"Who could want to?" answered Rustum, "but we're hearing about this sort of thing all the time. What are you policemen doing to let it happen?" Abu Ahad let the outburst pass him by, and a moment later his patience was rewarded. "I knew she shouldn't have kept the money in the house, especially with father being away."

"What money?" asked the inspector quickly. "Where is it kept? Can we see if it is still there?"

"Yes, of course. They always use the little loft over the kitchen, it should be there." Abu Ahmed fetched the stepladder from the kitchen balcony and Rustum climbed up it to disappear through a hole in the kitchen ceiling while Abu Ahad watched from below and steadied the ladder. A minute later he reappeared, with two plastic bin bags and very dusty knees. They put back the ladder and took the bags to the sitting room to check the contents, which proved to be 75 million lires in wads of one thousand lire notes. Abu Ahad was not at all happy to be responsible for such a large amount, and was glad to accept instead a signed receipt from Rustum to the effect that he was taking it for safe keeping. After that, Abu Ahad urged Rustum to go home and get some rest. The man was quite distraught, but Abu Ahad had other reasons for getting rid of him as well.

As soon as the young man had left, carrying the bags of cash in a large bin-bag and trudging down the stairs like his own grandfather, Abu Ahad went to work. With Abu Ahmed he had a good look at the window, but without touching it in case of fingerprints. Clearly the glass had been punched to make the hole which was big enough for a hand – Abu Ahad checked it. The bits of broken glass had almost all been projected over the marble surround and on to the carpet.

"Look here," he said, pointing to the pieces of glass, "if they had fallen a bit short someone might have heard them downstairs." At that moment a heavy lorry passed in the street below, drowning out Abu Ahmed's answer.

"What's that?" shouted Abu Ahad against the noise.

In a normal voice as the rumble of the lorry died away, Abu Ahmed repeated,

"I said that if something like that was going past you could take a sledgehammer to the window and nobody would notice."

"True enough," murmured the Colonel, almost to himself, and wandered regretfully through the house, the driver respectfully behind him. They were both looking for signs of disturbance, but there was nothing to be seen. The kitchen was clean, neat and deserted, not a cup out of place. The living room and front room were gloomy, tidy and growing even colder as the night settled in, but except where they had themselves dented cushions by sitting down, there were no signs of occupation beyond the coffee cup they had already seen. "She must have straightened up before she went to bed," he remarked.

"My wife does that, too," was the stolid reply.

The bathroom was next. Here there were only marks of Rustum's hasty passage, which had left a faint, unpleasant smell and a good few splashes around the hand basin. Abu Ahad wasn't unduly worried about the lack of signs, a strangling left no bloody traces to be washed off. He checked the bathroom cabinet, sliding the glass doors aside to reveal an obviously expensive collection of shampoos and face creams. Unlocking the medicine section (the key was in the lock) gave him nothing more than a box of paracetamol and a few patent medicines and cold cures. They looked at each other and Abu Ahmed shrugged his shoulders. "Nothing special here," he said, and they moved on to the back of the house.

The first door was at right angles to the bathroom, and opened to reveal the room that Abu Rustum sometimes used as an office, so Abu Ahad had seen it before. It was clean and not dusty, but felt unused and had clearly not been disturbed. Across the bottom of the L-shape of the hall they went into the room that had once been Rustum's and had been kept as a spare bedroom. There was the same feeling of ordered disuse and they could see nothing that warranted further attention. They were shutting that door when they both stopped and listened. They could hear the police sirens as reinforcements arrived and the clanging of the ambulance alarm as the driver joined in the general excitement.

"Idiots. Can't they ever keep quiet?" exploded the Colonel, at which the driver just gave the shrug he kept for rhetorical questions. He couldn't see that it made much difference, the neighbourhood would be ringing with the murder all evening anyway.

The master bedroom was at the top of the L-shape, and Abu Ahad turned on the overhead light and looked round carefully from the doorway. He set great store by first impressions and was annoyed with himself that he had not been sufficiently detached to make any useful observations the first time he had been there. Then something caught his eye and he walked quickly to the dressing table and bent down to squint along its surface. There were some new scratches sweeping in an arc from the base of the mirror to the front edge of the table.

He went even closer and bent down to have a better look, and his eye was caught by a bright sparkle near the edge of the fine blue Persian carpet. He reached down and peered at a large earring, a valuable one, too, if he was any judge. All the time they had been in the bedroom the sounds of the arrival of the police had been building up, now the doorbell rang, accompanied by hammering on the front door.

"Go and let them in before they knock the door down," he snapped irritably, "But don't let them touch anything. Start them off on photos and fingerprints on the broken window, and keep the ambulance men in the living room for now." In the few minutes he still had to himself he went back to the dressing table rug and scooped up the earring into a plastic envelope from a seldom-used set in his jacket, this he folded carefully and placed in his inside pocket.

He continued his careful walk around the bedroom until he came to the foot of the twin beds, where there was a quilted pink satin dressing gown crumpled on the floor. He picked it up carefully – it was both expensive and imported – and checked the pockets, which revealed nothing but a paper tissue. He noticed that the belt was missing, which prompted him to go to the head of the beds and, reluctantly, to lift the quilt up enough to check what he remembered from his first sight of the body. Yes, he was right. It was the dressing gown belt which had been used in the strangling. With relief, he dropped the quilt back and walked quickly to the door. There he was met by the police surgeon, a big, burly man who was none too pleased at being called from his evening surgery.

They shook hands and Abu Ahad led the doctor back round the end of the beds. The doctor lifted up the quilt, took one look and turned to him.

"Well, she's dead, anyway." Abu Ahad controlled his annoyance and did not reply. The doctor dropped the quilt back over the body and continued, "It looks quite clear but I'll have to check. The ambulance men can move her to the mortuary right away if you've finished with her." He started to move back to the door to call them in, but Abu Ahad stopped him.

"Just a minute," he said, "My men came at the same time as you. We haven't had a chance to take any photos yet."The doctor sighed.

"Can you hurry up? Or better still, can you send the body off when you have finished. I've a clinic full of patients waiting and I want to get back." Abu Ahad could see no reason why not, so the doctor walked briskly out, stopping only to give instructions to the ambulance men.

The Colonel took a last look round, checking again the dressing gown and the scratches on the dressing table top. He pulled out the envelope from his pocket and had another look at the earring, weighing it in the palm of his hand while he gazed absently at his reflection in the dressing table mirror. After a few moments he shook his head as if to clear it, and returned the envelope with the earring to his

66

pocket, then looked at his wristwatch and noted that it was already seven o'clock. He passed his hand over his face, then shrugged and walked through to the dining room to see if the Detective Captain and the photographer were ready to leave the window and to start the technical business in the bedroom.

It was the first time that Abu Ahad had worked with this particular Captain, Samir by name, who was a tough, fit-looking man in his late twenties. Abu Ahad had heard that he was very bright and ambitious, and other tales that he wasn't too particular about how he handled his witnesses. He thought he had better keep him in the background when it came to interviewing witnesses in this case, at least until he had some idea himself. A man like that could be very useful in getting information out of a certain type of witness but Abu Ahad didn't think that Im Rustum's friends were likely to be that sort, and he didn't want the Chief of Police on his neck for upsetting solid citizens.

The next thing to do was to send Abu Ahmed back to the Station to sign off for the night and go home, after which he wandered round the bedroom watching the routine work until it was finished. He had only had time for one cigarette, enough to make him long for a cup of coffee, when the Captain and the photographer both started to pack up their bits and pieces. The Captain looked glum.

"He's used gloves all the time, sir. There are lots of good polished surfaces, but only her finger prints, except on the man's wardrobe, and I bet those are her husband's. The window's the same – not a thing, just smudges, like gloves."

"Never mind, it's early days yet," responded Abu Ahad. He went back to the dressing table to have the earring photographed where he had found it before the photographer packed up completely.

After that it took only a few minutes to get the body sent off, and to post on guard duty the policemen who had arrived earlier, with his home number in case they should need him, before he was himself able to leave. He returned to the Station with the Captain and a driver he didn't know, so there was no chatting in the car. It had turned into a bitterly cold night and the wind cut round his ears as he hurried from the car park into the Station.

Once in his warm office he called for a glass of tea, sat down behind his imposing but dusty desk, and fished through the piles of paper on the top for a clean piece and a pencil. What he needed was a list. He always felt better when he could see things written down and classified – a useful habit at work, though it drove his wife crazy at home! This time he really needed a list in order to distance himself from the thought of Im Rustum who had so unbelievably turned into that horrid thing in the bed. The list he made first was one of questions:

1. Where had Im Rustum been the day before?
2. Who had known about the money?
3. Who had known about the jewellery?
4. Who needed money more than usual?

He looked at the last question and thought that it applied to just about everyone he knew at the moment, with money being tight all round. It could even apply to himself. However the list did give him the chance to tidy up his thoughts, so to speak, and gave him ideas for further questions, which he wrote down:

5. What, exactly, had the jewellery cost?
6. Which jeweller had made it?
7. Where had Abu Rustum and Rustum been last night?

As soon as they had a good description of the jewellery it should be easy to find out if it had been offered for sale yet, it was such a valuable set that it couldn't be sold too quickly or easily, especially with one earring missing. He looked at his list with some satisfaction and added:

Action – Contact the police in other cities to alert jewellers. He stopped for a moment to consider this, elbows on the desk and chin dropped onto his cupped hands, and then he put it aside and decided to concentrate on other positive aspects of what he could do.

By now it was eight o'clock and he should be going off duty. He was tired and hungry and he couldn't see any reason to continue before morning, so he put the paper into a drawer and thankfully left his office for home.

Abu Rustum came from Damascus as quickly as he could drive, and by ten p.m. he was pounding up the stairs to his house, grey-faced and sweaty. He put his key in the door, but before he could turn it the door was opened from the inside by a policeman.

"I'm sorry, sir, but no-one is allowed in," said the policeman, and another policeman, a little older, appeared behind him to give weight to his words.

"I'm Abu Rustum. This is my house. What's happening? Where's my wife?" The questions tumbled out. The older policeman came forward and ushered Abu Rustum into the living room, where he sat down on the settee and mopped his face with his handkerchief.

"He's right, sir. You really can't stay. Your wife isn't here now, they've taken her away. Colonel Abu Ahad wants to see you in the morning, but your son said you were to go to him tonight."

"What is this?" shouted Abu Rustum. "Where is Muna? Is she in hospital? Will one of you please tell me what is going on?"

The policemen looked at each other uncomfortably, then the older one studied the floor carefully as he said,

"She's not in the hospital, sir. She's in the mortuary. She was murdered last night."

"Oh, my God!" whispered Abu Rustum. His hands dropped to hang between his knees and the handkerchief fell to the floor. Then he straightened up with his mouth half open, apparently fighting for breath.

"Get him a drink of water, Aboud." The younger policeman rushed to the kichen and returned with water, which Abu Rustum drank gratefully.

"I don't believe it. Murdered. Here at home. I shouldn't have gone. Oh God, what have I done?" He gave himself a shake and seemed to remember he was not alone, for he continued, "I'm sorry. It's the shock. I can't believe it yet. Who is in charge of everything?" He was told that it was Abu Ahad, which seemed to comfort him a little, but there was nothing else the policemen could tell him except that Rustum had found the body and that he was to go there as soon as he could, as his own house was not available. Abu

70

Rustum shuddered at the thought of the bedroom, where his wife had just been killed, and was relieved to get away from the house which had become frighteningly not his own, with policemen and the feel of death in it.

It was as he was ringing the doorbell of Rustum's house that he really took in what had happened. By the time Rustum answered the door he could hardly stand upright, and he almost fell into his son's arms. They stood for some moments in the doorway, hugging each other and crying, until Rustum's wife, Ross, shepherded them inside and shut the door before the neighbours noticed anything.

She went to the kitchen and brought cups of tea with extra sugar, which she believed was good for shock. Her eyes were red-rimmed where she had been crying, but she was calm now, and she excused herself as soon as the men were settled with their cups of tea. It was a situation she would have found hard to handle at home in England, here she felt it was best to keep in the background and let the two men comfort each other. She was glad now that they had always been close .

Alone in their bedroom, she wandered around the room, picking up a hairbrush and putting it down, re-arranging the photos on the chest of drawers and, secretly rather ashamed of herself, began to entertain the thought that there would be some good things in the end. It would be nice to have Rustum to herself and not to share him with someone who had just assumed that mothers came first, and the money which would come to them would make life a lot pleasanter as well. She didn't know how this was organized in Syria, but there was sure to be quite a substantial sum for a beloved only child. She got into bed and drifted to sleep in minutes .

Rustum and his father sat up late into the night, talking and wondering. It was nearly morning, and the muezzin was telling the faithful that it was better to pray than to sleep, when Abu Rustum could be persuaded to put his head down on a pillow on the settee while Rustum found him a blanket. The son waited until he heard his father's snores, a comforting sound from his childhood, before going to his own bed .

Sunday Morning

Early morning saw Abu Ahad in his office, after leaving a message at the desk for Captain Samir to be sent to him as soon as he arrived. He took off his cap and unwound the long scarf his wife had insisted on. He dumped them on top of the grey metal filing cabinet, sat down at his desk and called for a glass of tea before reviewing the day's programme.

The first interview would be with Abu Rustum, which would be difficult and quite possibly embarrassing. He thought of asking Captain Samir to conduct it, but decided it would be better to do it himself. At that moment a policeman came in with his glass of syrupy black tea on a battered tin tray, and directly behind him came Captain Samir, who answered his "Good Morning" briefly and refused a glass of tea. Abu Ahad told him that he would be interviewing the dead woman's family and close friends himself.

"You might just go and see the neighbours downstairs. Check if they heard anything at all. From what I saw of the man, he couldn't have climbed the balcony, he's much too fat."

Samir gave him a look that said he really didn't need teaching his job, but asked mildly enough.

"What about the rubbish collector, sir? And there must be a cleaner of some sort. Do we have any details about them?"

They didn't, there had been no time the night before. Abu Ahad thankfully sent his junior off to Abu Rustum's house to find out, and then to talk to the neighbours.

At a few minutes to nine Abu Rustum and his son walked into the police station and were shown straight into the Colonel's office. Abu Rustum had shaved and borrowed a clean shirt from his son, but his face was grey and there were dark patches under his eyes. Abu Ahad got up as soon as his friend was announced, and they clasped hands then hugged each other without speaking. After that Abu Ahad asked Rustum to wait outside while his father was interviewed .

When they were alone and seated, one each side of the desk the way they had often had coffee together, Abu Ahad got down to business. He wrote his friend's name, Omar Dehab, Abu Rustum, at the top of the report sheet, and asked first for a list of Im Rustum's jewellery and the cash that had been in the house. He was told of the eighty million, less the price of the jewellery, that had been stored in the loft. Abu Rustum had also seen the jewellery before he left for Damascus, and told what he knew of his

73

wife's shopping trip with her friend, Selwa, which he had heard all about over lunch. Abu Ahad added Selwa's name and telephone number to the list of people to be questioned, and continued:

"When did you leave the house on Friday?"

"At about 3.30. I called at the garage to check the tires and fill up with petrol, after that I drove straight down to Damascus. I don't like driving at night so I started quite early."

"What time did you reach Damascus?"

"Oh, about 8 o'clock. I don't care to rush, and the road is always fairly busy at that time." Abu Rustum was slouched back in the chair, his left arm on the desk by his coffee cup and his right elbow resting on the arm of the mock-leather upholstered chair, while he absently counted over his bright turquoise worry beads with his right hand.

"Where did you stay in Damascus?"

At this question he stopped playing with beads and looked up at Abu Ahad before answering:

"At the Palmyra. I always do."

Abu Ahad asked a few more questions about whom he had seen in Damascus and then stood up.

"That's all for now, Abu Rustum. My policeman will type your statement and you can sign it. It should be very easy to check it out and then we won't have to bother you. I'll be glad to have one bit of the story tidied up".

Abu Rustum shifted uncomfortably in his seat, but made no move to rise. He sat up straight and looked uneasily from Abu Ahad to the policeman still on a straight chair in the corner, but now shutting his shorthand notebook.

"Just a minute," he said, licking his lids nervously and his eyes on the other policeman. "Can I talk to you privately for a moment, Abu Ahad?"

Abu Ahad saw and was surprised at the change in his friend. He still appeared old and shocked, but there was a flushed, fidgety look about him that made the Colonel sit down again, slowly and deliberately, before saying:

"Yes, er yes, of course you can. Leave us for a moment, Abu Juan." While the policeman left the room and shut the door Abu Ahad sat back in his swivel chair, rested his elbows on the wooden arms and put his hands together, fingertips to fingertips.

"Now, what is it?" he asked when they were alone.

"It's about the time when I got to Damascus," said Abu Rustum. "There's a bit of a problem with that. You see, I didn't actually sleep at the hotel that night. I just left my bag there in the morning before I went to see my customers."

Abu Ahad sat forward in his chair and rested his arms on the desk. He no longer looked like someone chatting to a friend, his face had become closed and official.

"Where were you that night, then?" The question was put quite quietly, the voice almost expressionless. Abu Rustum looked up at him, startled by his change in manner.

"I was in Aleppo," he said. Then he looked down at his hands and hurried on, "I was in the Hamdaniya. I was with my other wife."

"What!" Abu Ahad almost shouted. "What other wife?" Then he collected himself together and continued more

75

quietly, "Would you like to tell me all about this, right from the beginning?"

"I suppose I'd better. It's a bit of a surprise, I know. Do you mind if I smoke?" Abu Ahad motioned him to go ahead, but refused a cigarette himself. Abu Rustum lit his own with hands that shook a little, then drew deeply on it, settled into the chair again, and began, "You know Im Rustum and I only have Rustum? Well, he's a wonderful son, never been a moment's trouble, but he's always been closer to his mother than to me. He's always been more hers, if you know what I mean. And she never wanted any more. I wanted three or four, but she doesn't – didn't – like the mess they made, and she said she wasn't strong enough to keep on having children. She doesn't – didn't care very much for Rustum's little Omar to come and visit us a lot, now he can crawl around. She always said that foreign wives don't know how to bring up children properly, but he looks all right to me.

Anyway, about ten years ago it was really getting me down, and I married my foreman's niece. She'd been having a bad time - she'd just left her husband and she didn't have any children. Muna never knew anything about it because we just went to the Sheikh, we didn't register the wedding. In Hamdaniya I'm known as Abu Mohammed, that's our eldest, so people just don't connect me with Abu Rustum."

"But didn't she hear from the foreman?" asked Abu Ahad, by now fascinated by the tale.

"Not Muna. She's not interested in people like workers. They just don't come into her life. I don't suppose she would recognize the foreman if he spoke to her." He paused, and then added, "I don't suppose he would want to speak to her, either."

"Do you have any children by that wife? What's her name, by the way?"

"Her name's Fatmi, and yes, we do. We have five now and there's another due in the summer."

Abu Ahad sat back and stared at him, open-mouthed, for a second or two. Then he thought of another side to the question.

"My goodness, business must be good to keep a wife and five children as well as Im Rustum."

"I wish it were," Answered Abu Rustum. "You know how expensive life is now. It was all right at first, but it hasn't been too easy for the last year or two. Have you any idea how much they eat, and how fast they can get through shoes? Rustum was never like that. They're always playing football in the street or in the park with the other kids. Their mother is a wonderful manager and she doesn't waste a thing, but I sometimes wonder where all the money goes."

Abu Ahad smiled, and nodded sympathetically, amused to find Abu Rustum, whose elegant life had always seemed so far above such mundane details, was coping with the same problems as the rest of the human race. Then he said, very mildly,

"It must have been irritating to see Im Rustum with so much money when you were having trouble managing."

At first Abu Rustum answered quite casually:

"Oh, no. Not really. It's like two separate lives in a way. They don't connect with each other, they're so different, for one thing. Can you imagine Muna washing the floors herself? Fatmi really likes it – doesn't want anyone to help her." He smiled at the thought, seemingly completely relaxed and at his ease now that the confession of his double life was made. Then his face changed again, and he said :"Wait a minute, what are you thinking? I don't want her dead, if that's what you mean. We were quite happy and I loved her, I certainly didn't want her dead. I don't know what I'm going to do without her." His face had lost its grey, shocked look, he was flushed and angry now and he sat up and banged on the table with the flat of his hand and shouted, "Get that idea right out of your head. I didn't want her dead and I didn't kill her." He subsided into his chair again and added, "What sort of a friend are you, anyway?"

Abu Ahad sat watching him with an impassive, official expression on his face to hide the confusion of surprise, worry and suspicion that was flooding his thoughts. He answered, still in a quiet, professional voice to calm the other man down,

"I don't think anything yet, because I don't know anything. When you are ready we'll have the policeman back in to take the rest of your statement, and then we'll go ahead and check in the same way we'll check every other statement from every person we can find who knew her, until we find the person who did kill her." His voice rose as he added, "Do you really think I want to believe you could do such a disgusting thing, when we've been friends since Grade Three?"

78

Listening to him, Abu Rustum calmed down. The high colour seeped from his face and he sat hunched in the chair, the fist of one hand thumping into the palm of the other.

"Yes, I do understand. You're right. I'm sorry." So Abu Ahad rang the bell on his desk and recalled the constable to take the rest of the statement. This was to the effect that Abu Rustum had spent the night of the murder in the Hamdaniya with his second wife, and had travelled to Damascus early on the Saturday.

At the end of the statement the policeman left the room to have it typed out and Abu Ahad took the opportunity to explain that nobody could live in the flat for the time being. Abu Rustum could quite see that, but asked if he could pick up some clothes, and Abu Ahad readily agreed to this seeing no harm in it, and feeling it might be a way to approach a return to their old, easy friendship. He also agreed to say nothing to Rustum about his father's other life. He wouldn't have done so in any case, it wasn't his business, but he privately thought that Abu Rustum would need to be extremely lucky to keep his secret   much longer.

The question of the funeral had to be settled as well. It is part of the Islamic tradition that the dead are buried the same day, so it was unpleasant to have to say that the funeral must wait on the autopsy. However this was already in progress, and the doctor who had first examined the body had given Abu Ahad his private opinion that it was, as it looked, a simple strangling. If so, there was every chance that the body would be released by Tuesday, in time to be buried then.

Abu Rustum reminded the Colonel that Rustum was still outside waiting to be interviewed, and he thought it would be a kindness to the young man to finish with him as soon as possible.

"It has been even worse for him than for me, poor boy. Finding the body like that has upset him very badly, it was a horrible thing to happen to him."

"Finding bodies is never particularly nice"responded Abu Ahad, trying not to think about this one. "I'll see him straight away, while the whole thing is still fresh in his mind."

A few minutes later it was the son sitting opposite Abu Ahad in place of the father. Rustum was dressed, as usual, carefully and precisely from his city suit, with toning tie, to his well-shined black shoes. His face, however, did not match the rest of the picture, it was puffy and the eyes red-rimmed, as if he had cried a lot and slept very little. That, together with his hunched-up attitude in the chair, made Abu Ahad feel that he had seldom seen anyone so obviously and genuinely unhappy. He thought the best thing to do would be to get straight on with the questions so the man could get home again.

He started with the routine name, address, identity card, business etc., and continued:

"When did you last see your mother?"

"On Thursday. We went over after lunch and had coffee with her and my father. We stayed for about an hour, then we had to go home because it was time for Omar to have his sleep. My wife likes to keep to a routine for him, she's fussy about things like that. Then I talked to her on Friday afternoon, after my father had left, and she told me about the jewellery she had bought. I couldn't get over to her because Friday is my busy day. That's why I take my holiday on Sunday, although Mama always blamed that on having a foreign wife." A faint smile crossed his face at the memory.

"What is your job?"

"You know what I do. Oh, sorry, this is for the record, isn't it?" He sat up and straightened his tie, then started formally: "I import crystal chandeliers. I get them from Italy and Bohemia and I sell them here through shops in the city. They're very popular at the moment with all the big new apartments being built."

"How did you get started?

"It was around eight years ago, when I graduated. I wasn't really interested in going into the factory with my father, there isn't enough work for two of us, so my mother put up the money to get me started. Her cousin in Damascus introduced me to the people I needed to give me import licences and I was in business. It was quite straightforward to begin with, and I made enough money so that when I met Ross on one of my trips to Europe we were able to get married almost immediately. This last year hasn't been too good though, everyone is being a lot more careful with their money than they used to be. Still, I expect it is just a bad patch and we'll soon be over it – I hope so, at least."

Abu Ahad put his next question quietly:

"Where were you on Friday night?" Rustum looked up to protest, then shrugged his shoulders and replied,

81

"Yes, of course you have to ask me. I was with Ross visiting my cousin until about eleven, then we went home and I was there until nine on Saturday morning, as usual."

"How much did you know about the jewellery?"

"I knew she wanted to buy a big piece – she always says it keeps its value better, and she likes - liked jewellery a lot, but I didn't know exactly what it was. She told me on the phone on Friday that she had bought it. I know she got it from the same man who sold her a ring that was a present for my wife when Omar was born. She wanted us to go round then to see it, but we were busy so we put it off."

Abu Ahad cleared his throat, took a sip of water and returned to the questions:

"How is your business doing now? Most people are finding things a lot more difficult these days."

Rustum responded at once,

"You're right. It isn't as easy as it used to be. In fact I was hoping to talk to my mother about money for a new car. She always took an interest in the business and I need a reliable car to get around."

"Never mind," said Abu Ahad callously. "You'll get half of all her money now, all in one lump. It should be enough to tide you over."

Rustum stared at him, an open, surprised look on his face.

"Yes, I suppose you're right." Then he stopped, and continued quietly, "But I'd much rather have had my mother."

Abu Ahad let a few moments pass before standing up to indicate that the interview was over. The policeman in the corner shut his notebook with a sigh as they said their goodbyes, and Abu Ahad told Rustum that he must stay in Aleppo for the time being. When Rustum walked out of the office Abu Ahad noticed how much less cast-down he looked than when he had come in, even his step was firmer . 'Powerful stuff, money,' he thought to himself, cynically.

The police arrived at Selwa's flat at eleven and found her at home with Mahmoud, who happened to have no lessons that morning. Like everyone else in the neighbourhood, they had heard about the murder. It was a mystery how news like that got out, it was never on the television and seldom in the newspapers, but everyone always knew some version of the story – usually a more exciting one than the truth.

Mahmoud was inclined to be argumentative with the young police lieutenant who had been sent for his mother.

"Can't you leave her alone? Hasn't she had enough of a shock with that stupid rich friend of hers getting herself killed? Now you want all the neighbours to be talking about her being taken away in a police car!"

The lieutenant tried to be calm but firm when he answered that the colonel had sent the car merely to save Madame Selwa trouble, that the interview would not take long but must be done, and that Madame Selwa would be back home in no time. While he was explaining, Selwa was putting on her coat and adjusting her scarf – she had covered her head in public since her husband died – so Mahmoud had no choice but to give in. However he insisted on going with his mother, which was easy to agree to, as the lieutenant would have done the same in the circumstance. Men in Syria don't usually take kindly to their womenfolk getting involved with police stations unchaperoned, so they all piled into the police car, and a few minutes later were at the station .

Abu Ahad greeted her kindly when she entered his office, prompted partly by the way she looked so old and ill with shock. He ordered glasses of tea all round and chatted of this and that until it arrived. When they had all three been served, he overrode the younger man's objections and insisted that Mahmoud should drink his in the corridor so that he could question Selwa without interference.

Without her son to distract her, she took a few moments to put her neat bag and gloves on the desk, and timidly to readjust her scarf, then Abu Ahad motioned to her glass of tea and helped her to sugar.

"Thank you so much, Colonel," she whispered at him, both voice and hands shaking a little, "It's been such a shock to me, such a dreadful shock. Mahmoud doesn't mean any harm, he's shocked too, really. Of course he never liked her, but even so he's almost as shocked as I am, that's what's making him so cross."

"I quite understand, Madame Selwa." The Colonel's voice was at its most soothing and fatherly. "It's a horrible thing to happen to anyone, especially to a friend. Had you been friends for long?"

She sipped her tea, and when she spoke again her voice had steadied. "We've been friends since High School. We were always neighbours, but her father was richer than mine so she went to a private school when she was small.

From High School on we've been friends, and now this…"
Her voice wavered again, and Abu Ahad made comforting
noises and waited for her to steady herself, which she soon
did.

"We both married about the same time. She had a very
grand wedding of course, and Abu Rustum is a nice man,
but they only ever had Rustum. We had four altogether, the
three girls and Mahmoud, before Abu Mahmoud was taken
away from me, God rest his soul. But we managed very
nicely, and all the girls have good husbands, thank God."
Here she stopped, sipped her tea then got out a packet of
cigarettes. "Do you mind if I smoke? Do have one. No? Oh,
as you wish. Where was I? Ah, yes." She found her lighter,
applied it to her cigarette and continued, between puffs; "I
was always sorry for her with only the one, but Abu
Mahmoud wouldn't have it. He said that she couldn't do
with the mess of one, so how could she manage four, like
me. I must say he might have been right at that, because she
didn't really like the new baby very much. A dear little
thing, but the sort that gets into everything, you know". She
looked at him briefly and he nodded, he did know.

He decided it was time to interrupt the nervous flow of
words, so he asked:

"When did you last see Madame Muna?"

"When we went shopping on Friday morning. Not a
convenient day for me, being the holiday and the girls
usually drop in with their children. But Muna couldn't wait,
and she said they'd appreciate me more if I wasn't always
there waiting for them. I don't know. Anyway we had such a

85

nice morning, first the jeweller, then coffee at that place by the park, you know it?"

He did, it was very successfully catering for the middle-class female market by providing coffee, cakes and ice cream in a pleasant, respectable setting, and with no alcohol on the premises. His wife was very fond of the place too, and he had often wished he had shares in it.

The woman in front of him intrigued him. The general impression she made was of a flustered hen, continually moving her hands, waving her cigarette and moving around in her chair as the words came tumbling out. The almost-hidden hairdo, the respectable scarf, the well-cut coat and the polished shoes were the standard model for a woman of her age and class, but the defensive way she sat in the chair, the timid eyes and the nervousness were individual. Abu Ahad wondered if she was always like this, and tried to see this mouse-like female as the close friend of the cool, composed Im Rustum.

He was about to continue his questioning when he was interrupted by a peremptory knock on the door, followed immediately by the appearance of Mahmoud.

"Mother, are you all right? Are they being polite to you?" He glared at the Colonel and at the spectacled elderly sergeant whose turn it was to sit in the corner of the office, taking notes. The Colonel banged the bell on his desk angrily, and a policeman rushed in, unused to such a violent summons. The Colonel addressed him coldly ,

"Policeman, show this gentleman back to his chair in the corridor, and explain to him that I am not in the habit of permitting interruptions during interviews."

86

Mahmoud still stood there looking defiant, but his mother smiled up at him as he stood over her protectively, and said:

"Oh, Mahmoud, it is good of you to worry about me, but really you needn't. The Major is so kind and I'm glad to tell him anything that will help to catch the beast who killed poor Muna. Do be patient and wait outside for me – or if you like you can go home. Don't you have to be at school today?"

Deflated, the young man stepped back and walked to the door.

"Don't be silly, Mother. Of course I'll wait for you. I'll be outside the door." As he left the room he was further annoyed to hear his mother saying confidentially to the Colonel,

"You mustn't be cross with him. I'm such a worry to him now his father is dead. He feels so responsible, and these are such hard times for young men who have to get a start in life with nothing but their salaries."

Abu Ahad made sympathetic noises, took a sip of his tepid tea, and returned to the attack.

"You were saying, Madame, about going for a coffee after buying the jewellery?"

"Yes, yes. Where was I? I remember. We had coffee, but that was all, because we are both watching our weight. Oh dear, there'll be nobody to diet with me any more now." She turned from gazing into the air as she counted off the events on her fingers and looked across the desk at him. Her eyes had filled with tears and her face was lined, pink and crumpled. He thought it better to get on with the questions, and did so, ignoring her distress.

"Did Madame Muna take the jewellery out in the café?"

"No. Oh no. That wouldn't be very sensible, would it? Anyone might see it. She kept it in her bag, but of course we talked about it. She told me about the dress she's – she was," she corrected herself clumsily, "going to wear it with at the reception for baby Omar's first birthday next week - that's her grandson, you know. I suppose that's off, too, now. Well, it would have to be wouldn't it? We were in the café when she said she would bring it to the coffee morning at my house yesterday. We've all been friends pretty well since school and everyone wanted to see it."

He asked if there had been many people in the café, anyone she had noticed nearby, but all she remembered was that it hadn't been especially crowded and she hadn't been sitting near anybody who looked at all dangerous. Abu Ahad was tempted to ask her what a dangerous person looked like, but refrained for lack of time.

"After that we went home in taxis. We had to hurry because it was nearly lunch time. We heard the call for Friday prayers while we were having coffee. I had cooked the green beans before I went out, but the rice wasn't done, and Mahmoud had to be out early for a football match." She seemed to have finished, run down like a clockwork toy, and the sergeant rested his pencil on the desk with a quiet sigh of relief. Abu Ahad waited a moment, and then asked:

"Can you think of anything else? Perhaps someone who followed you?"

"No," she said. "Nothing like that. Oh!" She put her hand to her mouth, "I forgot to tell you. When we left the café we met a man selling lottery tickets and we bought one each. Muna said it felt like her lucky day." Again she seemed about to burst into tears, but she dabbed at her eyes with her handkerchief, muttered "Poor Muna!" to herself and continued bravely: "I like to have one when I remember. You never know, do you? It might be lucky, I won 500 lires once."

Abu Ahad had been slumping further and further down in his chair during this recital, his chin resting on his hand and his elbow supported on the wooden arm of this chair. At the last words he hauled himself up in his chair again, and said sharply:

"Do you have the ticket with you?"

"I'm sorry, no, I don't. It's in my dressing table drawer. I was going to ask Muna over to watch the lottery, it's on Tuesday, you know. Do you ever have a ticket?"

Abu Ahad smiled,

"I used to, but I never won anything so I gave up." He stopped and thought for a minute. He hadn't seen a ticket, but the house hadn't been searched properly yet. Whoever did the searching had better look out for it, just to tidy up the loose ends. "You can't by any chance remember the number, can you?" She thought about it, and then said:

"No, I can't be sure now, but if I go and look at my own I'll remember because it's the number after Muna's."

'It would be,' thought Abu Ahad, but he didn't say it. Instead, he took the earring from the locked drawer where he had been keeping it, placed it on the desk and carefully unfolded it from its wrapping without touching it. He didn't actually hope for much in the way of fingerprints, but was taking no chances.

As soon as she saw the earring, Selwa exclaimed in surprise and identified it as part of the set her friend had bought. Abu Ahad had been pretty sure of this anyway, but it was satisfying to have it confirmed. At this stage in the proceedings, anything which could be fixed was a help in clearing away the muddle.

The only questions left were soon asked,

"Do you remember what Madame Muna was wearing that morning?" Selwa wrinkled her forehead as she thought about it.

"Yes, I do. She was wearing her dark blue dress with the black buttons and the shawl collar. She had her fur coat on, and black shoes and gloves with her black bag. She didn't wear a scarf, though."

"And where were you on Friday night?"

"I was at home. The girls all came to see me with their families in the afternoon and I was very tired. Mahmoud was out with his friends so I watched a bit of television – there was one of those nice old Egyptian films on – then I went to sleep early."

"Thank you so much, Madame Selwa. You have been most helpful and we are very grateful."

"It's nothing," fluttered Selwa as she began to assemble gloves and bag. "If only you can find out who killed Muna."

"I'm sure we will. Don't you worry yourself about it. I'll get someone to run you home with your son. If you can remember anything else, just phone and ask for me". He

90

shepherded her to the door, and sent a policeman with her and Mahmoud to arrange a lift home for them. Mahmoud would also have to be interviewed, but he could see it as being a possibly stormy affair so he wanted to conduct that meeting without Selwa around.

The same Sunday morning the rubbish collector and the maid had each arrived at the flat at their usual times. The maid was rather scared about her unofficial holiday, since she did not enjoy the experience when she received the rough edge of Im Rustum's tongue. They were, one after the other, totally astonished to have the door opened by a policeman, and to be informed that there had been a murder and to be asked for their names, addresses and identity cards.

That was all that Abu Ahad had wanted said, but it so happened that the rubbish collector was a distant relation of the policeman, so it was only natural and reasonable that they should settle down on the front step of the flat and discuss the whole business from every possible angle over a cigarette. The rubbish collector then left, and he had barely had time to push his malodorous trolley round the corner when the maid arrived. She was so overcome at the news that she sat down on the top step and wailed – the policeman thought it was horror rather than grief so he didn't bother to fetch her a glass of water.

"Don't worry, Hadji, we'll find out who did it. The Colonel's working very hard on it."

She turned towards him. Her broad face had broken veins covering the heavy cheeks, and was now covered in easy tears. Then, leaning on his knee a wide hand, distorted and roughened by years of scrubbing floors, she said:

"Mind you, she was asking for it. Too rich by half and always some new bit of gold for herself. Do you think she ever gave me anything? Not so much as a bag of sugar or an old dress. And who's going to pay my wages?" The last came out on a higher, wavering note. A whole month's wages were more than she could afford to lose. The policeman was sympathetic, and suggested that she should ask Abu Rustum about that, which cheered her up. In the end she heaved herself off the step quite jauntily, and went to Rustum's house to offer her condolences and see about her pay.

Detective Captain Samir arrived at half past nine with a junior officer in tow, and took down the names and addresses of the rubbish collector and the cleaner. Then he strode off down the stairs to interview the neighbours, glad to have the chance of discovering evidence in what looked as if it was going to be an important murder case, before anyone else had 'muddied the water' for him. He was a young man in a hurry to get on, and his opinion of Abu Ahad was as low as it was high of himself, which was saying quite a lot. He prided himself especially on getting evidence from reluctant witnesses, though his shouting, bullying methods meant that his successes were limited to those witnesses who had no influence in the Police department. The Lieutenant with him was new to the Crime Division, and the Detective Captain planned on making this a demonstration of straightforward, effective police work.

In front of the door he smoothed his thick, black hair and his hand passed lovingly over his carefully groomed moustache on its way to straightening his tie. Preparations completed, he gave a sharp ring on the doorbell and followed it with a rat-a-tat-tat on the ornamental brass doorknocker. He stood back, a picture of brisk confidence much admired by the lieutenant, who had not descended the final step from the flat above, but was standing diffidently with his hand on the banister, his new trench coat unbuttoned and his hand-knitted scarf of glorious purple round his neck where his anxious mother had placed it carefully before he left home.

The small window set into the door was opened cautiously, and a thin, rather stupid-looking face appeared at the iron grill.

"Yes?"

"Open up," demanded Detective Captain Samir, in his most official voice, "This is the police, we have some questions to ask."

The response was not what he had planned. The girl's eyes widened, her mouth opened and she emitted the sound most easily written as "Eeeek!" Then she stepped quickly back and slammed the little door shut. They heard the lock turning inside, then the sound of the ubiquitous plastic flip-flops, as worn by the entire population of the country at one time or another, scuffing on the stone floor inside, while a frantic female voice called: "Im Abdul, Im Abdul!"

A little irritated, but not seriously discomposed, Samir turned to his junior and gave a superior smile.

"Women," he said, raising his eyes to heaven before resuming his attack on the door.

For a second time the small window opened, but this time the face that peered through was clearly that of the housewife. Her scarf was securely fastened over every strand of hair and her clothes covered by a long maroon dressing-gown which she kept wrapped over with her left hand while she held open the window with her right. She glared at them angrily.

The detective went back into his police routine of:

"Open the door. This is the police....," but he got no further because the woman opened the window wider, put her face to the iron grill and shouted at him:

"Certainly not! Who are you? How dare you ask me to open the door to a man when my husband isn't here? Would your wife let strange men into the house? And me a Hadji! What wickedness! How rude! Go away." She slammed the window in his face and left him red-faced on the doorstep. Before he had recovered enough to decide what to do, the window opened again and she hissed at him, "In case you were going to try bullying me again, just remember that my uncle is a Member of Parliament and he'll be really annoyed." With which remark she shut the window again, very firmly.

The lieutenant, who had watched the rout with jaw dropped in amazement, was trying not to laugh, but the captain was obviously so furious that he made an enormous effort and presented an impassive face until his boss had calmed down somewhat.

"If she's really a relation of an M.P. perhaps you had better leave her to the Colonel, Sir."

"Well, it's either that or break the door down, I suppose." Samir turned on his heel and walked crossly down the four steps to the main door, wishing he was with the security police who didn't have to put up with indignities like that. As he reached it the ginger cat from upstairs, already getting thin and dirty-looking, rushed past him into the building. In his general irritation at the world he swung out his foot to kick it, muttering "Daughter of sixty dogs!" a favourite local insult. The lieutenant wasn't too sure whether he was referring to the cat or to the housewife. However he was fond of cats himself, so he was glad that the well-polished shoe had not made contact with this one. He followed his mentor to the entrance of the building and they went off up-town to find the maid and the rubbish collector, who were much less likely to have important relatives.

The rubbish collector, by name Abdullah, lived in a very respectable working-class part of the town called Kalassi. This name is related to the word for limestone, and the district has been famous for its stonemasons since before Nebuchadnezzar sent for its workmen to build his palaces. The stonemason's trade was still well represented, but these days the low Arabic houses had largely been replaced by enormous blocks of flats which turned the streets into narrow canyons full of the sounds of motors and horns, street criers, loud music from video shops and the occasional braying donkey. Here people worked desperately to keep their fragile privacy in the tiny flats, and almost all the balconies were surrounded by large pieces of canvas, or anything else that had come available, in every condition of fade and tatter .

Samir quickly regained his poise in these surroundings. He lived in this district and knew its people. More important at the moment, he knew how to track down the rubbish collector in a city where the official names of streets were often unknown to the inhabitants, and most of the addresses were of the order of 'close to the Salem mosque' or 'opposite the Ghazal chemists.'

He blossomed under the admiring gaze of the lieutenant as, about half an hour later, they found Abdullah's house. It was midday and he was just back (early) from his day's work. He happened to open the door himself and invited them straight in. He hospitably sent off one of the children with instructions for glasses of tea while he seated them in the best parlour, on the hard, red satin armchairs and surrounded by enlarged and grainy photographs of defunct relations in ornately carved silver-painted frames. The room was also extremely cold.

The preliminary welcomes and enquiries after mutual acquaintances took some time, helped by Samir's family being long-time residents of the district. Eventually the tea was brought in by a heavily-scarved daughter, and the talk turned to the business in hand. Here Abdullah could not give much help. He had been at home on the night of the murder, with his wife and seven children, and had not noticed anything the next day except that no-one had answered the door, and that was not unusual. Samir was disappointed but not surprised. Abdullah must be physically strong, but the way he walked and sat suggested that years of carrying bins had given him enough rheumatism to discourage him from climbing over balconies. As soon as he could do so, very politely because every detail of the interview would be back to his father by suppertime and there would be trouble if he were accused of rudeness, the Captain nodded to his young companion and they stood up to go.

It was impossible to talk on the way downstairs. They were watched down, as they had been watched up, by children and adults who happened to be on the stairs, and by others who opened their doors to get a better look at the strangers than was afforded by the tiny security eye in each door. On the street, Captain Samir explained why he thought they could rule out Abdullah as both the robber and a source of information while waiting for a taxi, and the younger man tried to look mature and judicious as he nodded in agreement.

There were in 1995 about fourteen thousand taxis in Aleppo – more than in New York - and they are all yellow and very cheap to use. Within a few minutes the two policemen were on their way to the part of the town near the now unoccupied old prison. It was a warren of old Arabic houses, mosques, schools, religious schools and small shops. The main streets had been widened and blocks of flats built, but behind them the jumble of old buildings had been brewing for hundreds of years. Many respectable tradesmen and artisans still lived there – Aleppo people are as attached to their own districts as much as any villager to his village. However a lot of what had been at one time grand houses with fine carving over the doors and beautiful tiled floors were now occupied by groups of families who were sometimes, but not always, inter-related.

One of these houses was the one that they were looking for, and they eventually found the right door, of the ancient type of studded wood set in a blank wall and with a keyhole large enough for a palace key. This was not, however, locked, and they pushed it open and entered a wide courtyard with a dried-up fountain and an elderly lemon tree in the centre. All around were doors which had once led to different parts of the house, but each was now the front door for a complete family. During the day the women had a pleasantly social way of getting on with their work and each other, but the appearance of two men set them hastily tying up their scarves and scurrying to their own doors.

The maid was identified, and was as welcoming, as garrulous and as little help as Abdullah had just been. By no stretch of the imagination could either policeman see her heaving her bulky, rheumaticky body over Im Rustum's balcony. She would have had no way of knowing about the jewellery, of which, in fact, she seemed unaware, and she swore 'on the Holy Koran' that all her sons had been at home that night too, her husband, God rest his soul, having been dead these fifteen years, as was written in her Family Book (a sort of identity document) for anyone to see. The captain was inclined to believe her about her sons on the grounds that her neighbours would be sure to notice anybody moving in or out of the building at night.

Some time later, after they had heard all this and drunk the obligatory cups of tea, they were leaving the building as the husbands, sons and school children were coming home for lunch. Smells of cooking were another indication of time passing, so Captain Samir turned to his assistant, saying,

"Look, there's no point in going back to the station now, everybody is having lunch. You go on home and eat, and so will I, but don't forget to be back at the station for four o'clock. You have to learn to work at this job, no finishing at three o'clock then off home for us."

"Yes sir. Thank you, sir. I'll remember to be on time, sir," from the young man, who was so hungry that he was expecting his stomach to disgrace him by rumbling at any moment. He also knew that his mother was having a big cooking day today, and that was always worth being on time for.

"Don't forget", repeated the Captain, "You must be in my office at four, we have a lot of work still to get through today."

"Yes, sir. No, sir. Thank you, sir." From the policeman, who had already flagged down a service taxi (like an informal bus) and was backing into the street towards it .

Detective Colonel Bassam, otherwise known as Abu Ahad, went to the house of the murder as soon as he had completed the paperwork to do with interviewing Madame Selwa. Even so, it was almost 12.45 before he arrived, bringing with him enough men to search the flat properly. He had an appointment with Abu Rustum for one o'clock, so he could be present when his house was searched, but first he wanted to hear from the men on duty if anything had happened, and perhaps how far the Captain had progressed.

In the event, there was very little to tell. There was nothing at all to report about the night before, in the morning Captain Samir had gone downstairs to track down possible witnesses, and had had something of a problem in taking evidence from the woman who lived there. Neither of the men liked the captain, they had heard every word from the open security window and one of them had the gift of telling a funny story very well. However, out of loyalty to his staff the Colonel discouraged them from giving him more than the outlines of the story even though he would dearly have liked to hear more. He merely remarked that it would be just as well to go back when the husband was there, and she probably knew nothing anyway.

A brew of tea was gently simmering on the cooker, but Abu Ahad declined a glass. He left the men pouring the black fluid into glasses half full of sugar while he wandered about the house, just, as he thought of it, 'smelling the wind'. He was trying to come to it as if it were all strange to him, looking for something – anything – out of true. He wasn't particularly successful, so he was glad when the doorbell rang and he had to turn from 'tuning in to the atmosphere', and occupy himself with the tried and true route of routine enquiries.

Father and son had come together, both looking rather better than they had in the morning. Abu Ahad wondered if Rustum knew about his step-mother and his half-brothers and sisters yet, but it wasn't his business and he had plenty of more important things to think about. After greeting the two men, the colonel got straight down to work with the search team which had arrived a few minutes before. He had already decided to ignore the rooms which had not been disturbed, and to concentrate on the dining room and master bedroom. There was so little in the bathroom that he decided to include it, and the big cupboard near the bedroom door was locked and the key in its proper place in the dressing-table drawer, pointed out by Abu Rustum, so that could be left out, at least for the moment. It didn't interest him too much, as he could discern neat piles of towels and linen through the ripple-glass, far too tidy to have been disturbed.

In the dining room the men started work, looking for any bits of jewellery, the missing lottery ticket, or anything else they might notice. Abu Ahad wasn't hopeful of finding a button from the murderer's jacket, or even a handkerchief with his name on it, but the motions had to be gone through and he was genuinely interested in the lottery ticket. While the fingerprint expert went methodically over the doors and pieces of furniture all the way from the window to the bedroom, the other men examined first the balcony and then the inside of the room. One of the policemen who had been on guard overnight was sent to examine the patch of unused patio below the balcony, but Abu Ahad didn't hope for much. The men worked steadily through the dining room and into the hall, off into the bathroom and then along to the bedroom door, looking under cupboards and behind chairs. There seemed nothing to be found.

The bedroom was a more sensitive area, and Rustum and his father were called in after the preliminary search, which revealed nothing more than the scratches on the dressing-table that Abu Ahad had already seen. However, under the supervision of Abu Rustum, Rustum and two policemen moved one of the wardrobes away from the wall far enough for the colonel and Abu Rustum to get behind it – it was too heavy to move further than necessary. There was a small door, about 2 foot square, in the wall, unnoticeable at first glance as the wallpaper had been carefully matched across it. Abu Rustum explained that there were two keys, the other one should be on his wife's key-ring, and used his own to open the safe. It was three-quarters full of jewellery boxes – some red, black, blue or green leather, and others blue or green velvet. Most were unmarked, clearly bought locally, but one or two carried discreet initials which Abu Ahad recognized as from French or Swiss jewellers.

Abu Rustum wasn't sure exactly what jewellery his wife had possessed, but it seemed to be much as usual and, more importantly, it seemed not to have been disturbed. They replaced the boxes, locked the door and pushed back the wardrobe. Then Rustum showed them where his mother always kept her keys – and there they were, in the second drawer on the right of the dressing-table. Abu Ahad was startled and impressed. He thought wryly that no-one would be able to do that in his own home, his wife seemed to spend hours every day hunting for her keys, and they turned up in the most unlikely places, on top of the refrigerator or on the bathroom shelf.

Finishing in the bedroom took more than an hour, and as soon as possible Rustum left them to it. All the time he had been there the picture of his mother's dead face had haunted him and his own face had grown more and more yellow. Abu Ahad was sorry for him, but did not forget that a fair

102

proportion of the contents of the safe would soon be his. By the look of it, quite an inducement to crime .

After his son had gone, Abu Rustum opened and checked his own wardrobe, which he reckoned was as usual.

"Muna's wardrobe key should be on her ring. Ah, yes. Here it is." He opened the wardrobe door and then stepped back with a shocked expression on his face as a slight flavour of her scent lingering about her clothes wafted out to him. "I can't see anything wrong. You can see she's – she was – very tidy and organized." He gazed at the open wardrobe for a minute, then reached hurriedly for his handkerchief, covered his eyes and turned away. Again Abu George's sympathy was tempered by the thought of that other family in Hamdaniya who would soon be able to stop counting the pennies. He quickly brought Abu Rustum back to business.

"There is one thing I would like to know, old friend, Where would your wife have put a lottery ticket? We know she bought one just after she bought the jewellery, and it can't be very important but I like to have the loose ends tidied up and we can't find it."

"Did she?" Abu Rustum smiled slightly. "That's about the only thing she wasn't reasonable about. I always told her that it was gambling and a good Muslim shouldn't do it, but she wouldn't listen. She bought tickets quite often, then she and Im Mahmoud – Selwa – sat here talking about how they would spend the winnings right through the programme. I don't think they ever won anything, though." He paused,

"Now, where would she put it? The lottery isn't until Tuesday so it should have been put away. It should be in the drawer with her keys, or she might have left it in her handbag, she sometimes forgets things there. Let's see." He stretched up to the shelf at the top of the wardrobe. "The winter handbags at the front, the summer ones at the back in plastic bags. Look, here they are". He pointed to a row of expensive-looking handbags ranged neatly across the shelf.

"Selwa said she had a black bag," offered Abu Ahad, after consulting his little notebook. "Constable, fetch something to stand on. That dressing-table stool will do. Now, Sgt. Ahmed," as the stool was placed at the open wardrobe, "will you get up and pass me the bags that aren't wrapped up? That's right. One at a time."

He was interrupted by a quiet voice at his side .

"Excuse me, sir; I've been over all the surfaces. Here are the identity cards; I've checked the fingerprints on them against the ones in the house. There are only the family ones and one set of big ones, but the big ones are all over the kitchen as well so I think they could be the cleaner."

The fingerprint expert was a slight, neat man with very short brown hair and a carefully clipped line of moustache. He never appeared without a gleaming shirt and tie, and never, ever talked about his private life. Abu Ahad had worked with him for five years and still didn't know if he was married. On the other hand he did know that the man was obsessive about his fingerprints, and that his tidy person concealed an extremely methodical mind. Abu Ahad had never known him to be mistaken. The big prints would have to be checked, of course, but he was resigned to the belief that as far as evidence was concerned they had drawn another blank.

He turned back to Sgt. Ahmed and Abu Rustum, who were diligently checking the bags – first the black ones and then all the other winter ones. There were open handbags along the whole length of the dressing table, and the Sergeant was just stretching into the wardrobe for the last one.

"Any luck, Abu Rustum?"

"No, nothing."

"Never mind. How about trying the coat pockets?"

"I don't think she would, but – yes, why not?" Abu Rustum transferred his attention to the coats in the wardrobe while Sergeant Ahmed climbed heavily down and watched him, his hands on his hips.

There was no sign of the lottery ticket in the coats and they couldn't think of anywhere else to look, so they put the handbags back tidily and left. Abu Ahad locked the door of the bedroom carefully and dropped the key back into his pocket, and then he joined Abu Rustum and the small group of policemen at the front door. He was disturbed about the lottery ticket, and even more disturbed that the most probable people to have done the murder were the husband and the son – and they were both people he knew too well to be dispassionate about.

It was way past the two o'clock lunchtime his wife always hoped he would be home for, and he had to be back at the station by four thirty at the latest because the General who was in charge of the station had called a meeting, to be put in touch with progress. He should have gone straight back there to check over his notes, but the plaintive tone in his driver's voice when he said, "You'll be wanting to go home, sir, will you?" reminded him that he wasn't the only one who needed his lunch, and he hadn't the heart to contradict him.

He felt better as soon as he stepped through his own front door. The small folding-table was set up for him by the oil stove in the living room, and his dinner was on top of the stove keeping hot. His wife heard him and came through the archway from the dining room, clucking that he must be dying of hunger and hoping that the food was not all dried up. She saw him settled to his lunch and went back to the dining table where his four children were sitting, doing their various forms of homework. From Ahad, now in his first year at university, right down to Naji in third – or was it fourth? - grade who was being coached by his mother for a history test.

He wondered briefly if Im Rustum had ever bent her sleek, dark, well-coiffed head over Rustum's books, and found it hard to visualize. It must have happened, though, because she was very correct and that was an important part of a housewife's job. Mind you, he knew from complaining colleagues whose wives would not, or in some cases could not, do the job, how lucky he was that Im Ahad took all the work on herself; she left him free to be a busy policeman every day and a proud father when the school reports arrived. He looked fondly through the archway where he could see her back, now comfortably chubby, and the back of her head with her hair getting more and more ruffled as Naji struggled through his history.

In the reassuring atmosphere of home, a quick cup of coffee after lunch and fifteen minutes snooze on the sofa saw him fresh and ready to go when the driver returned to fetch him.

Sunday Afternoon

The old police station had no rooms that could be called pleasant, but the General's room was large and clean, and the oil stove was big enough to heat it. There was a tired-looking suite of armchairs in brown tweed grouped round the big desk, which was adorned with an intricately carved piece of wood inscribed "Police General Malik al Azrak" – presumably a present from a relation or a grateful client.

At the other end of the room four men were seated around a scratched table. They were the General himself, Abu Ahad, Captain Samir and Lieutenant Ahmed. The meeting had started at five o'clock when the General had arrived back from another meeting, and by half past five any casual observer could have seen that it was not going too well. They were all sitting back in their chairs looking glum, cigarette smoke filled the air and the table was littered with papers and empty tea glasses .

The General was nearly at the end of his term in Aleppo before being moved on, he hoped, to Damascus, so he was more than usually anxious to get a quick result. He had learned from experience that Abu Ahad was reliable, so it was not aggressively that he asked;

"Are you certain that we can't arrest the husband and the son together? If we charge them both, one of them is sure to admit it. In God's name, who else could it have been?"

Abu Ahad was worried. "I see what you mean and I suppose you're right, but I'd rather wait a bit longer. After all, it only happened less than forty eight hours ago...." He stopped, aware that it sounded lame.

"Excuse me, sir," from Captain Samir, "Can I raise two points?"

"Go on"

"First, there is still the neighbour downstairs to be interviewed. The husband was away this morning so I decided not to disturb the wife." He ignored the astonished expression on Lt. Ahmed's face and continued, "By now the man will be there and they can be questioned properly. Secondly," he continued, "perhaps the colonel would prefer the idea of taking the two men in as suspects if someone else were to do it. It is embarrassing for him to have to arrest his friends, I can see that." He sat back with a satisfied smile on his face, and at that moment Abu Ahad would gladly have committed murder himself. Instead he answered the General's enquiring look with a quick nod of the head and looked away.

"It's no good, Abu Ahad; we'll have to bring them in. I'll put someone else onto this case and they can do it."

"Sir! No! I'd prefer to stay just until they are brought in. The least I can do is tell them myself. I suppose we'd better get on with it." As he began to stand up he looked at the general, who shook his head, amswering,

"I don't think so. Don't worry, I'll send someone diplomatic to bring them in without a fuss. There's just one thing I need you to do now. That's to interview those downstairs neighbours. They know your face so you may

108

get a bit more cooperation from them." This was said with a straight face, but Lt. Ahmed wondered how much his boss knew about the morning's fiasco, and still more did he wonder how he knew it. "Oh, and before I forget, can you let me have the ear ring and the receipt for the money you were talking about, and anything else you have collected. Send them to me with all your notes".

Correctly interpreting this as a dismissal, Abu Ahad was left with no choice but to salute, say "Yes, sir," and leave the room. The trouble was that in his own mind he wasn't sure enough of his friends' innocence to be able to fight very hard for them. He had a gut feeling that they hadn't worked together so one of them must be innocent, but he couldn't swear to more than that. Oh well, it was out of his hands now.

His last job, before formally resigning the case and returning to the mounds of paper about other matters which had already piled up on his desk, was to go and see Im Rustum's downstairs neighbours. Six o'clock in the evening was a good time to do it. He would catch the husband after his siesta and the wife would almost certainly also be at home. Accordingly, he went there with his driver as soon as he had sent to the General everything he could find relevant to the case.

When he returned to Exhibition Street – probably for the last time, he thought gloomily – it was already quite dark, and now it was raining as well as cold. They hurried to the building and rang the ground-floor bell, hoping it would be answered quickly. A child answered the bell and the buzzer on the door sounded to let them in to the building and, as they approached the door of the flat, the boy they had seen the night before opened the security window, so Abu Ahad explained who they were and asked politely asked to see his parents. The family was obviously expecting them, for the father, now fully dressed, came up behind the boy, opened the door and welcomed them into the front parlour. This room, overfilled with heavily carved furniture and framed photos of dead relations, was only a degree or two warmer than outside, but at least it was dry. They sat down and gratefully accepted the offer of coffee.

The husband identified himself as Hassan Abdul, and automatically reached into the breast pocket of his shirt to show his identity card, which was as automatically checked.

Yes, they had heard about the murder. No, they had not heard anything strange. At this point two children could be heard fighting in the passage outside the door, and it was clear that almost anything could have happened upstairs without being heard. Then the wife brought the coffee in, served the visitors and sat down on the edge of one of the chairs, nervously touching the front edge of her scarf with capable, work-roughened hands to check that her hair was hidden. She confirmed that they had been at home on the Friday night, and that the oldest of their six children was not quite fourteen years old "and doing very well at school." She was unable to tell them much about Muna.

"She didn't like us being here, we aren't her sort of people. When she saw me she said hello, but not in a way you like to hear, looking down her nose. Abu Rustum is nice though, always so polite and helpful, and Rustum is all right too, but he's always rushing around. It must have been

110

a shock to his mother when he married that foreigner – all short skirts and blonde hair. She could have picked almost anyone for him, but the boy went his own way, just like his father," she finished spitefully. Abu Ahad let the last remark slide over him, but noted that Abu Rustum's second marriage was not the secret he thought, even if Muna had never known about it.

It seemed that these people were unlikely to have any connection with the affair. They could account for their time between home and Hassan's work, and their children were too young to have been involved. For form's sake Abu Ahad had them called in and asked them if they had seen anything, but they were much too helpful, offering the sight of the butcher's boy and a man in a funny hat, to be hiding more than the usual childish secrets.

Monday

Monday was not a good day for Abu Ahad, but it was a much worse day for Rustum and his father .

Abu Ahad was relieved to have been taken off this case. He had been far more upset at finding the body of Im Rustum than if she had been a stranger, and his suspicion that either Rustum, whom he had seen growing up, or (and more likely) Abu Rustum with whom he had been at school, had done the deed made it difficult for him to be objective. The only thing he could do now was to make sure that both men were treated with respect at the station, and that they were supplied with tea, coffee and, for Abu Rustum, cigarettes.

The two men had both been horrified to be arrested on the Sunday evening. They had spent the night in a cell in the police station, where Rustum had refused to accept the idea, which Abu Rustum saw as inevitable, that he was a suspect just because he stood to inherit so much.

The next morning they were questioned by Captain Samir, supervised at times by the General himself. The Captain was not violent, but he tended to try to browbeat witnesses at the best of times. He was also scathing in his attitude towards Rustum, whom he saw as a spoilt rich boy who had never had to work for anything. In the course of the questioning he managed to make sure that Rustum learned about his father's other wife, and about his own five half-sisters and brothers, and felt a degree of pleasure at the shock and disbelief he saw in the other's face. Abu Rustum had known that the story would come out as soon as he realised that he and his son were suspects, however the worst part of the day for him was when he and his son were together for a time, but Rustum would not look at him.

After several hours of questioning, alone and together, the General decided that there were no reasonable grounds to keep them. There was no direct evidence against them, and they were too well-connected to be treated lightly, so he sent them home with orders to report to the police station every morning, and left them to sort their personal problems out. Before they left the station they had to give in their Identity Cards, taking receipts stamped at the station in their place. It is not advisable to travel without these cards in Syria, in fact it is impossible to use inter-city public transport without them, and so they were effectively confined to Aleppo.

Ross, dealing with an extraordinary situation in a country far from her Surrey family, had made sure that both Rustum and his father had legal help, and was totally sure that Rustum could never be violent, but even so it was a great relief to have him back unharmed. He was so distraught that it was some time before Ross could get any sense out of him. He came into the flat, wrapped his arms around her and leaned his head thankfully on her shoulder. She could feel how cold he was, and that his whole body was trembling so she hurried him into the living room and called for the maid to put the kettle on. She had never seen her cheerful, sociable husband like this, and it was frightening. She placed a blanket over his knees and left him with little Omar climbing on him, saying, "Poor Daddy. Cuddle".

A tea-glass of hot herbal tea, the woolly blanket and the sympathy of wife and son did a lot to restore Rustum's balance. Neither adult wanted to talk about Im Rustum in front of the little boy, but Rustum could not resist telling his wife about his father's other family. Even that, horrifying as it had been at first, when told to his wife soon became embarrassing rather than a reason to cast off his father for ever.

When she finally understood the story of Abu Rustum's other family she was shocked too, but much more interested and even amused. She had always seen Abu Rustum as part of the backdrop to Rustum and his mother, but after two and a half years it was still a new country and a new culture for her so she was prepared not to judge too quickly. This was helped by the feeling she had always picked up from her mother-in-law that Rustum had married beneath him and his wife was only just passable.

She passed her hand over her well-groomed hair and looked round her prettily-furnished room. 'Well', she thought, 'I am not the only one who thinks she wasn't an angel.' That thought was too catty to entertain for long, and she returned her attention to Rustum, who was a much healthier colour again. Clearly it was much too soon to ask about a new car, but there was no harm in making discreet enquiries, also, by summertime it would be perfectly correct for them to take a really nice holiday. It was comforting to think that the police had a much better case against the father than the son.

Abu Rustum was greeted by his family in the Hamdaniya with shouts, kisses and hugs from his children, while his wife there was affronted that anyone could imagine he would do such a thing. Nor could she understand his distress at Rustum's reaction, only feeling that it was about time he knew, and he would soon get used to it.

While she finished cooking the lunch and set the table she was wondering how soon there would be some extra money, because she was well aware that Im Rustum had been far richer than her husband. Would they get the house? Or would that go to the son? She promised herself that when the money did come she would take the children on a shopping spree, and would buy the most expensive clothes she would find for them. During lunch she made the children sit and eat quietly because their father was upset, but her own head was full of exciting plans for the future.

The two wives in different parts of Aleppo were quite prepared to accept the new reality and enjoy the advantages it could bring so they each slept well, though neither of the husbands slept much that night.

Tuesday

The lottery always takes place on Tuesdays on a special television programme at seven thirty. This Tuesday, Selwa settled herself on the settee in plenty of time with her ticket, a cigarette and a cup of coffee. However, as the programme was introduced and the usual five children began to spin the wheels, each of which would show one digit, she was overcome with tears that Muna wouldn't ever be there again to check her own ticket. She had to get up to find the box of paper tissues and missed the one and two digit numbers that won their holders small prizes, but she was safely back in her seat for the larger prizes.

The number of wheels being spun each time increased steadily, and the prizes went up accordingly. 500, 1,000, 5,000, 10,000, 25,000 lires. Selwa became engrossed in the programme, busily checking her ticket, puffing at her cigarette, sipping her coffee and occasionally wiping her eyes with a tissue as she watched. The previous two numbers had been for 50,000 and 100,000 lires – not enormous prizes but not to be sneezed at. The children took their places and pulled the back of the wheels for almost the last time, the wheels went spinning round and the numbers clicked past the window on the front of each wheel. Selwa leaned forward and watched intently as the wheels slowed, then one by one hesitated and stopped. The final digits began to appear, 2-7--, so far it could be hers. Another number appeared, 2-75-, surely this time it was possible. 2375-, only one number to go and her ticket still had a chance. Then she screamed and knocked her coffee cup over as the last number slotted into place – 23753 – hers was 23754 and Muna's ticket had won. The shock left her shaking and breathless, far too upset either to watch the last number for the biggest prize or to switch the television off.

Mahmoud came in a few minutes later and found her still on the settee, tears streaming unchecked down her face and her coffee spilled on the carpet. He rushed over to her and put his arms around her. "Mama, Mama, what is it? What has happened? Are you ill?" She reached over to the little table for the box of tissues and sniffed,

"No, dear, it's nothing. It's nothing like that. It's just…" She started crying again but stopped quite soon to continue, "It's Muna's ticket. She won. And she's dead and she doesn't know." She paused and noticed the coffee stain on the floor. "Oh, dear, look at that mess on the carpet. What can I do to get it out? Coffee always leaves a stain. Oh, dear, dear, poor Muna. Think of her winning the lottery at last, and being dead."

She was bending down and fussing over the drying coffee stain on the carpet as she talked, dabbing at it with tissues she was dragging from the box, so she didn't

116

notice Mahmoud straighten up, staring at her. His face was first white, and then red and furious and he interrupted her ramblings with :

"Are you telling me that Sit Muna's ticket won the prize?"

"Yes, dear. Not the main prize, she – it won the 500,000 lire prize. I didn't think to look what number won the first prize. Isn't it sad? She's won the money and she's dead."

"That woman," he exploded, "even when she's dead money comes to her. It's all her fault. If she hadn't been there you'd have bought that ticket and you'd have won."

"In the name of God, what are you talking about?" His mother looked up at him, a truly horrified expression on her plump, tearstained face. "That's got nothing to do with me. Anyway, but for her I'd have been at home cooking lunch and I wouldn't have bought a ticket at all." She pulled another tissue out of the box as her eyes filled with tears again, "It was only last Friday. There hasn't been such a horrible week since your father took ill and died so quickly, God be merciful to him." She sniffed and then she sat up straight, put her hands square on her knees and said, almost fiercely, "And don't you talk about her like that. She was my friend, and now she's dead." She got up, collected the coffee cup and the ash-tray and positively marched to the kitchen, indignation in every line of her back. Mahmoud watched her with his jaw dropped, startled out of his own miseries by what was, as far as he could ever remember, a unique display of temper from his gentle mother.

117

Wednesday

Selwa telephoned the Colonel at his office early on the Wednesday morning to tell him about the winning ticket. She didn't see how it could help but she thought she should tell everything she knew, and also the Colonel had been very kind. When he received the news, Abu Ahad did not trouble her by telling her that he was no longer involved, he just passed the information on to the General.

When that was off Selwa's mind she went back to her cooking and to supervising the cleaner, Rahzia, with the feeling that she had done something useful, which cheered her up so much that she found herself singing quietly as she worked.

At around ten o'clock the doorbell rang, it was the cleaner's boy with the dry cleaning from Saturday. She thanked him and went to take the clothes from him, but he pushed an envelope into her hand first, and he looked so disgustedly at it that she took it, and then the clothes, without a word. She shut the door behind him and took the clothes to lay them carefully over the back of the settee in the living room, which gave her a free hand to turn over the envelope and read the name written on it in pencil. It was addressed to Mahmoud, and when she turned it back again she saw that the flap was partly stuck down. Mystified, she took it to his room and placed it on his desk, but she picked it up and put it down again several times, before leaving it because Rahzia called her.

She didn't forget the strange incident, but household jobs and the presence of Rahzia kept her busy for the morning, and she was so tired when the other woman went home at two o'clock that she had a short snooze on the settee. However she could not settle, too many disturbing things had happened for her to relax, Mahmoud was busy all day and she didn't expect to see him until quite late in the evening. She wandered back into his room and picked up the envelope, realizing that it was not very well sealed; in fact it was only stuck down right at the centre. A few minutes later she had decided that it was her duty as a mother to find out what the problem was, and she slipped her finger under the flap of the envelope and eased it open.

At first there seemed to be nothing inside, but she peered in and saw – a lottery ticket. This was the problem! She knew that the cleaner and his assistant were very strait-laced and surely did not approve of gambling, and she understood now the disgust on the boy's face. She smiled to herself and slid the ticket right out to see if she could remember if it had won anything, and the smile became rigid on her face.

This was Muna's ticket. It was the winning ticket, with the number just before her own. At first she started to cry quietly, but then she panicked, and pushed the dreadful piece of paper back into the envelope, licked the flap to stick it down and abandoned it on Mahmoud's desk, almost running to get out of the room. She went back to the kitchen and started the ironing, blotting out the sight of the numbers on the ticket.

As she worked with her hands at the routine tasks they knew so well, her mind was working away on its own.

She had never been stupid. In school she had always done very well, but like many other girls of her generation she had been carefully trained to be obedient, so few people knew of her intelligence. From babyhood she had been a good little girl for Mama and Baba (Daddy), then for her teachers and eventually for her husband. She found it both natural and agreeable to be told what to do and to be protected like a child. However her brain had insisted on staying alive and disturbing her with occasional flashes of understanding that what she was being required to do was futile or unnecessary, and now it would not stop worrying away at this new problem.

Fortunately the new season's cheese arrived at six o'clock, and she tutted and scolded at the boy for bringing it when she was alone. She had no choice but to struggle and pull the 20kilos of white sheep's cheese, cut into cubes and packed in plastic bags, from the front door to the kitchen. Then she had to place the pieces individually in layers with lots of salt in the large plastic baskets specially kept for the purpose. By the morning most of the water in the cheese would have drained away and she and Rahzia would drop the pieces a few at a time into boiling brine to sterilize them. Then they would flavour them with aromatic seeds and pack them away in the freezer to eat for the rest of the year.

She didn't finish until nearly seven o'clock, when it was time to wash thoroughly before she prayed in her special long skirt and white cotton scarf. Taking them off at the end, she folded them carefully with her little prayer mat, and was left with the evening to live through. There was a tight feeling in her chest as she walked slower and slower through all the rooms, shutting the shutters and the curtains against the night. She could feel herself being pushed towards a terrible idea, and part of her mind was resisting as hard as it could.

The television didn't hold her attention for long - yet another serial where a poor but honest doctor would take twenty six episodes to win his rich but pure bride, whose father was rich but corrupt. The actors seemed to be wearing the faces of the people she was thinking about – her son, her friend, her son's girlfriend – finally she switched it off and sat on the settee with tears rolling down her cheeks yet again. She was more deeply unhappy than she had ever been before in her life.

She sat for a while longer, gazing at the pale flames visible through the small window at the front of the oil heater. Part of her mind was treading the old, accustomed paths – 'Mahmoud is upset. Mahmoud looks sick. He shouldn't be out in the cold'. That part said, 'the world is normal, the fire is warm. Rhazia must sponge over this carpet when she comes tomorrow.'

Meanwhile a horrible, heavy sensation was closing in around her chest and stomach. 'He did it. Mahmoud did it.' At last the words forced themselves in a whisper from her mouth.

"Mahmoud killed Muna!" At that point the pressure of the knowledge overwhelmed her. She rushed to the bathroom and was comprehensively sick.

When she was sure that she had finished she leaned against the cold white tiles of the little bathroom, shaking and quietly crying. Her legs were trembling so much that she let herself slide down to crouch on the icy floor. There she wept almost silently for the horror of her baby boy's metamorphosis into a murderer son, for the years of struggling to manage since her husband's death, and for Muna, who had been her anchor through those lonely years.

Eventually she had no more tears left to cry and she looked around wearily. With difficulty she pulled herself upright against the washbasin, and waited an agonizing few minutes while her left leg pinned and needled itself back to life. Slowly she cleaned up after herself then, stiff and aching, returned to the warm living room. Almost absently she lay down on the sofa and pulled the old quilt over herself, letting its familiar smell of satin cover and cotton stuffing take her from consciousness of her suffering to a few moments of troubled sleep.

It was after ten o'clock when Mahmoud returned to the house, and he went straight to his room to change into his pyjamas. He picked up the envelope on his dressing table and frowned at it, wondering where it had come from. He turned it over and noticed that it had been sealed then opened again, and he opened it up and peered inside. His face went a yellowish colour and he felt sweat all over his cold body when he recognized the lottery ticket inside. He pulled it out with fingers shaking so hard that at first he could not get a grip on it. His legs went weak and he sat down suddenly on the edge of the bed .

The scene in Im Rustum's bedroom came alive before his eyes. The slight smell of perfume in the room. The quiet, careful opening of dressing-table drawers to pick up some of the millions which must be there. The jewellery gleaming slightly in the hall night-light, reflected in the dressing table mirror. The small scraping noise it made when he swept it up, together with the piece of paper underneath it. That had what woken her up, and she sat up and looked at him, saying, "Mahmoud! What's going on! What are you doing?" He had panicked, grabbing a pale belt thing, pulling it frantically from the soft garment it had been on and rushing at her to stop her calling out.

The following few minutes insisted on pushing their way back from the subconscious where he had been struggling to keep them. He had shut his eyes and pulled and pulled despite all the horrible choking noises. He knew it took only a short time to die like that, but it had seemed endless before the sounds stopped and she went limp. After that he had still not been able to open his eyes as he held on ever tighter to make sure she was really dead. When he was quite sure, he dropped her back onto the pillow and then he had to open his eyes to look around for the quilt to cover up the terrible thing she had become. That sight had been coming back to him every night as he tried to sleep.

Now a rush of fury brought his strength back with it. That rich female, with everything she wanted and swimming in money, was going to win in the end. In increasing anger he remembered that when he had finally got home that night, creeping in so as not to wake his always-anxious mother, he had wrapped the jewellery up carefully in an old T-shirt then stuffed it at the back of the cupboard part of his schoolboy desk, still full of old textbooks and notebooks from his college days. The piece of paper he had recognized as a lottery ticket, stuffed back into his pocket and forgotten. Even when he realised his mother had sent the jacket to the cleaner he had only been relieved, until the evening of the lottery itself and the unimaginable bad luck of it being the winning ticket, compounded by his mother remembering the number.

Since he was a little boy, the youngest child and the only son, he had always worked off his temper by shouting and screaming at his mother, and after his father's death there was nobody to stop him. Thus it was natural for him to storm into the kitchen where his mother was now fiddling about nervously, woken by the sound of the front door as he came in, shouting at her that his bad luck was all her fault. However this time he was deeply frightened and that made his anger even less controlled than usual so he did something that he had never done before. He raised his hand and went to hit her, and she was so shocked that she just stood there, so totally miserable that she was no longer crying.

Seeing her face, he did not hit her but changed the blow to a shove to her shoulder. However he was a very strong young man who spent his days teaching and practicing basketball and football. His push was more than enough to knock his small-boned mother off balance. She fell back and the heel of her slipper skidded on the floor, bringing her down with a crash on to the old-fashioned stone-tiled floor. Mahmoud grabbed at her to break her fall, but missed and only succeeded in changing

124

the angle, so that she caught the side of her head on the edge of the raised tiled area under the cooker.

The silence in the kitchen was total, then Mahmoud crouched down over her calling, "Mama, Mama, wake up!" But nothing happened except that, with as little complaint in death as in life, she sighed once and stopped breathing. At this further disaster, Mahmoud sat down beside her on the stone floor and wept his heart out. He was weeping for his mother and for the nightmare that his life had become in the last few days, and for the hopelessness of his position. Before he had had a bleak future in terms of money, but now he had no future in any terms.

After about half an hour he had cried himself calmer, and then as he sat by his mother's body sobbing and shivering on the chilly floor, 'what ifs' started to present themselves. What if he got rid of the body and said she had 'gone to visit her friend in Lebanon'? What if he reported her to the police as a missing person? What if? The most important thing was not to have her body around. He chose not to remember that she had daughters who would soon start looking for her, who had not always believed his stories in the past – they could not imagine that he would kill her!

He got up stiffly and looked down sadly at the quiet body on the floor. She had spent all her life being gentle and meek, she didn't deserve what had happened to her, or what he was going to do. When he reached the sitting room a shivering fit came over him and he reached out his hands to the oil stove to try to get warmer. The kettle was simmering there, but he couldn't face going back into the kitchen to get what he needed to make a hot drink.

Suddenly the telephone rang and he jumped. He really did not want to talk to anyone, but the only way to stop the noise was to answer it. It was a friend of his called Sami, and when he heard Sami's voice a plan sprang, complete and apparently perfect, into his head. Never mind that it would only give him a day or two – the future would have to look after itself. He took a deep breath and tried to make his voice as normal as possible.

"Hello, Sami. How are you? Yes, I'm fine thank you. How is your fiancée? Oh, good."

"Sami, I'm very glad you called, I was just going to call you. I wonder if you can help me. I have to get some olive oil from Afreen tomorrow very early. It's for my mother and my aunt and it's been waiting since the harvest in October. Do you think I could borrow your pick-up truck to fetch it? Thank you. Thank you very much. When do I need it? Well, they really want me to go there very early in the morning. Yes, tomorrow. Is that possible? It would be a great help. Thanks again."

"The only problem is that I've got to leave at six thirty in the morning and I know you sleep late. Would you mind if I take it now? Yes? Great! I'll be around in fifteen minutes. Goodbye."

As soon as he put the phone down he rushed to the bathroom to wash his face and tidy himself up. The yellow look of his face and the dark circles under his eyes shocked him when he looked in the mirror to comb his

126

hair, but he was beginning to feel in control of his life again.

At Sami's house he had to drink coffee and make polite conversation for a short time, but an hour after the telephone conversation he parked the truck outside his own flat, as near to the main door of the building as he could get. Now he only had to wait until everyone was asleep, then he could carry his mother – no, not that, the body - down to the truck. The new reservoir off the Afreen road was about an hour away and would be deserted at night. If he wrapped her – the body – in a sheet and put some stones in it that would be the end of the story. The reservoir was already deep and getting deeper every week as it was steadily filled up by the small River Afreen.

There are many varieties and degrees of religious feeling amongst the people of Aleppo. The man who kept the small laundry and dry-cleaning shop nearest to Selwa's house was an extremely conscientious and also a very rigidly religious person. He had always had a respect for Im Mahmoud, and was disappointed when he found the lottery ticket in her son's pocket. Clearly the young man was living wildly, and it was a pity such a nice lady had to put up with it. When he sent the ticket back it was to embarrass her son, and to remind him that it was very wrong to gamble. He had sent it in a sealed envelope so that the boy's poor mother would not be upset.

Then he started hearing the gossip about the missing lottery ticket, and when it turned out that the murdered woman had actually had a winning ticket it he could no longer avoid hearing about it, however distasteful it was. Various customers told him all they knew about it, and then gossiped between themselves in front of him and his apprentice. He had picked the boy because he felt that this one had the same point of view as he. Thus neither of them took any personal interest in the lottery, but by the end of Wednesday morning they had managed to remember several of the numbers on the ticket, and had convinced themselves that it must have been the one everyone was talking about.

The apprentice was all for rushing to the police at once, but Abu Sayid, his boss, did not want to get mixed up with the police before he had thought about it After his lunch he decided to read some special verses of the Koran before he had his afternoon rest, to help him to decide what action to take, and was rewarded with a dream of blood and disaster worse than he could ever remember. So when he shut the shop late that evening he went straight to the police station.

At first he had difficulty in getting anyone to listen to him, and he was about to give up and go home when a policeman he knew recognised him. This man had views similar to his own on the state of the world and what things were coming to, and often stopped by his shop for a glass of tea if his duties took him in that direction, so he listened carefully to Abu Sayid's story .

Then everything began to happen more quickly. He was taken into a small room by Captain Samir, who spoke scathingly to him until he realised the possible importance of what he was hearing. After that he was seated, given a glass of tea and questioned and questioned until his head was spinning.

What day had the ticket arrived? Was he sure whose jacket it had been in? What was the number of the ticket? Why had he remembered it? How did he know it was important? Where was it now? The questions went round and round, and were repeated in front of the General. In the middle of the questioning his wife phoned him on his mobile, but shrieked and shut the line when he said he was with the police. Around midnight he was thanked and sent home abruptly, and as he left he saw two police cars rushing off, alarms sounding and lights flashing. He hurried home in the rain before anyone could change their minds and want him back.

In the flat, Mahmoud had taken a white sheet and wrapped his mother's body in it in the traditional way, looking at her as little as possible. On a cold, damp winter evening during the week very few people were out of their homes after eleven o'clock and now it was almost midnight. The building seemed quiet and he decided to risk moving the body. Theirs was the flat nearest to the front door of the building so he swung the bundle on to his shoulder and walked boldly out. There was nobody around and he managed to sling it straight into the back of the pick-up truck, although he was upset to see the sheet getting wet and dirty in the small puddle of rain already there. He walked to the front of the truck and got in as calmly as he could, started the engine, and drove away just before the police cars skidded into the street, sirens blaring and lights flashing as if they were making an American police film.

The policemen jumped from the cars and rushed into the building to hammer on the door of Selwa's flat, but got no answer. The neighbour across the passage came to the door and said that both mother and son should be in by now, but could not help in any other way. As it was a ground-floor flat all the windows were protected with heavy iron bars so there was no easy way in. Captain Samir was almost beside himself with frustration, but for the moment all he could do was to leave two policemen on guard and go off to get further instructions from the General.

Meanwhile Mahmoud was beginning to think that his luck had changed as he drove out of the city onto the road that went northwest on the Afreen road and to the reservoir. The rain was making the roads slippery, but he drove carefully and still managed to travel quite fast. All went well for the first ten miles, until there was a police check-point. They were probably checking for drug-smugglers as they were trying very hard to stamp out the trade that passed through Syria from the East on its way to Europe, but Mahmoud was in no position to have the truck searched. Instead of slowing down he put his foot on the accelerator and drove through the group of Customs Officers in the road, making them jump for their lives. They of course assumed that he was smuggling drugs and started to shoot over the top of his truck, which unnerved him so that he swerved from side to side on the wet road, and as the pick-up slid over to the left side of the road it was hit a glancing blow from an enormous truck coming the other way from the Turkish border. The truck driver was so busy controlling his vehicle on the wet road and trying to make out what all

130

the shooting was about that he didn't even notice the bump, but it made the pick-up roll over. The body shot out and came unwrapped from the sheet, and Mahmoud slammed against the door, then against the windscreen and back against the door. The last thing that he saw before he died was his mother's body draped across the side of the road.

The Customs police were astonished and then horrified when they reached the truck, and they phoned both the traffic police and the detective branch. Very soon Captain Samir and the General were there to inspect the bodies and to try to puzzle out what had happened, and by morning they had come to a story that was fairly close to the truth, though they would never be certain of all the details.

Rustum and his father had their Identity Cards returned, and were left to sort out Im Rustum's estate and their relationship with each other. Abu Ahad was relieved to find neither of the men were murderers, and the General gave him the job of explaining everything to them. However the hidden second wife left him with the feeling that the man who had seemed to be his friend had just too many secrets, and they didn't see much of each other afterwards.

The people who felt the simplest emotions when the truth was, more or less, uncovered were the two wives and Captain Samir. Both wives were, of course, glad to have their husbands home, and each was secretly planning how to spend the money that would soon be coming her husband's way. Im Mohammed was thinking in terms of a bigger flat and private schools for the children, while Ross was more inclined to a new car and a holiday in Europe.

Captain Samir's feelings were not so positive. He had seen the case as a chance to make his name, and had taken a personal dislike to Rustum on sight, so he was angry that the case had fallen apart and thoroughly cross that Rustum was walking away untouched. He wasn't, perhaps, the most logical policeman in Aleppo.

NILE STREET

Bruised. Bruised body, bruised mind, bruised heart. Impossible to decide which hurt most. Susan sat in the park while Tarek rolled his ball round the empty bandstand. She was sitting rigidly erect with her hands clenched and pushed hard into her pockets. All her will was concentrated on not allowing tears to appear in her eyes.

"I will not cry. I will *not* cry," she chanted silently to herself, over and over again. Slowly the warmth of the November afternoon sunshine, and perhaps a sort of trance induced by the repeated phrase, calmed her a little, and she sat back on the green bench and began to look around. The deciduous trees were all looking dried out and untidy, waiting for the winter rain to come and strip them of their yellowing leaves, but the tall evergreens – could they be cypresses? – were dark and restful to the eyes, and made free and grand shapes against the skyline.

She no longer felt as though she might burst into uncontrollable tears, but as the tension left her, her thoughts moved onto another track.

"How can he be like that? What can I do?" To each question, finding no answer, she returned again and again. The thoughts seemed to be darting around inside her head of their own accord, and were only disturbed when she went to pull her handkerchief from her pocket and the pain from the bruises on her arm made her wince.

Her husband, Ahmed, had been hitting out at her on occasion since just before Tarek was born, three years ago. However in the last year it seemed to be happening more frequently and with less provocation. Also he was being less careful about what Tarek saw, and on one or two occasions, when Ahmed had started to shout at her, Tarek had crept away, white faced and large eyed. She had found him later, crouched in the far corner of his bedroom, cuddling his knitted rabbit.

Susan always told herself that it was not that Ahmed was a cruel man. He was a competent and kindly lawyer who worked hard to extract justice for his clients from a system which did not make it easy. He was also an extremely conscientious father, although he demanded standards of behaviour from Tarek that she felt no three-year-old should really be expected to reach. He often slapped his son quite hard for what seemed to her very minor offences. The times when he struck her were always occasions when some small domestic accident had occurred, such as losing her key, or locking herself out of the house, and, on one occasion, having the parked car scraped while she was having coffee with a friend. He would panic, and soon there would be a row, even if its immediate cause might be quite different.

Today they had all been together in the kitchen, ready to eat lunch there. She had been lifting a hot dish from the oven when Tarek had walked past and bumped her just enough to make her lose her grip. The dish had slipped noisily onto the pull-down door of the oven and some of the gravy had spilt on the floor, while a little splashed on her skirt. Then Ahmed's nervous shout of,

"Be careful! What have you done? What's happened now?" had almost made her drop the dish in earnest. She had tried to answer calmly, but had felt the familiar tightening of fear in her stomach and it was all she could do to get the dish safely to the table. He had been silent during lunch, helping himself without comment while she tried to talk as usual to Tarek and maintain the appearance of calm, even though her throat became progressively tighter with tension, so she could barely swallow. However the effort was worthwhile, as Tarek did not seem to notice anything, and she breathed a small sigh of relief as she saw him settling for his afternoon sleep, his eyes already almost shut.

Walking as casually as she could back into the living room, she saw Ahmed was looking at some papers, which twitched as she passed, but she reached the kitchen without any other notice from him. There she lit a cigarette and inhaled deeply before starting to make the Turkish coffee. She arranged the tray, with full, tiny cups and a glass of water, and was thinking that at least she hadn't made a mess of this job, as ready-ground Turkish coffee was only one step more difficult than Instant, when she heard her husband's voice behind her at the kitchen door. She nearly dropped the tray, coffee, cups and all, on the floor.

"So you have to fill the place with smoke as well," he said, his voice ominously quiet. "Do you realize you could have killed that child before lunch?" She put down the tray. She wanted to protest, opening her mouth to speak and spreading out her hands, palms upwards, in a helpless gesture, but he gave her no chance.

"You want to kill him, I can see. You aren't fit to be a mother and you never will be again. I won't allow you to have any more children, you're wickedly careless. People like you should be in prison. Go into the other room with the coffee, and for God's sake don't spill it." All the time he was speaking his voice was rising until he shouted the last words. Susan no longer wanted any coffee, she knew she couldn't swallow it under his glowering eye, so she said, with a placating smile,

"No, love, I don't want any now. I'll just clear up in here while you have yours quietly by yourself so you can get on with your work. There's the tray." She pushed it gently towards him .

He looked at her speechlessly for a moment, while his face flushed and his eyes closed to narrow slits .

"You will drink your coffee." He hit out at her and caught her left arm, which he held on to in a painfully tight grip. "You will act properly. The proper thing to do when you have made coffee is to drink it!" He was shouting now and his face was close to hers, while he was shaking her by both arms, like a rag doll. "You're a crazy female, wasting coffee you made yourself. You're just like all the other women. Your life is all waste and mess. You are useless." As he shouted the last words he let go of her left arm and punched her shoulder, which pushed her back against the chair. She half-missed it and fell to the floor, pulling the chair over herself as she fell. She managed to pull herself up against the table and gasped out,

"I'm not crazy, I'm not! It's you who's crazy. There isn't anyone else like you here." She could say no more as she was fighting against the tears which flowed so easily when she was upset, and which she knew would only enrage Ahmed even further.

"Oh no, I'm not mad. I'm only trying to make you live an orderly, decent life, and I will, whatever you think. I won't break. You'll be in the lunatic hospital before you drag me down with you." With this he took his coffee, turned and stalked back into the living room, while she picked up the chair and sank down on it. She propped her elbows on the kitchen table and dropped her head to rub her eyes with her knuckles .

Presently she got up to start clearing the dishes, and became conscious of her aching arms, shoulder and ribs. She rubbed at her shoulder as she surveyed the kitchen, and debated with herself whether to do it or to go and rest for a few minutes first. The sound of impatiently rustled papers in the living room decided her against going through there to their bedroom, so she started collecting the plates.

It always pleased her how quickly the dishes could be done, and how pretty and neat the kitchen looked when they were all stacked, clean and shiny, on the draining rack above the sink. By the time she was finishing off by polishing the glasses and cutlery to prevent them drying with water spots on, she felt a lot better, and caught herself humming a tune from the morning's radio. Realising this, she was suddenly overwhelmed with unhappiness, and had to struggle against tears again   .

After this episode Susan and Ahmed were very careful with each other, speaking politely in front of Tarek, but it took them several days to relax into normal friendliness and to act as if nothing had happened. Susan occasionally reflected that this was one of their problems, that they never referred to their arguments or to Ahmed's violence. They both pretended it had not happened and let it sink into the past, chiefly, she thought, because they were both so horrified by their behaviour that neither of them could bear to think of it objectively, much less to discuss it.

Anyway, on the few occasions that talking had seemed imperative to Susan, and she had convinced herself that they could discuss it quietly, had even planned whole conversations with Ahmed's assertions and her balanced replies – all sweet reason, she could not screw her courage to the point of opening her mouth for the first vital words. As she sat there, knowing that the time was right to speak, her stomach tightened and her knees went weak, and she knew that she never would speak first.

The face they had always presented to the world was of a pair of kindly, friendly people enjoying a fairly happy marriage. Each secretly dreaded more than anything else that other people would suspect what a miserable mess they were making of their life together. Maintaining this front was often quite a strain, they were always elaborately polite to each other in front of their friends and Ahmed's relations, and on occasion Susan had blessed the local custom which honoured her as a modest woman when she wore long sleeves in very hot weather to hide bruised arms. Sometimes the strain did show. Occasionally Ahmed would speak to her in a peremptory voice, issuing orders as if she were a servant, or she would spend a whole evening carefully avoiding the necessity of speaking to him. Short, awkward silences would make holes in the general conversation, and slightly puzzled glances would be exchanged among whatever company they were in.

This year the warm weather lasted until the end of November, by which time the farmers were praying for rain and everybody was feeling irritable with the dust which blew everywhere. The few showers which came in October and November only damped the ground and laid the dust for a few hours before the boisterous wind dried it again and tossed it about, leaving a constantly thickening film on the furniture and windows.

Susan was more and more anxious about provoking a row with Ahmed. The wind and the dust was making housework a misery and affecting all their nerves. Tarek did not look well, his large eyes seemed to be getting larger and darker in his rather pointed little face, although Susan was constantly being assured by her friends that it was only the weather, and that this sort of weather was very hard on small children.

The nights had been getting steadily cooler since the middle of September, but one morning Susan woke feeling unusually chilly. She rose and opened curtains, windows and shutters to see why, and was delighted to see that it must have rained heavily in the night. The roads were covered in muddy pools and a few drops were still falling.

She was leaning out to enjoy the smell of the rain, and to catch a few raindrops on her face, when she heard Ahmed's voice behind her .

"What on earth are you doing? Shut that window! Are you trying to catch pneumonia?"

She closed the window quickly and turned back into the room, and identified the sensation that had woken her. It was dampness, beautiful, cool, healing dampness. Her face already felt less tight and dry and she imagined each separate cell in her body absorbing moisture and expanding like a prune in hot water. Well, perhaps a dried apricot sounded more attractive. She frowned briefly at the squeaking wardrobe hinges when she opened it to find her winter dressing gown. It never seemed worthwhile oiling them at the end of the summer, but the change in the weather made her feel brisk and positive, and she resolved to go round all the hinges in the house with the oilcan this morning.

Over breakfast she saw that the weather had affected them all the same way. They were sitting at the table a few minutes earlier than usual, and Ahmed and Tarek chatted while she brought the eggs to the table and then poured the tea. Tarek attacked his egg with an enthusiasm that had been lacking for some time, and after breakfast she could hear Ahmed humming loudly to himself as he shaved. Then Tarek ran to her, laughing, to have shaving foam wiped off his face,

"Daddy painted me! Look, Mummy, Daddy painted me! Now he's going to put cologne on me when he's finished, so I can smell nice, like him." He darted back

140

into the bathroom and she could hear their voices as they talked and laughed together.

She decided that at last she could put the carpets down without being thought eccentric. In fact, as she thought about it she realized that carpets were being spread over balconies on all the surrounding buildings. As soon as her cleaner, Aysha, arrived they dragged the carpets from the summer storeroom over the bedroom corridor out onto the balcony. They hung them all side by side over the balcony railings then Aysha took the old-fashioned cane carpet beater and started banging away like all the neighbours, to get rid of the last of the olive oil soap which had been protecting the carpets from insects all summer, while Susan got on with the next part of the job, the final washing over of the floors before the rugs were laid.

Ahmed had promised to bring home a spit-roasted chicken, so she had no cooking to do, and by lunchtime the carpets were all laid, the air smelt faintly of soap, and she had even managed to oil the squeakiest of the hinges. Tarek had thoroughly enjoyed the bustle and excitement, and was jumping up and down on his bed, shouting, "See me!"

The next milestone was Christmas and kept Susan busy. There was so much visiting among the English and American wives, exchanging recipes and tracking down or borrowing from each other such things as glace cherries, treacle and Christmas cake decorations. She and Ahmed did not quarrel at all, although it was a week or so before she realized that the peaceful atmosphere in the house was merely the absence of quarrels. Ahmed must have noticed it too. About a week before Christmas they were driving away from an old school friend of his whose wife Ahmed found a constant source of irritation, when he reached over while still peering through the frosty car window and grasped her nearest knee, saying:

"I'm glad that I'm married to you and not to someone like Amira. I don't know what I'd do if you ever got fed up enough to leave me. I hope you don't." He quickly released her knee and grabbed the steering wheel with both hands hissing "Dog, son of a dog!" as a cyclist riding an unlit bicycle swerved out of a dark side road almost under his front wheel. When they had both recovered from the shock she answered,

"Ahmed, I couldn't leave you. I love you and I don't want to not be near you. I couldn't be happy away from you." She could not say any more. She felt so full of happiness the she was almost choking with it, that he wanted her to stay so much. In her lower moments she had wondered if he wanted her around just to save the bother of a change. Together with this she felt an enormous tenderness for the man beside her, she knew he felt things very deeply and also that he hated to express his deepest feelings. For him to have done so must have required a very great effort and she found herself near to tears.

Outside the house she had started to reach for her bag and gloves when Ahmed briefly touched her cheek. She looked up at him, and at the expression of gentleness and tenderness on his face she felt her own face breaking into an involuntary smile. She leaned towards him but he hurriedly drew away and grinned at her in mock horror.

"Sue, remember this is Syria. What would the neighbours say?" She giggled and he went on, "Just go up and tell mother we're back and I'm waiting to run her home. It'll only take five minutes, and you can be making yourself beautiful for me until I get back."

"You mean 'more beautiful', don't you?" she answered pertly as she collected her belongings and stepped out onto the pavement. She called a cheerful goodnight to the watchman in his cubby-hole inside the main door, and went up to their apartment to wake her mother-in-law, thank her and pack her off home as quickly and tactfully as she could manage.

Christmas and the New Year passed in the usual bustle, with visits to and from their own friends interspersed with polite but somewhat constrained visits from Ahmed's relations, who came to acknowledge 'her' feast. She appreciated the kindness that motivated them to come, but found the visitors trying as they always seemed to come when Ahmed was out, and she had to do her best to make polite conversation until he returned or they chose to leave. One particular fat old uncle slipped from his place as favourite relation on Christmas Day when she had to ply him with chocolates and Turkish coffee, and then to sit chatting to him in the front room, while the Christmas dinner was in urgent need of attention in the kitchen. By the time he had finally heaved himself out of his chair and tottered benevolently on his way, she was so irritated that she had to count to ten several times to resist pushing him through the door.

They were invited to a New Year party given by Margaret and Hanni, one of the other couples they occasionally visited. It was the first real party they had been to for a long time and Sue was looking forward to it a lot. In the morning she left Tarek with his grandmother while she went to the hairdresser round the corner to have her hair done. As she walked in through the door of the salon she could tell that she would be there for the rest of the morning.

Syria is not a country where appointment systems work very happily, and the almost universal practice of hairdressers is to deal with any customers who arrive on a 'first come first served' basis. This morning, with parties everywhere tonight, a lot of other people had come first, so Susan, after acknowledging the hairdresser's hurried welcome, sat in a corner and watched the goings-on. She had a book with her for if she got bored or needed something to hide behind, but at first there was quite enough of interest in her surroundings to hold her attention.

As she sat down she nodded to the other women who were already waiting on a row of chairs down one side of the white and grey salon, and greeted more enthusiastically one of them whom she recognized as a neighbour. There was a slight movement along the row as one or two women leaned over to neighbours to ask who the blonde foreigner was, and some nodding of heads and quick, curious glances in her direction told her that they were being informed who her husband was, how many children she had and, as far as was publicly known, what her

144

mother-in-law thought of her. As a newcomer this had irritated her to the point of exasperation, but she had grown to accept it and was now able to ignore it and watch the hairdressers at work, having nodded and smiled politely at those customers whose eyes had accidentally caught hers while they were having a good look at her.

All the chairs of the salon were full and all the staff working hard. Customers had been in earlier in the week to have colouring done or touched up. Grey was not an acceptable colour and had been covered with shades of henna red, and many girls with lovely dark eyes either had their hair lightened all over or had lots of blonde streaks put in, to give an all-over impression of being fairer than their true colour. Now the final work was being done, and most women had magnificent heads of hair for the hairdressers to work on. The majority of the older women were going for conservative, formal styles, but a few of them and the younger ones were walking out with exact copies of the most exotic styles to be seen on the most popular American actresses. The time passed very easily until it was Sue's turn, although it was almost three hours later that she left the salon, quite tired from the effort of trying to understand the gossip going on around her. She stayed at her mother-in-law's only long enough to collect Tarek, have her hair admired and make sure that her mother-in law would baby-sit for them.

By almost ten o'clock that evening they were ready to go. Susan felt very pretty, her hair style suited her and she was wearing a smoky-blue dress that matched her eyes. When they were leaving the house she gave Ahmed a sidelong admiring look, he always managed to be dressed absolutely correctly and today she thought he looked even more handsome than usual. As she looked up at him she caught his eye and saw he was appraising her too; they both laughed.

"Hurry up. We'll miss the party," he said.

"It's all right. It really only gets moving at midnight," she smiled, and they went out together to the car. The New Year looked hopeful.

Spring came suddenly that year, as it often does in Syria. One morning in early March Susan got up and opened the shutters to find the sun pouring light and warmth from a cloudless blue sky. For the last few months, life had been peaceful. She had looked forward cheerfully to each day as she had woken up, and now she was suddenly ridiculously happy, she wanted to dance around the bedroom, singing.

Smiling to herself at the thought she went and looked in on Tarek, who was sleeping neatly curled up with his head on the pillow and his knitted rabbit in his arms. She wondered in passing when he would be old enough to part with it for a day or two, as it was seriously in need of a wash. Then she went to the kitchen to lay the table for breakfast. As she squeezed the oranges, she thought they had better enjoy them while they could as they would get very dry as the weather got warmer.

She made Ahmed's morning coffee and included a cup for herself, then dug out an embroidered tray cloth she had worked at school, which had somehow managed to get itself packed when she came to Syria. Next came the glass of water which is always served with Turkish coffee, and she thought that though it was a pity she hadn't a posy of flowers on it, the tray still matched her mood.

Stepping carefully over the edge of the Persian carpet, she crossed the living room and managed to get into the bedroom without spilling anything. She put it down gently on the bedside table and shut the bedroom door quietly so Tarek could have his sleep out .

"Wake up," she said to Ahmed, rubbing his shoulder, "Coffee's ready."

He opened his eyes, looked at her and at the tray, then smiled sleepily and said,

"So am I." He reached up with one arm and pulled her down towards him, but she kissed him and pulled herself away, laughing, and said,

"Which do you want, me or the coffee? Because the coffee will get cold if it has to wait. Anyway I don't think I like hedgehogs very much."

The answer was a grin, and he pulled himself up to a sitting position, so they drank their coffee comfortably in the morning sunshine, chatting quietly. When he finished his, he put the cup down carefully on the tray and reached out to her again.

"Come here," he said, so she put down her cup and obligingly cuddled up to him. "Do you want a hedgehog now, or do I have to shave first?"

"Well, if you go and shave you're sure to wake Tarek, but I'll still be here tonight."

He gave her one of the occasional sweet smiles which seemed to make her heart stop for a moment,

147

"Sue, that's the lovely thing about being married, to know there will always be another time and we will always be here. It makes up for everything bad that happens."

Susan cuddled up even closer to him answering,

"You know, I'm feeling quite fond of hedgehogs."

During the morning Susan got a lot of work done, encouraged by the sunshine. Tarek had relaxed a lot in the last few tranquil months, growing and putting weight on at last. He had even considered her suggestion this morning that his rabbit might enjoy a wash, after having it carefully explained that Rabbit would not be hurt by the experience.

Ahmed's mother came to lunch, and chatted to her son in Arabic far beyond Susan's comprehension. She did not mind, as the older woman turned to her occasionally to compliment her, in carefully simple phrases, on her cooking. There had been a certain degree of hostility between them at first, but that had worn away in time to comfortable, fairly friendly, incomprehension. Just now Susan was busy making sure that Tarek ate all his dinner with the minimum of mess, and in pressing her mother-in-law to extra helpings of everything, against her protestations of having tasted each dish and eaten enough. This custom usually irritated her, but today she felt too happy and generally contented for anything to annoy her, and even managed to infuse a degree of warmth into her voice.

They drank coffee in the sitting room, and Susan sat back dreaming as she sipped at hers. She avoided looking at Ahmed's mother, who was still chatting with her son, her coffee cup in her left hand and a cigarette in her right hand. As she spoke, she gesticulated with her right hand, occasionally dropping ash on the well-polished furniture, though she most often managed to get it into an ashtray on the little carved table beside her chair. The sunlight caught the scarlet nails and heavy rings which adorned her plump, well-groomed hands, and now and again drew a gleam from the chunky gold bracelet she wore, while this, and the necklace which decorated her ample and well-tailored bosom, chinked and clattered slightly as she moved in her chair. When she finished her coffee and put down her cup she put her left arm around Tarek, who was fascinated by her. He sat as close to her as he could, and watched silently as the cigarette smoke collected round her head and drifted slowly across the room.

The talking continued as Susan cleared the dining table and tidied the left-overs into the fridge. They barely noticed when she collected the coffee cups and replaced her mother-in-law's full ash tray with a clean one, so she decided to wash up while she could. She had got everything washed and drained before Ahmed put his head round the kitchen door for her to come and say goodbye to his mother. He left with her to drive her home on his way to his office, and Susan told him that she was going to see Janet, who she often spent the afternoon with.

Tarek had almost grown out of his afternoon sleep and today he was full of energy, so as soon as Ahmed and his mother had gone she called him to get dressed straight away for going out.

As they walked along the street she pointed out to her son how the buds were beginning to break through on the trees lining the pavement, and told him he would be able to run in their shade when the sun got too hot in the summer. He was always fascinated by the half-wild and extremely shy cats that abounded here, as in all Middle Eastern cities. They too were enjoying the warm weather, and most were sunning themselves with one eye half-open to watch for danger. Tarek attempted to approach each one they came across, but the reaction was always the same. The cat would watch with narrowed eyes and twitching ears until Tarek, hand outstretched and calling "Pussy, pussy," was a yard or two away. Then its nerve would break and it would dash for cover under a parked car, across the road, or slink over the nearest wall as if its striped or parti-coloured body contained no bones at all.

The distractions made progress very slow, but this did not trouble either of them as they pottered along the road to Janet's. The traffic was getting heavier as the afternoon wore on, and the occasional school bus roared past like a juggernaut, crammed to bursting with children. Susan had often wondered how parents could possibly allow their children to travel in them, but then again, she had never actually heard of one crashing. They reached a very busy corner where two wide avenues met, each with a row of trees down the middle, together with several smaller roads. Susan took firmer hold of Tarek's mittened hand and was just about to cross when she heard someone call.

"Sue, Sue."

She turned to look and saw Elizabeth, who lived a little further up and who was also visiting Janet. She waved to her with her free hand. Suddenly Tarek, pulling his hand away and leaving her clutching his empty mitten, called 'Pussy, pussy', and dashed out into the street towards the central trees.

With horrifying suddenness there came a jumble of separate impressions in Susan's mind. Tarek running across the street with one hand held out to the cat he had seen. The bus swinging round the corner, catching him with its bumper and flinging him into the air, the arc he described as he was thrown clear, and Elizabeth's face, eyes staring and jaw dropped in a scream.

So fast that it seemed as if it must be happening to someone else, Tarek was lying crumpled in the road, the traffic had screeched to a stop and people were pouring out of their cars. The bus driver was sitting on the kerb, white faced and shaking and explaining to a growing audience how he couldn't stop, couldn't help it. Susan was kneeling beside Tarek, who also had a crowd around him, and Elizabeth was standing beside them looking dazed and with tears pouring down her carefully made-up face.

Somebody phoned the nearby hospital, and very soon an ambulance arrived, together with a police car. The policemen pushed their way through the crowd and looked at Tarek, but when various people explained that his mother was a foreigner, they just checked which hospital the ambulance men had come from, then waved them on to move the little boy away.

The next few moments were to remain nightmarishly clear in Susan's memory for the rest of her life. The ambulance swayed, so she had to cling on to the edge of her seat as they swung round corners, while the siren contrasted with the silence and stillness of Tarek's small, blanket-covered form, even his face was turned away from her towards the cream-coloured wall of the vehicle. At the hospital he was quickly wheeled away on a stretcher, while Susan was taken aside by an anxious young doctor who extracted from her Ahmed's name and office number. When she tried to ask him about Tarek he would only say "Insh Allah, God willing, God willing", before leaving her .

She sat stiffly upright in the same chair for what seemed a long time, barely aware of her icy cold hands and feet, and the fading light outside. At different times people looked through the glass panel on the door with expressions of anxious sympathy. Once a nurse brought her a glass of hot, very sweet black tea, and tut-tutted over the coldness of the hand which took it. The only time she roused herself was when Ahmed came in, he had already seen the doctor and he looked her coldly up and down, said,

"How could you do it to him?" After that he stood in silence with his hands behind his back, occasionally swaying backwards and forwards on the balls of his feet.

The doctor entered and snapped on the light, which made her jump then shade her eyes with her hand, and Ahmed left the room with him. When he came back a few minutes later he just said, 'My son is dead. You've killed him".

Susan put both hands to her face and was surprised to feel the wetness of tears. The doctor bustling in behind Ahmed seemed to notice nothing strange in the atmosphere, and was voluble in his explanations of the great efforts made to save the little boy's life. She rose to her feet and walked beside Ahmed, who punctiliously opened doors and stood aside for her but would not look at her. The lump that had been gathering in her chest seemed to rise to her throat and to make her incapable of speaking, almost of breathing.

At the hospital entrance they saw Janet and Mohammed. Janet was crying, her usually tidy hair streaked damply across her forehead, and even Mohammed looked very close to tears. As soon as Susan and Ahmed approached, Janet ran to her and put her arms around her. She told her that Elizabeth had been so distraught that her husband had taken her home, and a small part of Susan's brain commented that of course it was Janet who was left to pick up the pieces. Then Ahmed took his wife's arm above the elbow, rather more firmly than was comfortable, and they all moved towards his car, Janet's arm still round her shoulders.

When they reached the car Ahmed, who had not spoken a word since they had left the hospital, turned to Susan,

"Come on, we have to go home." She looked once at his face, closed and pale with shock, and recoiled from him. She could not face the coldness of his voice, or the elegant apartment with Tarek's toys in his room and his clean plate and Donald Duck mug in the kitchen. She was also, behind the blank confusion in her mind, physically scared of being alone with her husband. All their recent friendliness and closeness had disappeared; the terrible accident had shut him back into himself, away from her and refusing to let her approach. She started to sob loudly, and could not stop herself.

"You're being hysterical. Get into the car and stop drawing attention to yourself. It's time we went home." She knew that she could not possibly, so she turned to Janet,

"Don't make me go. I can't go there tonight." They made a small group at the kerbside. Ahmed stood half looking at her with the passenger door open for her. Only his drooping shoulders betraying his misery. Susan stood, resting her head on Janet's reliable comforting shoulder and saying almost to herself, "I can't go home. Not tonight. You don't know."

Tears were streaming down Janet's face and she was absently stroking Susan's hair, to comfort her as if she were a small child, while she looked over her friend's head to see what her husband would do. Mohammed was both extremely upset and very embarrassed. He put his hand on Ahmed's shoulder and let it fall again, and made a helpless, shoulder-shrugging gesture.

Janet took the initiative, saying,

"Ahmed, please let Susan come to us tonight, and perhaps you can come too? We can give you the boys' room and then you can go home in the morning, when you're past the first shock."

Ahmed looked at her bleakly,

"No, thank you. Janet, but Susan must do as she wishes. Are you coming back with me or not?" He turned to his wife. She managed to look back at him more calmly, but answered,

"No, Ahmed. I can't. Not tonight."

With conscious and obvious effort he pulled himself up as straight as usual and turned to Mohammed.

"Thank you for coming to help. It's what Susan wants so she'd better stay with you tonight. I'll phone you in the morning. I think I'll sleep at my mother's. There'll be the funeral and everything." He turned quickly away, closing the passenger door on the empty seat. Then he walked round the bonnet of the car, got into the driving seat and drove away without looking round again.

Janet and Mohammed led Susan the short distance to their house and let themselves in. Mohammed's sister had been babysitting and came forward with sympathetic questions, but he shushed her and she went with Janet to clear their youngest boy's bedroom and make up the spare bed. While they were occupied in moving the little boy to his big brother's room without waking him, Mohammed relieved Susan of her coat and persuaded her to sit down. Then, quite quickly, reaction to the shock set in and she started shaking. At first only her teeth were chattering, but soon her whole body was shaking and she was sobbing so hard she felt she would choke. Mohammed took her hand to steady her, but when he felt how cold it was he was thoroughly frightened, and hurried from the room in search of his wife, blankets and hot tea. Janet dashed in and told him which blanket to bring, instructed his sister to make tea and sent him to the flat downstairs to their neighbour, who was a doctor.

As soon as the doctor heard what had happened, and examined her briefly, he ordered her to bed immediately. Mohammed's sister appeared, scared but fascinated by Susan's strange behaviour, bearing a cup of sweet black tea and a hot water bottle which was tucked in bed beside her. Then the doctor fished out two white tablets from his bag, which he waited for her to swallow with her tea before leaving her alone in the room. The door was ajar and she could hear subdued voices in the hall, then the opening and closing of the front door. A feeling of warmth began to steal over her from the hot bottle, and her mind refused to accept the facts of the afternoon. She felt as if she were a small child, being cared for again, and that when she woke up everything would be as it ought. Tarek's little white face in the ambulance and Ahmed's cold closed face in the hospital were just a dreadful nightmare from which she must surely awake. The pills worked quickly and she was already feeling a bit dizzy when she heard Janet whisper,

"Are you all right now, Sue?" She just had the energy to answer,

"Yes, thank you. Night, night," before the warm blackness swamped her and she fell into a deep sleep.

It is Islamic custom to bury bodies on the day of death, but Tarek had died too late in the afternoon for that, so he was buried the next morning, All their friends and relations went to pay their respects at Ahmed's house, while Susan slept on at Janet and Mohammed's, surfacing just enough to be aware of people talking around her before slipping back to sleep. At their apartment, Ahmed sat in the front room with the male mourners while his mother presided over the ladies in the living room. At first Susan's absence was accepted as natural distress, but by the third and final day of the formal mourning sympathetic visitors were enquiring of Ahmed and his mother if she were ill. His mother glossed over the women's questions with ease, but Ahmed's stony face and awkward manner when questioned by the male visitors was not so effective a bar to gossip.

Susan continued to live in a sleepy, drugged state for several days longer, and the doctor caring for her managed to convince the police that she could not appear as a witness in the case against the bus-driver. At last, a week after the accident, she woke to find Janet sitting on the bed, shaking her shoulder gently and calling her name.

"Good grief, I thought I'd never wake you," said Janet. "I've been here for ten minutes; I was beginning to think you were really ill." Susan tried to speak, but a yawn forced its way out first.

"I'm sorry. Why, what time is it?" she asked, then "What day is it?"

"It's Wednesday, and you've been here for six days. Mohammed and I are getting worried about you. You've been asleep on and off all the time."

Susan felt headachy and had an enormous thirst. Then she suddenly remembered how she came to be in a strange bed in someone else's house.

"Oh heavens, when I'm asleep I forget what happened. Is it really nearly a week since then? What has happened?

157

Please tell me and don't take any notice of the tears. I can't help them, but I am listening. Do you have a tissue?"

Janet took both her hands,

"Careful, Sue. You've had a very bad time but the worst part is finished. Would you like a cup of tea or something, and then some breakfast? You've hardly had anything these last days. We only managed to wake you up enough to get some soup into you, and then you just fell asleep again." She got up to get the tissues from the dressing-table and handed the box to Susan, who pulled a handful out to scrub her damp face.

Janet tried again.

"Sue, you know Tarek is dead and he won't come back, but Ahmed is alive and he is by himself. He has telephoned every day to make sure you are all right. He wants to come and see you as soon as you are awake. I don't know what was the matter with you both at the hospital, but he is awfully lonely now."

"Yes, I suppose he ought to come, poor thing. He's had a horrible time too," said Susan, "But there are a lot of things nobody knows about, and I don't know if we can ever sort ourselves out now." She stopped a moment and sighed, then went on, "Thank you for being so kind, I think you saved me from going crazy by letting me sleep. I feel as though I can manage now."

Just at that moment Janet's younger boy, Zaki, a few months younger than Tarek, crawled into the room, pushing a car along the floor and making brrrm brrrm noises. He looked at Susan, gave er a wide smile,and said,

"Hello, Auntie Sue. I want to play with Tarek. Why are you sleeping in my bedroom?"

Janet hurried him out to play in the living room, then came back to Sue, who was sitting up with her arms crooked round her knees and the tears running slowly down her face to drop unheeded from her chin.

"I'm sorry, Sue. Look, you will have to stop crying because we don't know what to do with you. Would you like that cup of tea?"

With a great effort Susan pulled herself together and stopped crying,

"Yes, please, and do you have any hot water? I'm sure I could be more normal if I were clean. Then I must see Ahmed. If he telephones could you ask him to come here, please?"

"Wouldn't you like to speak to him yourself?"

"No. I don't think I could, just yet. When he is here it will be easier."

"Yes. Well. I suppose so." A pause, then a consciously positive, encouraging voice "Well, there is plenty of hot water. Which do you want first? A bath or tea?"

"I'd rather shower first and wash my hair."

Susan was quite surprised that she could carry on fairly normally on the surface. She was able to isolate a large, uncomfortable lump in her mind, knowing that to examine it closely would be impossibly painful at the moment. It was composed vaguely of Ahmed, Tarek's death, and what to do next. When Mohammed came home to lunch he was relieved to find their visitor at last behaving in a normal way, and looking as clean and almost as neat as usual. This·

did not, however inspire him to conversation and he confined himself to a few hearty generalities over the lunch table, then discovered an urgent appointment elsewhere for the afternoon.

In another part of town Ahmed's mother had mentioned Susan several times to him at first, but he had refused to discuss either his wife or his son, so now she, too kept to commonplaces when he was there. She was deeply sorry for her son, and very upset to have lost her grandson, but it was not her way to interfere with the decisions that men made. A strong man should be able to control his own life, and certainly should be able to control his wife. This afternoon he had been sitting over his after-lunch coffee, only half listening to her and worrying away with the rest of his mind about Sue. He had been having his meals with his mother each day, and at four o'clock he abruptly got up and said goodbye so he could call Janet from his own home before going to the office.

He felt cold and sick when he picked up the receiver, and was unnerved to see his hand was shaking as he reached down to punch in the number. Each day had taken Sue a bit further from him and shut him up more firmly inside himself, so he was almost frightened when Janet answered his question about Sue with,

"Yes, she is much better and she wants to talk to you. Can you come over?"

"Perhaps we could talk on the phone?" he ventured, fighting to keep his cool, composed front.

"No," answered Janet. "I know she wants to see you. Mohammed and I both think it would be best for her. It really would be kind if you could come." Cornered, Ahmed's instinct was to play for time.

"Can I come this evening, at about eight? I'm busy until then and I want to say thank you to both of you as well."

"Don't be silly," from Janet, "there's nothing to thank us for, but we'll be glad to see you." As soon as she put the phone down, Janet took a deep breath, went into Sue and told her the news. Then she bustled off to round the children up for a walk before Susan could protest.

The afternoon passed very slowly for several people in Aleppo that day. Janet took the children to the big park, which was some little way from the house, and dawdled as much as she could. Susan waited in bed until the house was empty, then slowly showered again and dressed. After that she made herself a cup of tea and sat in the kitchen reading some old English magazines she found there. Mohammed, in his office, spared a few moments to think of the evening, but being comfortably sure that 'these things always work out in time', he was able to get on with his work quite happily.

Perhaps the most to be pitied was Ahmed. Every time he noticed the hands on the clock in his office he felt a choking sensation of cold fear in his chest. His clients found him abstracted and unhelpful, and it was fortunate that they were still feeling sympathetic towards him about Tarek's death.

When eight o'clock struck Mohammed was unaccountably delayed at the office while Janet was ostentatiously putting the children to bed. Thus it was Susan who answered the door to Ahmed and who led him

161

into the front room, normally reserved for the most formal of visitors. They sat down awkwardly on opposite sides of the room and each tried to think of something to say. Sue indicated the cigarettes next to Ahmed's chair and he was able to fill a few minutes in clumsily taking one, lighting it and drawing a first breath of smoke.

"Sue."

"Ahmed." They spoke simultaneously, and stopped.

"Have you been very busy?" Sue finally managed.

"Yes, quite. No. Not really," he replied, obviously at a loss and completely unlike his usual, calm self.

"The funeral must have been dreadful. I'm sorry you were alone," she ventured, screwing the paper tissue in her hand tighter and tighter until it started fraying into small pellets.

"Yes."

He answered briefly and stopped.

"Are you staying at home or at your mother's?" she tried.

"At home. I didn't want to upset mother too much. She was very good about the funeral and everything." He looked directly at her then for the first time since he had arrived, and asked "Are you coming home?" The bleakness in his voice was matched by his face, which was closed and cold as if the human being behind it were no longer there, and Susan was frightened.

"No," she whispered, "I daren't." As she said the words the muscle at the corner of his left eye began to jump, and he clasped his hands together across his knees until the fingers were white. However his voice was quite calm when he answered,

"You must do as you wish. Do you want to go to England?"

"I don't know. I haven't thought."

"Well, you had better start thinking. You know where I am if you want an exit visa and a ticket. There are your clothes as well. Or if you change your mind...." The sentence was left unfinished, hanging in the silence as Ahmed got up. "I'll go now. Say hello to the others for me."

He didn't notice her whispered 'Goodbye', which faded on the empty air as he left first the room and then the flat quickly and quietly.

Going down the stairs his face felt like a mask, and the only thought in his mind was that everything he really wanted was gone. He had only just managed not to beg Susan to come back – but that was, of course, unthinkable. The car was a haven in the dark, and then the dam burst and tears rolled down his face. He was not just crying for Tarek, but for all the things that had gone wrong with his marriage.

It was with a strange feeling of relief that he felt his shirt growing damp and chilly as the tears dripped off his chin. He drove a long way round to his own house - not 'their' house any more – and before he reached home he had control of himself again. He reached across to the glove compartment and grabbed some tissues to wipe his face so the doorman would notice nothing.

That night Susan sat up in bed with her arms wrapped round her knees, trying to think. She had been desperately shocked at the way that Ahmed had aged in the last week, and deeply frightened by the blank front presented to her when she said that she was not returning. The days of hibernating in Janet's house had done her good. Her mind had been clearing itself while she slept and cried. She remembered how charming and caring Ahmed had been, and how she had loved his smiling face. She supposed he too must see the change in her – whatever he had seen in her in the first place. She was sure that the mess they had made of their marriage was neither his nor her own fault entirely, it was that together they made a fatal combination.

There was no choice. Neither of them would now be strong enough to break the violent, destructive pattern of their life together. Perhaps a firmer woman would make Ahmed take control of his feelings and not allow the small seeds of panic to grow into this monster. She couldn't stretch her imagination to any other man for herself, just now she only wanted to go home and wait until the pain was less. People said she would feel better one day, though she didn't believe it.

In the morning she persuaded an extremely reluctant Mohammed to leave a quickly written note at Ahmed's office, and that evening a messenger brought her passport with an exit visa. The same envelope contained a one-way airline ticket, a door key and a note in Ahmed's writing saying that she would need her clothes. The next day she steeled herself to return to the flat when she knew it would be empty, and stuffed the first clothes she came to into a large grip which was in the wardrobe. Then she left quietly, turning her eyes away from Tarek's bedroom, thankful that the door was shut.

The ticket was for the day after, so in the early morning Mohammed took her to the airport and she left.

COFFEE MORNING – March

There should have been a big coffee morning to celebrate Ross' thirtieth birthday. The women didn't bother with other birthdays, or every coffee morning would have to be a celebration, but every ten years there was a cake with candles and a gift.

In the event, the celebration was postponed and they went instead as a group to pay a condolence visit at Susan's house on the third day after Tarek's death. Janet, with Elizabeth as moral support, had been there on the day of the burial and had sat amongst the other women in black, everyone either crying or trying not to. Ahmed's mother had sat at the head of the room, scarved and reading the Koran, and each woman who entered the house approached her and said,

"His years be with you" before shaking her hand, being kissed or being hugged according to how close they were.

Janet and Elizabeth had arrived at the open front door at the same time as a large group of women, and heard each one say,

"Where is Im Tarek?" Then it was their turn to greet the older woman; although she knew both of them she merely inclined her head slightly at their greetings and shook their hands briefly. This was unnerving, but they found places towards the back of the rows of white plastic chairs which now filled Sue's sitting room, and sat there while all around them women counted off prayer beads and whispered to each other.

The correct length of stay for people not connected to the family is about half an hour, so promptly after that, after surreptitious checks on watches, Janet and Elizabeth joined the slow-moving group of women who were shaking Ahmed's mother's hand again and leaving.

Silence had been correct inside the house, but down the stairs and out into the fresh air, Elizabeth ran one hand through her hair and exclaimed'

"Heavens, I'm glad that's over. She's scary!"

"It must be really bad to go through that without Susan," responded Janet, "and of course Ahmed is her only son, I think her daughters are all married and living abroad. But I didn't tell you about what happened at the hospital." She filled Elizabeth in on how Susan came to be at her house and finished, "It's so sad. You could see that she was scared of him – I never realized and she never said anything. Anyway, Mohammed was so good, he calmed Ahmed down, and he told me that Susan can stay as long as she needs to."

Elizabeth offered to come and visit her, but Janet responded,

"Thanks, but she's had some sedatives and she's fast asleep. When she wakes up I'll call you."

They separated, Janet to look after her family and her visitor, and Elizabeth to phone around with the gossip.

The day of the funeral was counted as the first day, and the third day is traditionally the day for every woman who wishes to pay her respects to visit the home of the bereaved in the morning. This meant that all of Susan's friends were socially bound to go, though they all knew that something strange was going on, and that Susan was, in fact, asleep at Janet's house.

It was embarrassing that she wasn't there, but her mother in law received them graciously, though she had aged visibly and her hands were shaking over her beads as she prayed quietly with the other women. They stayed the required half an hour, sitting silently after subdued greetings to other women they recognised, then left as unobtrusively as possible. They were all shocked, but could say nothing inside the house. Outside, they collected in a quiet group and talked over what they knew.

When they were on their different ways home, Ross walked along with Janet. They lived quite near each other, and socialized in the same group as Susan and Ahmed so they knew more than any of the others about the family.

"They always seem quite happy when we see them," from Ross.

"Yes, I know what you mean, but I don't think they would let anyone know if they weren't" replied Janet. "And do you remember when Susan came to Elizabeth's in October in long sleeves when the rest of us were all boiling hot? I thought she looked strange at the time, but you know how it is. There is always so much to do with the house and the children that you let things go."

"Well," from Ross, "She wouldn't have welcomed it if you had tried to find out what was the matter. I always think that if people want help they'll ask for it, and if they don't, it means they want to be left alone."

Janet glanced at Ross and noticed again the self-confidence which showed even in the way she walked, so different from Susan's slightly apologetic manner and closed expression.

"Yes, perhaps you're right." But she thought, 'I hope you never have to find out that you can't control everything!'

MOHAFAZA

Elizabeth lived in a large and beautifully furnished flat in one of the most exclusive parts of the city. Most of the neighbours had been there for years, and considered themselves to be superior to the rest of the city. They were the old Aleppo families, and rather looked down on the new people who had swelled the city to ten times its size in the last few years. Other families might be good enough to marry into if they had enough money, but all the dignity would come from the Mohafaza

Her husband was a physician, son of a famous physician who had gone into partial retirement when his son, Bakri, came back from England with his fresh clean FRCP in his briefcase, his fresh blonde wife on his arm, and the belief that it was his duty to protect his wife from the world. Elizabeth revelled in his protection and in the status she enjoyed as his wife. With the other English women she was extremely kind and helpful, and mostly avoided pointing out that her husband was rather better, richer and generally more satisfactory than any of theirs.

Life had been made easy for them, there was this flat waiting in the family building and a place in his father's clinic. Even the hospitals where his father worked were quite content to accept the son as he steadily took over his father's work. Eventually his father had retired completely, and he died some years later, leaving his wife to be cared for by her sons.

When they first arrived, Bakri asked Elizabeth to make the flat as English as possible, and she had managed to produce almost a replica of her parent's comfortable home. Chintz covered sofas in the living room, carefully-made dark wooden furniture for the dining room and a totally English bedroom. There he promised her that he would take care of her as long as he lived, and that she needn't worry about anything because that was why they were married .

"You are my silver princess, and you will have a perfect life here. I don't want you to worry about one little thing, it's my job to make sure nothing that can hurt you ever comes near you." She was overcome by his caring, cried a little on his shoulder, and took the philosophy as the basis of their lives.

Twenty five years had passed since they had arrived. Bakri's practice was as large as he could manage. These days he often suggested other physicians when he was busy – a risky thing to do where the market was so restricted and there were so many young doctors struggling to make a living. He was tolerant of the youngsters, and enjoyed the idea that he was a generous colleague, which he found not too difficult as he had a private income from family land to cushion his life. Also he could not conceive that anyone might be better than he, or might become more successful. At fifty five he felt himself to be at the height of his powers, his life under satisfactory control on every front, professional and domestic.

Their two boys had not followed him into medicine – it was no longer so easy to get into the Faculty, and anyway neither of them particularly wanted to – but they were both busy studying different types of engineering at the new German University near Homs, and that was prestigious enough to be satisfactory. The older, Jamal, was exactly the son anyone would want, he often thought. He worked hard and already had some of the self-assurance of his father. Sayed, younger by a well-planned two years, was much less predictable. He was bright enough to pass exams easily, but didn't seem to understand that he had a position to keep up. His daughter was still young enough to see Daddy as a synonym for God, and was a constant joy to him, while his wife was always there, always competent and always did and said the correct things .

The first small cloud for many years appeared on his personal horizon as a call from Homs from Jamal, telling him that Sayed was getting too friendly with a very fast-living group, and had come back to their flat drunk.

"Baba, I had to put him to bed. He was singing and shouting so the whole building must have heard him. I didn't know what to do."

"Don't worry I'll deal with it. And you were right to phone me here in the clinic and not at home. We don't want to worry your mother."

"Thanks, Baba, I knew you would know what to do. Tell Mama we'll be home for the weekend in another three weeks. Bye."

172

With a sigh, he called Sayed that evening and made what he termed to himself the 'heavy father' speech, pointing out that he was paying for their education, and if their behaviour was unsatisfactory he would be forced to cut off funds. Sayed's voice told him that he was furious to be corrected like that, but the words were polite and apologetic, and Bakri hoped that was the end of the problem.

The same week his brother phoned him from his mother's house, begging him to come immediately as she seemed to be very ill. Again, he was at the clinic and rushed straight out, telling his nurse to cancel his appointments. He drove the half-mile home as fast as he could in the increasingly dense traffic and ran up the two flights of stairs to his mother's front door. He arrived and found his brother looking white faced with worry and Elizabeth almost in tears.

"Thank God you've come," she said, in a choked–up voice. "We didn't know what to do." She continued more calmly, "Annas called me up here because he was scared about your mother. She was talking to him when her cup of coffee dropped from her hand and she looked at him as if he wasn't there. Then she 'woke up' and was cross with him for letting her spill the coffee. When I arrived she looked a bit pale, but she seemed all right. What do you think it is?"

Bakri checked his mother and found she was fine again, but he felt sad because he knew without any specialist diagnosis that it had been a transient stroke, and he also knew that the days when he could take his mother and her health for granted had just ended. He left her watching television, tutting over a fashion show with models wearing almost nothing, with Elizabeth sitting beside her until his sister could get there from further out of town, and trod heavily downstairs to his own house. It was that week that he realized that his hair was now more grey than black.

After that, life settled down again for a few weeks, but his routine now included checking his mother's blood pressure every day – which she thoroughly enjoyed – and making sure she took the medicine which was now necessary. Elizabeth went up to her every day in between his visits, which left him free to concentrate on his work.

At the clinic, he made sure to call either Jamal or Sayed each day before he saw any patients, so he could be sure that Sayed was behaving himself. Late evenings saw him at home snoozing in front of the television, out with his wife dining with other doctors and their wives, or entertaining the same doctors and wives to supper at his own home or at restaurants. Occasionally he even took Elizabeth out to supper on their own – she deserved to be cared for, and also he was aware that it was good for his image (he didn't use those words, but said to himself that it was 'the right thing to do').

Meanwhile Elizabeth had her own life during the day. She had to organize the work of the house, not the cleaning as she had an Indonesian 'treasure' for that, but there was always cooking as she preferred to offer visitors her own handiwork. She also helped out at a children's charity twice a week, and enjoyed time spent with her English friends. Mariam, too, took up some of her time and a lot of her attention, it was her job to bring the girl up to pass her exams, go eventually to university and then to marry someone suitable, and she took the responsibility seriously.

There was a good weekend when the boys came home, with their washing, from Homs. It was satisfying for their father to sit at the head of the table at lunch with all his family around him, and comfortable to play cards all together in the evening. Jamal was clearly happy in his own way, and there was nothing to complain of in Sayed, though he was not, perhaps as open and ingenuous as he had been .

Elizabeth enjoyed having the house full again too, she noticed the emptiness when they were away even more than her husband did. She threw up her hands in mock horror when they dumped their dirty washing at her feet, and she was busier in the kitchen than she had been for some time. However she revelled in the sight of the two young men sitting at the kitchen table and telling her the news, one head of black curly hair and the other of straight brown hair. It seemed as if they were the same children who had done exactly that when they had come home each day from school, though common sense told her that students are not like schoolboys, and they don't tell their mothers everything any more.

She felt a strain between them as well, that was new, but when she asked what was the matter she was met with blank looks and denials from both of them, so she gave up. No doubt it was something trivial – a student thing of

175

some sort. No need to spoil the weekend for it. Meanwhile, she had prepared food she knew they loved, and the cake tin was full of freshly-made cakes that she and Miriam had made together.

Like Bakri, Elizabeth felt especially comfortable sitting round the kitchen table on the Saturday evening, playing cards. They had a private, family version of Whist which always produced laughter and accusations that Elizabeth was cheating herself to let Bakri win –as in fact she often was – and ended with cups of tea and large slices of fruit cake before Mariam had to go to bed. Later that night, when Elizabeth was drifting off to sleep as she waited for her husband to come to bed, she was vaguely aware of raised voices from the sitting room, but they were not loud enough to disturb her.

In the big, comfortably furnished room Jamal was telling his father how embarrassing it was to have a brother who people talked about. How his friends drove cars with the speakers up too high so everybody turned to look at them as they passed, and how "my brother", he couldn't say his name, he was so angry, "was going to clubs and meeting the sort of girl you don't want to know about, Baba."

Sayed was equally angry, the more so because he was on the defensive, and raised his voice at Jamal, shouting,

"Just leave me alone. I haven't hurt you and I don't think I need you to tell me how to behave." He turned to his father and continued, "Baba, have I failed any of my exams? Have I overspent on my allowance? I don't see

176

why I can't have some sort of a life even if Grandfather here thinks everything is beneath him."

Half an hour later Bakri had managed to calm both his sons down. He had sympathy with both points of view, Jamal was perfectly right in wanting to avoid a scandal, but he could remember kicking over the traces himself as a student in Egypt so it was hard to condemn Sayed. Sayed agreed to be a little more discreet, and Jamal, while still maintaining that he was right, grudgingly admitted that his brother wasn't actually doing anything too dreadful yet. They went back to Homs the next afternoon after a large lunch and with bags of food and clean laundry, saying goodbye to their mother, father and sister apparently as friends, and life in the household returned to normal.

March was a very busy month for Bakri. There seemed to be a constant stream of traffic accidents to be dealt with, and many of them, or their families, asked specifically for him to care for the victims once the surgeons had patched them up as best they could. He often thought that if his neighbours could be persuaded actually to use the seatbelts in their cars, and the young men would sacrifice their macho image to crash-hats when riding motorbikes, there would be a lot less business for him and a lot fewer tragedies for their families. He complained about this again, after having yet another youth die while the surgeon was trying to stick him back together.

"They just don't think!" he said forcefully over the lunch table.

"No, dear, but you do as much as anyone can," was the response. "You can't change the world all by yourself. Don't forget that we are out to supper at Dr Omar's this evening. We should get there by nine-thirty; I said we wouldn't be late."

He promised to be home early and set off for his clinic in a cheerful frame of mind. The weather was pleasant, his patients were all doing reasonably well and Omar was a close friend, so the evening should be good. He even found a parking space close to the clinic, a fairly unusual happening.

A week later, towards the end of the month, he had just arrived at the afternoon clinic, this time with his head full of worries about two of his patients, when the phone rang, and he was surprised to see the call was from Jamal because his sons almost always called later in the evening. 'Oh, dear,' he thought, 'what's the matter this time?' but he didn't expect it to be more than the usual storm in a teacup that he was becoming accustomed to from Jamal.

"Baba, thank God I've got you. I need to talk to you." He didn't need to add 'without Mama knowing', and Bakri replied at once,

"What's the matter? Tell me what the problem is."

"Baba, it's Sayed. He's in prison and I don't know what to do."

"In the name of God, he's where? What are you talking about? What on earth has happened?"

"He was out with his friends again last night, I told you they were really bad people but you wouldn't listen. Well, last night – no, early this morning, it was about three

178

o'clock – he phoned me to go and help him in the police station in the middle of Homs. I got dressed and went as quickly as I could, but he had been arrested and they would only let me talk to him for a few minutes. They say he was in a car that killed someone, and that they were all drunk, the Police are really mad at them. Please can you come and sort it out?"

Bakri did what he had trained himself to do as a young man and took a deep breath to calm himself down.

"Was your brother driving?"

"No. I'm sure he wasn't. It was a boy called Wasim's father's car, a BMW, and he wouldn't let anyone else drive it, I'm certain."

"Thank Heaven for that. Now I'll have to close the clinic and tell your mother I'll be away, so I can't be there until tomorrow morning. In fact, I won't start out until daylight, there's no benefit in arriving at night, so I should be at the university by about ten thirty. Can you miss lectures tomorrow to take me to the police station?"

"Yes, of course. Thanks, Baba. Is there anything you want me to do now?"

"Find out who was driving the car, and who else was in it. If you can find their parents it would be a help as well."

"I'll do that straight away." Then his voice wavered and sounded much younger and less certain, "Don't be too long, Baba. Goodbye."

For a moment Bakri rested his elbows on his handsome and well-polished desk, letting his head drop into his hands. Another problem. Surely he knew someone in

179

Homs who could help? Oh, well. He wiped his hands over his face, sat up straight again and pressed the bell fixed in the floor just where his foot could find it.

The nurse entered, plain, square, reliable and thoroughly scarved, to hear him,

"I'll start seeing the patients now. Have you got the notes sorted?" as he had done for the last many years.

"Yes, doctor," the routine, reassuring response, "These are for the first patient. Do you want to see him now?" She looked again at him, noticing him as a person for the first time, probably, in years. "Are you ill, Doctor? Do you want me to cancel the clinic?

"No, no. I'll see them if they've come to see me. Don't worry, I'm fine." He managed a smile, and a slight movement of his head in her direction suggested that she got on with her job.

Fortunately for his peace of mind, it was now the end of the month, and there were not too many patients, the non-urgent cases would be back after pay-day on the first of April. He saw the last one through the door out of his office at eight-thirty, and walked right round to a lawyer friend, leaving the nurse to do her usual efficient job of clearing and tidying after him.

His friend was busy with a client, but by nine o'clock they were discussing possibilities over a cup of coffee. His friend was inclined to take an optimistic view of the affair.

"If Sayed wasn't driving?"

"No, no, Jamal is sure he wasn't."

"Then it wasn't his fault. You shouldn't have any problem getting him out of it, alcohol isn't illegal. Now if it had been drugs it would be a different matter."

"No, no. He doesn't take drugs, I'm sure of that." He hoped that what he was saying was true, but had a sudden flashback to his son's resentment when asked what he did do. Please God he wouldn't have to deal with that.

His friend continued,

"If you don't want to go yourself, I know a good lawyer there, he's a cousin of my wife's. He can sort it all out for you without any trouble."

"No. I'd better go myself. I don't want any problems later and I'd rather make sure everything is covered. But thank you, and perhaps you can give me his name. I'll need someone when I arrive."

The name was written on a slip of paper and handed it over.

"Here you are. Don't forget, if you have any problems there just phone him and he'll help. When are you setting out?"

"As soon as I can. Tomorrow first light I should think. Thanks again, I'll keep you in touch with what happens."

He excused himself and set off home trying to think of a convincing reason why he should be going to Homs at such short notice, without alarming Elizabeth or putting the idea of accompanying him into her mind. All the way home he was trying out different scenarios in his mind – he had been called to an old patient – there was a conference he had forgotten about – his cousin had come from America for a few days – they all had advantages and disadvantages, but he settled for the old patient, as that gave him good reason to be too busy to take her with him.

In the event, he had been wasting his time. When he walked in through the front door, Elizabeth and Mariam were bent over Mariam's French book, trying to do a difficult homework together. They looked up and smiled at him as he went past, then went back to it. He went to their bedroom, and took ten minutes off, stretched out on the bed with his arms above his head before returning to them to ask Elizabeth to pack a bag for him.

"Where are you going? You didn't say you would be leaving us, has something happened?" He mumbled something about a patient, and she immediately said,

"Oh, dear, what a pity. I can't come with you because Mariam has tests all this week and I really should be with her. Will you be all right on your own?"

"Yes, of course I will." He was very relieved, "It's nothing really, I should be coming right back. It wouldn't be very interesting for you anyway. Do you want me to bring you anything?"

"Not really, just come back quickly. Are you going by bus or driving?"

"I'll drive, it makes me more independent when I'm there."

"Must you? That road is so dangerous. Please drive carefully."

Mariam abandoned her homework and added her comment as she came round the table to him,

"Baba, don't drive too fast. They're always having accidents on that road. Are you sure you don't need Mummy? I can stay upstairs with Nana if you like."

"No, no, I'll be fine. Your mother needs to be here with you, that's what mothers are for." He ruffled her hair as she put her arms round him. "You take care of your mother, and don't let the cat steal too much while I'm away!"

She reacted as he had hoped, forgetting his journey in annoyance at the slur on her pet.

"Baba, that's not fair, he doesn't steal. Cats just eat what they find. We shouldn't leave things out because he doesn't know it's wrong." Her face was quite flushed, so he laughed and hugged her.

"I know he's the most remarkable cat in the world. Good night now, Mimi, I probably won't see you in the morning. Do you want anything from Homs?"

"No thanks, Baba, I can't think of anything special." Then she looked up at him slyly, "Unless you see some extra special cat food?"

"Off to bed with you," he laughed, "Good night."

The next morning he set off before it was fully light. He had not slept well, but had lain awake listening to Elizabeth's smooth breathing, worrying about Sayed and hoping that his wife would not find out and be worried with him. The alarm going off was a relief, meaning he could get out of bed and start doing something. Elizabeth made his coffee while he showered and shaved, and put into the car the bag she had packed for him the night

183

before. Very soon he had kissed her on the cheek and driven away from the house.

The main road took him through quiet streets out onto the Damascus road, where he was able to drive much faster, though he didn't rush too much for fear of meeting a farmer saving a lira or two in petrol by driving his tractor the wrong way up the road to his fields instead of going further along the dual carriageway and then doubling back. He was too worried by what he might find to enjoy the greenness of the fields on both sides of the road or the blue sky with the puffs of white cloud.

Circumventing Hama on the ring road, half an hour later he was approaching Homs and the traffic was increasing. Now he should be taking the big Homs ring road to go out on the West side towards the university, but he felt he deserved a break, and he was also increasingly worried about what he would find when he arrived. A breakfast of olives, cottage cheese, apricot jam, fresh bread and hot black tea revived both his body and his mood, and he covered the last stretch with very little delay.

While in the café, he took the chance to call Jamal and they arranged to meet outside the University campus. He was still a hundred metres away when Jamal spotted him and came hurrying towards the car, white-faced and anxious.

"Thank God you have arrived safely," he said, the polite formula getting more emphasis than it usually did. "I've already phoned the police station, but they didn't want to let me talk to Sayed. I kept telling them that he wasn't driving, but nobody listened to me." The young man

184

was almost in tears, and his father patted him on the shoulder.

"You know you did the right thing phoning me. I'll take care of it now if you show me where the police station is – it isn't a place I usually visit." He smiled at his son, who managed a watery smile back.

"Yes, Baba, I'll show you. It's back in the town centre." They got back into the car and retraced the route to Homs, then Jamal gave his father directions and they stopped outside an old building which Jamal told him was the right police station.

Inside, the doctor was treated with great respect and courtesy when he asked for help, so it was the more noticeable that the atmosphere cooled when he told them his business. The Desk Sergeant looked uncomfortable, and immediately sent a young policeman to see if the Colonel was busy. Thus, a few minutes later Bakri and Jamal were sitting on prickly upholstered armchairs in the Colonel's office. Bakri settled himself apparently at his ease, looking every inch the senior man, in control of the situation.

After the introductions and polite remarks necessary to any social or business situation in Syria, Bakri approached the business in hand,

"Colonel Nazir, please can you tell me how I can get my son back? I don't understand exactly what he is being held for."

The Colonel coughed behind his hand, from embarrassment rather than any physical reason and answered,

"I'm afraid your son was involved in an incident yesterday afternoon, and we can't ignore it. We are preparing the cases against all the young men involved at the moment. I'm sorry, but there is nothing to be done just now."

Bakri took a deep breath, and motioned for Jamal to keep quiet.

"I understand you have your procedures, but perhaps you could tell me exactly what happened."

"Your son – Sayed, I think – was in a car that killed an old man crossing the street. When the police got there they found all the people in the car were drunk, and when they asked for papers and information two of the young men started fighting them." Bakri managed to hide his relief that at least his son was not facing a drugs charge.

"Was Sayed driving the car?" The Colonel shuffled through the papers before answering.

"No."

"Was he one of the ones fighting the police?" This was a genuine worry, as he knew that Sayed was quite capable of getting angry quickly, and fuelled by alcohol might easily have become aggressive.

Again the shuffling of papers, then, "No, it seems not."

"In that case, do you have reason to hold him any longer? I don't think it is illegal to be drunk as he wasn't driving, and you say he didn't resist arrest. I'm sure you can see that I want to take care of my son and am shocked that he was drunk and put himself in such a difficult situation. If you could let me take him home, I will guarantee that he doesn't leave the country, so if you need him again you can find him."

The Colonel was impressed by Dr Bakri, who was using all his solidly respectable personality to produce just such a result. He decided on the easy option and asked the men to wait outside while he phoned the General. Bakri politely agreed and requested permission to see his son, all the while Jamal remaining silent.

A policeman was called to take them to the cells positioned below in the cellars, and a heavy iron door was unlocked to let them enter. In the small, stuffy room were Sayed and one of his friends, both looking tired, dirty, shocked, a little bruised and generally the worse for wear. They looked up as the door opened, and as soon as he saw his father, Sayed heaved himself up off the thin mattress on the floor and flung himself into his father's arms. He managed not to cry, but it was a near thing.

"Baba, I'm so glad you've come! It's been horrible. Wasim was driving too fast and then we hit this man." Sayed shuddered, "You could feel the thump right through the car, I thought we were going to go off the road. And then the police came and everyone was shouting, and Wasim and Abed were fighting them. And they said we were all responsible and I didn't know what to do. How can we keep it from Mama? I can't bear for her to know. What's going to happen?"

Sayed ran out of words and breath, and his father was able to put him on one side and shake hands with the other boy, Hamoudi, who was obviously equally upset and waiting for his own parents to arrive. It occurred to him that these two had already been separated from the others, as facing less trouble, and he felt a little more optimistic.

In the event, after guaranteeing his son's return with a sizeable bail, and leaving Sayed's identity card at the station so he could not leave the country, and effectively would have to stay either at home or on the university campus, Bakri was able to pack both of his sons into the car by two o'clock in the afternoon. He was furious with Sayed, but didn't want to make a fuss in public, nor did he want to encourage Jamal, who was obviously itching to shout at his brother. For the moment it was better to drive quietly away and find a restaurant for lunch, at least after a drive back to the university campus to allow Sayed to shower, shave and change his clothes, which were certainly out of keeping with those of his meticulously neat father and brother.

Lunch was a sombre affair, with all of them aware of the death that Sayed had been passively involved in, but Sayed looked a lot better with a good meal inside him – young men are seldom put off their food by disgrace. Then he delivered the two boys back to the campus, Sayed very chastened by events, and Jamal persuaded to be magnanimous about the whole business, partly because he was fond of his brother and had been shocked at the sight of the prison cell and also because his father had hinted that he would be most displeased if he acted in any other way. He warned them to behave as normally as they could, otherwise their mother was bound to find out and to be very upset. This was an effective guarantee of good behaviour, as all their lives they had been careful not to upset her.

At five o'clock he was driving back north along the Homs ring road, with the possibility of being home by half past seven, so he stopped to phone Elizabeth and told her to expect him for supper.

When he arrived home he just said that the case had been less difficult than he had expected – in fact, the literal truth – and he was glad not to have had to stay the night. The next day he surprised his nurse by arriving at the usual time for his clinic, and had a peaceful day with all his patients proceeding as they ought. He called the boys, and found Jamal very sorry for Sayed, and Sayed extremely apologetic and subdued.

He and Elizabeth were due to go out that night to supper at a restaurant with a large group of friends, and he was home on time, to find Elizabeth dressed and finishing her makeup while Mariam sat on the end of her bed, admiring her mother.

"Doesn't she look lovely, Baba? That's my favourite dress."

He looked round from his wardrobe, where he was choosing a tie to go with the suit and shirt laid out for him on the bed.

"Your mother always looks beautiful, but yes, it is a nice dress." He smiled at Elizabeth and said, "I like your hair, dear."

Elizabeth glowed at the praise, and preened herself in front of the mirror,

"Thank you dear, you always make me feel good."

189

COFFEE MORNING – June

The last of the monthly coffee mornings before everyone started to drift away on holiday was at Janet's. She saw Sami and Solah off to summer school and the daily woman getting on with the cleaning, hindered by Zaki, then rushed to the kitchen to check on the cakes, the coffee and the cold drinks for her visitors.

Ross and Chris came together in Ross' new car. The murder of her mother-in-law had been followed by a series of scandals. Her father-in-law's second wife and a whole collection of half-brothers and sisters for Rustum had hit hardest, but Rustum was adjusting to it, although he didn't want his son to be too friendly with them. However the money he had inherited had provided a large new car for each of them, a Sri Lankan maid to do the housework and to look after Omar when his mother was busy, and the prospect of longer and more expensive holidays.

The day was hot enough to make the air conditioning very welcome to Elizabeth, who sank into an armchair when she arrived. She savoured a cold drink of fruit juice and the cool room after the walk from her house that she inflicted on herself even in the hottest weather in the sacred name of exercise. Now she looked round her friends and reflected that it had been a more eventful year than most.

Ross appeared well and prosperous now. The horrible murder in her family, and the gruesome death of the murderer and his mother had shocked away her image of efficient successful affluence for a very short time in February. Now at the end of June she had regained her balance comletely, and when the year of mourning ended, which her husband insisted on keeping to the last day, she would be ready to start entertaining on a lavish scale. Meanwhile, the black, grey and navy clothes that Rustum insisted she wear for this year were extremely well cut and sported very famous labels.

Elizabeth looked fondly at Janet as she came in with the coffee pot. She felt comfortable with Janet, always reliable and uncomplicated, living peacefully with her pleasant husband and children. Janet had had all that trouble with Susan and her little boy who was killed by the bus, and had dealt with it so calmly. Mind you, her husband made a difference. Elizabeth was sure that her own Bakri would have been very difficult to live with if she had landed a crying woman on him for a week or however long it had been. He would have insisted on her returning to her husband, which was right and proper she supposed, but doubtfully.

Susan still kept in touch with Janet by the occasional email, but when Elizabeth or Janet saw her ex-husband in the street he gave no sign of recognizing them. It was probably natural in the circumstances, and easier than having to talk to him.

Janet came and sat beside her for a minute and asked her about her holiday plans.

"I think we are going to Turkey for a few days once all the exams are over. We probably won't go to England this year, but my parents are coming over in October, so it doesn't matter. What about you?"

Janet answered happily,

"Oh, we're all going together for August. Mohammed booked the tickets a month ago, didn't I tell you? My sister has finally decided to marry again and she wants us there. The problem is what to take as a wedding present. I can't think of anything she wants that she doesn't have already, especially from the choice I have here." She got up again to start serving coffee and cakes, and Elizabeth sat back and sipped her coffee.

Alone for a moment, she looked happily around the room at her friends. These were people she was comfortable with. This year they were a small group, but there were certain to be others because there were always single young men going to English-speaking countries to study. Some went straight from school and more went to do post-graduate work, but they were there for the most critical years of their lives. If they had not married girls from home they were fairly sure to get involved with girls from the country where they were studying, and some of those would end up coming back here with them. She hoped the glory days of fifteen years ago would return soon, when there were so many women at the coffee morning that they overflowed into the living room and the dining room. Who knew how many would be here by September?

AFTERWARDS

Prologue

This is a story based round my experiences in Syria in 2013. The events inside the house are fiction, but I have put in many things I believed to be accurate news at the time. 'Only the names', as they say, 'have been changed to protect the innocent'. The point of view is that of Elizabeth, so this is not an objective view, however it is one which is seldom heard in the West, so may be enlightening.

Since I left, the ISIL set of fighters has brought more distress to the area, not least to the majority who are truly horrified to be identified as belonging to the same religion as people who seem to them to be God-defying terrorists.

Aleppo, 2013

February 17th

I wake up, stretch and reach out to ruffle Bakri's hair. I feel round his pillow, and pull my hand back quickly when I remember that he'll never be there again. He's gone. I don't want to open my eyes and see the bedroom we've shared for almost forty years. It's a strange, scary place without Bakri to bring it life. I struggle with the urge to scream that it isn't fair, it isn't true, but I know that it is true, and that I mustn't make a noise because my poor Mariam will hear me and be even more upset than she was yesterday at the funeral. There was enough shelling last night to disturb anyone's sleep, so if Mariam can have an extra few minutes now she should be left to it.

Shells criss-cross the city every night. For those living within half a kilometre of a gun emplacement, and that's most of us in this beleaguered quarter of the city, the thud – whizz of the outgoing shells has become a background noise, even the house-cats take little notice – the flick of an ear or an enquiring raised head before going back to sleep. It's only in the areas where the shells are falling that the night is horrible, spent in uncosy cellars hoping and praying that there will be an escape route when the shelling eases at daylight.

Yesterday morning there were just a few people walking across Sa'adullah Jabri square, by the main post office. In normal times it would be crowded with all sorts of traffic, pedestrians moving on this main north-south road where it crosses an equally important east-west route, while cars, trucks and motorcycles slowly honk their way along the one-way system round the central area full of people lounging about or boys playing football. But now, snipers shooting from the rebel east side of town at anything moving mean the benches in the middle are empty. The eastern side of the square has been blown up by a car bomb so the road is shut, and those people who have to use the square to get somewhere tend to stay on the north side, where they are not such easy targets.

Dr. Bakri had to cross the square every day to get to his clinic, though, being in the Minsheah area close to the rebels, he cut down his hours because, despite his good reputation, patients were not happy to take serious risks to see him. Most doctors in the area gave up and saw all their patients in hospitals or even in their homes, but Dr. Bakri was not going to be dictated to by people he despised. He knew how much money the government had put into the system and was convinced that anyone who was prepared to kill people in order to change it was beneath contempt.

Each day at nine o'clock sharp he marched across the square as if he owned it, and several times he had heard the whistle and crack of bullets as he made his determined way, but the odds were against him and this time he heard nothing, feeling only a thump on the side of his head. He was dead before he hit the ground, and didn't know that the other people crossing the square ran to him, doubled over trying not to be hit themselves. Then, when somebody recognised him, they started shouting that the doctor was dead. There was hardly any blood on the ground, he had only taken the one shot, and he almost didn't look dead when the shooting stopped, the ambulance arrived and his body was moved.

"He can't have known anything about it", they said to me. "He died instantly". They told me that at the Razi hospital, where I rushed to see him as soon as I heard of the 'accident', though he was already dead. Their words were designed to comfort, but at that moment I didn't want hear them. I felt cut off from them all, in my own bubble, waiting for Bakri to wake up and get on with our life, until Mariam came as fast as she could, and hugged me and we leaned against each other and she cried. Then Mariam insisted on taking me back to her own husband and family in Shahba Jedid, and putting me to bed in the spare room I often occupied when Bakri was away and I took the chance to visit her and our grandchildren overnight.

I was only able to rest for an hour or two because funerals usually take place on the day of the death and I had to be back home. It was after the midday prayers, though neither of our boys could get back to Aleppo to attend. Fortunately, Bakri has plenty of cousins who could be at the mourning, and these days it's all too usual for families to be broken apart and unable to get together. Mariam and I sat in my formal sitting room with the folding doors open onto the everyday room so there would be plenty of room for all the women mourners who would come at the time when Bakri's body was taken to the mosque for prayers before the burial.

Assia knew what had to be done. She came to live with us when our last Indonesian maid went home and there were no more coming because of the fighting. Assia's family have mostly been killed during attacks either by the army or the rebels, so she was glad to have a place to stay, and now she could safely be left with the arrangements. The front door was open and the traditional triangular frames covered with flowers were arranged on the stairs. Even in these strange times the wreaths filled the stairway, and more were being brought every minute, it seemed. She must have started work as soon as I left for the hospital because she had rolled up the antique persian rugs in the front room, moved the silver vases and and the crystal bowls, and pushed the pretty chairs to the sides of the room, making space for the stacks of white plastic seats for all the mourners who were sure to come. It didn't look like my flat when I returned, but I was grateful she had taken charge.

A special van is always used to carry bodies to the mosque and then the graveyard. It drew up on time, its loudspeaker giving out the Koranic verses appropriate for a death, and I thought my own heart would stop beating when I heard the shuffling footsteps of the pall bearers carrying the open coffin with Bakri's body. I heard them edge the box out of the study near the door, where he had been overnight, and I needed to say good bye to him, even though I had to push through the women quite roughly, with Mariam trying to tell me I shouldn't. How could I let him leave our house for the last time without kissing him goodbye? Every day of our marriage I kissed him goodbye until now. I had to do it, to say goodbye to my rock for almost 40 years. I had to know he was truly leaving and would not just open the door one evening and ask what was for supper.

There was a further time of distress when my brother-in-law came back. The funeral cortege had been stopped at the dividing line between the army and the rebels, and the family told that only he and the driver of the hearse would be allowed through to the graveyard, so the burial had been hurried and lacking in the ceremony due to such an eminent doctor. This was the final straw for me, and the tears which could not come before started flowing down my face, though I managed to keep silent and not to lose control of myself completely.

Now I have to get out of bed and dress in black, which Bakri hated for me. I am a natural blonde, well, I was blonde until the last few years and I still keep my hair that colour, and he loved my blonde hair and blue eyes to be set off by pastel colours. But today it has to be black to be ready for the second day of mourning. Like the first day, when women started arriving as soon as his death was announced on our local minaret, the women will come from about ten in the morning until about two thirty, then the men will come in the evening. The men are not my problem. I shouldn't see them or be seen by them, and Bakri's brother and eldest cousins will be there to receive them in the room the women use during the day.

Mariam puts her head round the bedroom door, her face pale but as composed as she has almost always been, even as a child.

"Mum, you're awake. Did you sleep?" mostly, I had. The dreadful morning before and then the exhausting day of the funeral accepting the condolences of so many relations and close friends of the family, added to a stray sleeping tablet I found in my bedside drawer, meant that I don't remember much after getting into bed, except feeling too sad almost to breathe. In the early morning there must have been an explosion quite near, because I woke up again and listened to the shelling, but then I must have dropped off to sleep again, and now it's daytime and this nightmare is still going on.

I don't want to move. Every part of my body feels heavy in the bed, and I'm sure that the effort of getting up, let alone dressing and sitting in the front room for another day, is beyond me. Then Mariam comes and sits on the bed beside me.

"Mum, if you want to stay in bed today I'll look after everything and tell the visitors that you're ill."

This gives me the reason I need for moving. I can't let her do that alone. I pull myself up to a sitting position and put my arm round my daughter – the one of our children who never has caused problems and is always there to help.

"No, dear. I'll get up now and we can have a cup of tea together before the women start arriving."

"Well, stay in bed for now, and we can have it here." Mariam goes to the bedroom door and calls,

"Assia, can you make two cups of tea and bring them here, please?" There is a faint answer from the kitchen,

"Yella, (which means, roughly, OK) I'll be there in a minute."

The tea comes and we sit quietly to drink it. I am still in bed, wrapped up against the February cold, and Mariam is in the big blue velvet-covered armchair where her father always drank his morning coffee. Neither of us wants to talk about him because we can't do so without crying, and his death has pushed everything else out of our heads.

During the morning we sit on the largest of the settees at the end of the room furthest from the door, and greet each of the women who enters and makes her way through the crowd of chairs to kiss us and to murmur the correct geeting, "May life be yours", while the Koran is playing on a quiet CD, and the women already seated pray for my Bakri's soul.

They mean so well, clicking their beads as they count the hundreds then thousands of ejaculatory prayers – "God is Great", 'There is no God but God, and Mohammed is His prophet' – or silently reading sections of the Koran, so they can calculate how many times the whole book has been read for him, but I am too exhausted to pay much attention, though Mariam and I are both wearing scarves out of respect for the Koran. However, even I, exhausted and shocked, am calmed a little by the atmosphere of prayer which envelops the room for most of the morning.

I find time to be relieved that the electricity is on this morning so the room is warm enough. So often we have to wrap ourselves up in all sorts of woollies if we want to be

200

comfortable, and all of mine are colours that would cause scandal if I wore them today. I only have black clothes at all because they are necessary when I have to go to a funeral or a condolence visit, I never ever thought I would be wearing them for Bakri.

There's a phone call from Jamal at about midday and I have to make my apologies quietly to the crowds of women in black and take the call in my bedroom. He's working in Dubai now and he's been trying for 24 hours to get through, but the telephone lines from Aleppo are down to everywhere except Turkey so he's had to get his call put through via a friend in Ankara. This means it isn't very clear, but he's able to find out how his father died and what has been done. He wastes some of the precious minutes asking why his father took such a risk, but then remembers what he should be doing. He promises me that he will come as soon as he can, and tells me not to worry about money.

I put the phone down, reminded that for the first time since our marriage I will have to be responsible for the finances of the house, which is a daunting thought. Bakri always told me that I was not to worry about anything, so I didn't, and that whatever I really wanted I must have, which was a pleasant way to live. I was his silver princess and he looked after everything. Now I remember that he kept cash, both liras and dollars, in the safe behind our bed-head but I know I will have to wait until everyone except Mariam leaves before I check to see how much, or little, I have to manage on until I can use the money in his bank account. It is another blow, but this time I am rather ashamed of myself, because the tears I'm trying to control are for me and not for my dear Bakri.

Sayed phones as the last of the visitors is leaving. Unlike his older brother, who spoke calmly and tried to reassure Mariam and me, Sayed sobs down the phone about how his father was the only head of the family and what will they do now he is gone? I have to exert myself to calm him, but it takes the last of my energy and finally Mariam takes the phone from me and speaks to her brother. She asks him when he will be home, because we know he's in Beirut, but he can't give us a date, only promises us he's thinking of us all the time and it will be as soon as possible.

Finally, it seems like years later, there's only Mariam and me left in the house, even Assia has gone out to see some relatives. Mariam makes me a mug of tea the English way, waits while I take a couple of paracetamol tablets and sees me into bed before going home for a few hours to catch up on her own children who've been in the care of her mother-in-law and her cleaner. She'll be back to sleep over with me, but for an hour or two I have the silence and solitude that I desperately need. There are sounds of shelling, and sometimes the thump of something heavy being fired, but it's not very close, and is also in the opposite direction to Mariam's flat, so I'm able to sleep despite the noise.

Life is not happy here. For months the pavements have been full of bombed-out shopkeepers trying to earn a living with the remains of their stock. The schools, university residences, mosques, churches and partly finished buildings are crammed with displaced families who are being fed each day (mostly) by lots of volunteer organisations like the Red Crescent, the Red Cross, the Jesuit Refugee Service and small spontaneous groups. They are supported by donations from countries as far away as India, but not from Europe. It is embarrassing – or it was before I had other things to worry about – that there is not so much as a packet of soup or a tin of milk from England for the poor people who have stayed here. The British Government seems to be supporting the rebels whatever they do.

February18th

Today is the last day of formal mourning, and it is the tradition that women who are not especially close but wish to pay their respects should come. I am so tired that it is difficult to murmur the correct greeting and to remember those faces I should know. There should also be a family meal at the end of today's mourning, but the only decision I have made in these last few days is not to have it. Mariam agrees with me, and we are sending the money that would have been spent to one of the food kitchens, a local convent, where they always need extra supplies.

February 19th

After the funeral and the three days of mourning with so many people in the house, I've got to adjust to such a new life. Before, Bakri organised just about everything, from the place we lived and the friends who visited right down to what vegetables came into the house. I loved being protected and cossetted, only occasionally did I feel rebellious and then only for a short time. Now I must set to and organise my own life. Each day I have to decide to get up in the morning and to go to bed at night.

The news is bad again today. Assia came early and was followed by a nurse from the hospital where Bakri worked. This woman always had his admiration because she is married to a complete disaster of a man, and manages to raise their children, five I think, on her salary as a nurse, while he sits at home watching television or plays cards with his friends at a coffee shop. They are Kurdish and living in a Kurdish quarter called Sheikh Maqsoud, where they have a tiny house that she has managed to buy in the rougher side of the area. Today she hugs me and tells me how much she misses the doctor, and she is crying, which is pretty much what I expect from most of the nurses who visit me. But from her it is a surprise. Her life has always been so hard that crying is something she just doesn't do – I expect she would have collapsed years ago if she had indulged in tears. Now she tells me news which really does shock me.

One of the Kurdish political parties, I always mix them up, has sold out to the rebels, who have taken over the roadblocks which kept them out. She tells me that a lot of money changed hands, and that the people who were paid have run off to Turkey. I don't know how much is true, but certainly she is one of a very large number of residents who have left. Now she has taken her children to the hospital where she works, and they are living in an empty ward at the top of the building. She tells me that a lot of the people were spitting at the new guards on the roadblocks, and she saw her husband there as well. Apparently she told him to go and get himself killed because he'd always been useless and now he was disgusting as well. She's a brave woman, she could easily have got herself shot on the spot.

February 22nd

Mariam is worried that I am getting depressed – I think I have the right to be a bit depressed, but it is nice of her to care. To take my mind off my troubles, and everyone else's too, she has brought me a sack of lemons to make lemon squash for the summer. There are twenty four kilos of lemons, so I should be kept from worrying quite effectively, bless her.

First I have to wash the lemons, then there is the job of taking off the zest from some of them and storing it in the fridge in some juice. This is hampered by the fridge being off more than it is on, but the weather is cold enough that it will probably be all right. Juicing twenty five kilos of lemons when the electricity is so unreliable is another challenge, but when the power disappears half way through the job I am so 'in to it' that I curse, drag out the old hand press and carry on. The beautiful lemon smell is certainly cheering, and I'm feeling much less depressed by the time I measure the sugar into the big bowl I've used for this job since the children were small. Now I have to keep stirring the sugar and lemon mixture until all the sugar has disappeared, then there is a lovely squishy job forcing the

205

lemon flavour out of the zest and pouring it into the squash and it will be 'job done'.

The flat is so cold that I have to move the bowl from window to window to get a bit of warmth from the sun, but at least it makes me remember to stir the mixture, and I suppose it counts as exercise as well. I look at the clock when I finish to see how long I have before Bakri comes in, and everything is back. He isn't coming in. Ever. The afternoon stretches in front of me.

February 25th

I hate the telephone this morning. The news about Sheikh Maqsoud seems to be even worse than I first heard. Yara phoned today and told me that one of their workers has just escaped from his flat there. Last night he heard a noise in the street and looked out to see his neighbour who was a sergeant in the army, but only working in a military office, pulled out onto the street and beheaded in front of his two small boys and his pregnant wife, who promptly miscarried. Their worker grabbed his own children and slipped away with his wife and their identity papers. They got to a bridge where they could see an army tank, and were taken on board with another family, and delivered to a nearby Christian area. By this time it was about three in the morning and they were all exhausted, but they had nowhere to go except Yara's home, for her husband's help. Fortunately they saw a light in a church when they were on their way, and got a place to sleep there.

Yara's husband is trying to find them somewhere to stay, but our side of the city is so crowded with people who are frightened either of the fighting or of the rebels that he's got a hard job to do and she thinks the man will try to get to his relatives in a Kurdish village near the border. He was so much in a rush to leave that he remembered the family papers (life in Syria without your identity card and family book is almost impossible) but forgot quite a large wad of money he had stored against an emergency like this. I hope he isn't silly enough to go back to try and fetch it.

It puts my own problems into perspective. Bakri died so quickly that he can't have suffered, I am safe in my own flat and the children are all safe. Jamal is away in Dubai where he's been for quite some years now. He's a 'merchandiser' for a big company there, which he explains to me fairly regularly but I never really grasp. He's not married though he's well into his thirties now, but I think he's been too busy with his career.

Sayed has not done so well. He has always been the one we worried about, and I know his father smoothed one lot of trouble over for him when he was a student, though nobody told me the details.After he finally graduated he worked for the national oil company near the Iraqi border– not very well paid – but that job got too risky and he came back to Aleppo last year and was helping Mariam's husband in his factory and living here with us. He didn't much like the routine, and when his girl-friend's family went to Canada he really lost heart. Then Adnan had to close the factory and just now he's working in Beirut, but he hasn't been there long and I'm not sure what he's doing. I know he was hoping to marry Suha before all this trouble started, and I'm so sad for him. He's always been a bit erratic and the one I worried about, but perhaps he's found a good job and will be able to settle down in Lebanon.

Mariam was her father's delight. She seemed to be on the same wavelength as he, much more than the boys. Perhaps it's because she is six years younger than Sayed so she was like an only child, where Jamal and Sayed are so close together that they were more like twins. She married against her father's wishes – nothing but a doctor who was also a prince on a white horse would have really suited him – but eventually he put a good face on it for the wedding and soon got to like Adnan, even though he is from a business family not a professional one, and didn't finish his university degree while Mariam finished very well and will do her Master's degree when she has time.

March 2nd

I have to be home all day, and most of my friends have left so I'm beginning to get interested in the flat again. Really, there isn't anything else I can do because the only women still here that I used to be close friends with are so committed to one side or another that I can't bear to talk to them, or so sad that we can't help each other.

I wander from room to room in my pyjamas, a cooling mug of coffee in my hands. Everything seems so dull and depressed and I realise it is because there are so many extra bits and pieces in each room that Assia's best efforts aren't enough to keep the rooms shiny and clean the way they always were. I'll have either to do more myself or put a lot of the photos and pieces of silver and china away.

Side tables full of photo frames, and cabinets stuffed with pretty souvenirs of anniversaries and holidays are irrelevant now Bakri isn't here, and they collect dust and dirt.

The air in this part of town was getting dirtier and dirtier each year as the city grew round us so rapidly, but all the poor refugees from other parts of town have made the problem so much worse. They are living all over the place, and their rubbish spreads around them and brings flies and horrible smells even into this flat. I know the dustbin men are doing their best, but somebody told me that the big recycling plant was blown up last year by the rebels and the landfill holes are too far out of town to be safe, so I can't imagine what they are doing with the trucks of rubbish. The result for me is tarnished silver and china ornaments which feel slightly sticky to the touch. I go to the kitchen and swap my mug for a big enamel tray, to make a small start on clearing what our more affected friends called my 'objets d'arte'. Everything will have to be cleaned and then packed away somewhere, but I'm not yet sure where that will be – in the small loft, I suppose.

Clothes don't take up any time because I only have a few black things to wear and I can't face putting on any other colours. Mariam says I could wear grey, but when I opened the wardrobe to think about it I could remember buying the pale grey jersey and trousers when Bakri and I went to the Carrefour shopping mall for the last time before it was attacked. I believe it has been destroyed now. Such a pity. It was the first mall in the city, with escalators and pretty shops and cafes. Bakri and I went there to shop in a real supermarket and to have an evening cup of coffee, and we found the sort of clothes we like there as well. I don't think I can wear that outfit yet. Today, actually getting out of my pyjamas, into the shower then into day clothes takes all the energy I can still find. Often I don't bother until I am pushed into moving by thinking about the worry I'll cause to Mariam if my darling daughter finds me sitting about, unwashed and undressed, when she drops in for her daily visit.

March 7th

Slowly the days fall into a pattern. I am alone at night, at my own wish, and then early in the morning Assia arrives from the cousin's where she is staying now, and the day gets going. Mariam usually comes by in the morning, and always brings the children over for an hour in the afternoon, breaking up the long stretch till bedtime is back. The first week I slept badly unless I took sleeping tablets, but then I began to worry about becoming addicted so I put up with a few nights of sleeplessness until my sleep came back.

I had forgotten about the viber facility on my phone and it was a shock when it started to ring this afternoon. It kept on ringing while I tried to press the right picture on the silly little screen, but I'm glad I persisted because it was my sister, Jenny. She had been trying for ages, but mostly there hasn't been any internet at the times she could ring. This time she was lucky, and I was happy to hear her voice, though as usual she was scolding me – but that's sisters for you, especially older sisters! The conversation went something like this:

"How are you? Are you well? What's happening? Are you safe? We see dreadful things on the TV every day."

"We're all well and we're not in danger" (under my breath adding 'I hope').

"When are you coming home? We're waiting for you."

"Well, I'm keeping the four months in the house for Bakri's memory."

"You're *what*! Are you crazy? You should be coming here where it's safe."

I know she's worried about me, and I'm happy that she cares, but reality here is different from there. I absolutely want to do this for Bakri. It is the last thing I can do for him, and I feel that then I will be free to go away. At least, I think that's what I feel. Sort of paying my dues. It just wouldn't be right to up sticks and go straight away, but how can a worried sister understand that? She always tried to organise my life until I met Bakri, and she wants to keep me safe now he isn't around any more. I am slightly shocked to realise that before I was married I managed to go my own way, and I often ignored her and my mother's advice.

When I think how I travelled to Australia for a year, and cycling and sailing holidays I went on either alone or with friends they didn't approve of, I wonder at myself becoming so dependent on Bakri and feel slightly and surprisingly annoyed with him. I manage to stay calm and eventually she rings off, threatening to come and collect me as soon as she can get a visa, but that shouldn't be any time quickly as the Syrian Embassy in London and the British Embassy in Damascus have both been shut down.

Miraculously, the electricity is on for most of the day, so I get some washing into the machine and it gets to the end of the cycle. Result! As I'm hanging it on the balcony, keeping out of sight as much as possible, I feel homesick for England and for Jenny, with her cheerful husband, their well-organised life, their pension plans and their paid up mortgage. When Bakri was here I didn't even imagine that I would feel this way, but now I feel so vulnerable.

March 10th

I didn't sleep well last night. First of all I couldn't get to sleep, then when I finally dropped off Jeannette rang me from France. She was just thinking about going to bed and thought of me. Thank you, Jeannette! She doesn't seem very happy in France but she thinks her husband is very selfish to want her to come back. I try to sound sympathetic because I know her marriage has never been ecstatically happy, but it is hard not to tell her that she is lucky he is alive to want her here. When she finally rings off I lie there, wide awake and so alone in this big bed. In the last few years, when Bakri was away for any reason, I went with him or stayed with Mariam and her family. Now I have to get used to this space with only me.

The nights are cold and I can't put the heating on because I can't get enough fuel, so Assia went around the pharmacies yesterday until she found a supply of hot water bottles. She bought ten of them, his whole stock, and gave me two, Mariam three (for the children) and her family the

212

rest. God bless Assia! She's made it possible for us all to sleep well.

March 14th

The internet was on today when the electricity came so I was able to have a look at my emails and there was a surprise waiting for me. Janet had sent me a message saying that she heard about Bakri and was very sorry. I expect she heard from her husband's family because it must be ten years since they left. We've kept in touch with Christmas letters, and Bakri and I visited them a few times when we were on holiday in England, but when they moved to Sweden we didn't get over there.

I read the email again, carefully, and get the feeling that she is worried that I can't cope with life without Bakri. 'You were so close. What will you do without him?' Perhaps I'm too sensitive, but it sounds to me as if she thinks I will just fold up and die. I suppose I would have expected that, too, but now he's gone and I haven't folded up, I'm still here. It's a bit astonishing that her email, which I'm certain was very kindly meant, makes me rather irritated. And even a little bit more positive about the future. I start to write a message back telling her that though I am sad I am perfectly all right and will be able to get my future sorted very well, thank you. Then when I read it back I realise it sounds really quite nasty so I delete it and decide to wait a few days before answering. I learnt a long time ago that waiting before writing is often a good idea!

March 15th

Bakri has been gone for almost a month. It doesn't seem possible. Last night I had such a vivid dream about him that I knew he was there. We were going up the grand staircase into the dining room of the Aleppo Club in the centre of town and I could feel his hand resting on the small of my back, the way he always escorted me. I can't remember which dress I was wearing, but we were going to dinner with somebody and we were looking forward to it.When I woke up I still felt happy until I realised it was only a dream. Realising again that he has gone is almost as bad as the first time.

In some ways our life before the troubles began all seems like a dream now. We seem to have had parties all the time, smart clothes were very important and we both took travelling and shopping for granted. Then it all stopped quite quickly as the rebels got nearer and nearer to town. The last few weeks before he had his accident I almost didn't leave the house as he was frightened I would be kidnapped because I am his wife. Being blonde didn't help because it made me more noticeable, but at least he never suggested I should start wearing a scarf!

March 16th

I wake up with a splitting headache because the noise last night was so bad. Bang, bang all night, with an explosion near enough to shake the building and make the windows rattle. I phone Mariam to make sure she's all right and she hasn't had nearly such a bad night. I expect it was an attack on the Governor's official home tound the corner, or the Security Police office up the road.

Assia arrives earlier than her usual nine o'clock – it used to be seven thirty on the dot, but why bother now? - and tells me that the roundabout at the top of the rise, away from the security police but near the university, was hit. Heaven knows who they were really aiming for. I still have enough paracetamol left in the medicine box so two of those and a cup of tea are all I want before I go back to bed and leave Assia to her own devices.

April 3rd

Today it was my turn to comfort Mariam. She came alone because she was so upset and she and Adnan try hard to keep a good atmosphere in the house for the children. She told me that one of Adnan's workers from when he used to have the factory came to him very upset yesterday evening.

The man's nephew, only about thirteen years old, was living with his mother on this side of town and trying to make a living for them by selling bread. He decided that he needed a trolley which he remembered leaving in their flat on the other side of town. Of course his mother was horrified that he wanted to cross the 'line', but he reckoned that he was too young and too poor to attract attention so he went. Then he disappeared, and reappeared, dead, on a battlefield. This fits with other rumours that children are being used as 'cannon fodder' by the less pleasant parts of the opposition. I comfort her as much as I can, and we have mugs of instant coffee from what is becoming my

215

precious store before she calms down and goes back to her family.

I know the rebels have plenty of reasons to be angry, but what good does it do them to break innocent people's hearts like this? The 'good' part of their movement must be very depressed at what the 'bad' ones are doing. It seems that there are so many splits in their groups that almost anyone can try to make a fortune by whatever means come to hand.

April 8th

The days are getting longer now we are into April, and that makes staying home a little less dreary. It is also nice that the weather is much warmer so I don't need to worry about keeping warm during the day, though the evenings are still chilly. It used to be my favourite time of year. I don't know how I'll manage being here in the middle of December, alone and with the shutters and curtains closed by five o'clock.

Being alone in the flat at night makes me a little nervous, so I usually leave the sitting room door slightly open in case there should be any strange noises – the idea of something happening in my flat and me being unaware of it is too creepy to think about. So far there has been nothing to hear, nor have the police or anybody else I might be scared of rung the doorbell or knocked at the door.

This evening I am sitting watching a television programme. The electricity is off again, but dear Adnan, Mariam's husband, has got me some petrol to run our little

216

generator so I don't have to sit in the dark. It is a 'nature' programme, but I'm not so much 'watching' it as 'sitting in front of' it', my thoughts are so far away that it could be almost anything in front of me. I am sitting with the cup of herbal tea I always make myself before bedtime, and trying to summon up the energy to take a shower because the electricity was on today long enough to heat the water.Then I do hear a noise, the noise of a key in the front door. For a moment I am frozen to my seat, but not knowing is even worse than looking so I go quickly into the hall to find out what's happening. The door opens quietly, while I am so scared that I think I'll die, and Sayed is standing in front of me. I rush to him and hug him.

"Sayed! At last! I've missed you so much. Why has it been so long? The road to Beirut has been open for at least a month. I know it's a long way round, but you should have come." Then I stand back from him. The first thing I notice is the dirty smell, and when I really look at him I see that his clothes are filthy and he surely hasn't shaved for days.

"Good grief, Sayed, what has happened to you? Were you attacked on the way? Where is your luggage? When did you leave Beirut?"

Sayed smiles down at me, the tallest in the family. He takes after my father. But his face is thin and pale and his shoulders stooped, not at all like the smart young man who is my son.

"I had to come and see you, but I can't stay very long. I don't want to get you into any trouble, or anyone else in the family. I haven't brought anything with me."

"What on earth do you mean? Come in and sit down. When did you eat last? Do you want to have a shower first? I've never seen you so dirty."

"Is there any hot water? A shower is exactly what I need before I tell you all the news. You don't have any food ready, do you?"

I become the archetypal mother and get busy fetching him dry towels, then going into his old bedroom to hunt up some clean clothes among the things he left behind. As soon as I hear the shower starting I hurry to the kitchen to heat up the food left over from today, which I had planned to finish tomorrow. Thank heavens I've got a new tank of gas for the cooker, because the other one is hooked up to the little heater in the living room to replace the central heating that won't work without electricity. Sayed is lucky to find a tank-full of hot water and I can wait another day for my own shower.

Finally, he is sitting beside me on the settee, clean, and with a tray of food on his lap that he's clearing as fast as he can, and I can ask him what's going on in his life for him to turn up in this condition. Between mouthfuls, he explains that he has to be careful because the security services are looking for him. I can feel myself going cold at the thought.

"Oh, Sayed, what have you been doing? You know we don't get mixed up in politics. Your father always stayed away from both sides. What have you done?"

"Mother", he says, trying to be patient and wiping his mouth with his knapkin, "I saw too many things. I couldn't stay out of it any longer. You wouldn't want me to be too

218

scared to do what is right, would you?" I look at him and think, "Yes, I do want you to be not involved, and I don't care if it's because you're scared", but I say nothing. The room seems colder, and I turn to Bakri in his usual chair, to demand he reins in his son, but of course he isn't there.

Sayed goes on,

"I was in Damascus to see Omar about two months ago. Do you remember him? He was at school with me and he used to come here a bit." I nod. I can remember a shy, rather intense boy who never spoke directly to me, though he seemed polite enough. "Well, when I saw him he told me that he was helping people who want real changes in the country, but he was beginning to think that he was being watched. I left him, thinking it was his imagination, but he disappeared the day after and nobody knows where he is. So I had to start to do something myself." He stops and looks at me. "Cheer up, Mum, I don't go around throwing bombs or anything like that. They don't think I'm reliable enough to let me into the big plans."

His words horrify me in so many ways that I sit still and silent, unable to move or to speak. I have the unreal feeling that if I say and do nothing this dreadful scene will never have happened – I suddenly remember feeling the same way when I was very small and my mother was shouting at my father. This time the feeling passes quickly, but that isn't any better because I have no idea, not a single speck of an idea, what to do. The small gas heater hisses away quietly and the room is quite warm, but I am chilled to the point of shivering. This sort of thing was always

Bakri's job – though if he were here this particular sort of thing would not have happened, he would have stopped my silly son in his tracks before he got in so deep. I know he says he's not very involved, but that's like the old joke of being 'only a bit pregnant'. Each side here is so entrenched by now that anyone identified at all as belonging to 'the others' is likely to be murdered by the rebels, before or after torture, or to 'disappear' into the arms of the security services.

Everyone knows that the security services are very active just now, but the people I know mostly see that as a direct response to the threat that the opposition is bringing to the country. It's an open secret that the rebels are being financed by Turkey and Saudi Arabia, and that a lot of them are not Syrian or even Arabs. The 'alternative government' in Istanbul is a nasty joke. Too many of them are either suspect themselves or have been out of the country for so long that they're completely out of touch with what's happening on the ground. Bakri used to laugh at all of them. Meanwhile, most of my neighbours believe the popular TV channels that are paid for and controlled by outsiders who want to damage the country, though before he was killed, Bakri used to point out all the times that most of the 'reporting' had been untruthful propaganda.

Now, while I am sitting here beside my dear, unconsidering son, all the ramifications of his actions slowly unfold in my head. Everyone knows that people who help the rebels are going to disappear. Horrific photos appear every now and then of tortured bodies thrown into mass graves and, even if they are manufactured pictures

220

most of the time, I'm not so stupid or self-deluding to believe there's no truth in the stories. How has my precious little boy managed to put himself at so much risk? I pause and my hand seems to lift itself in front of my mouth. I realise that this is not the worst of the case. The security services have a nasty habit of taking in all the friends and connections of suspects. How many friends is he compromising? Good grief - my heart's beating so fast that I can hear the pounding in my ears - they could come for Mariam, perhaps, or for her husband!

This is no good, I have to get control of myself or I'll go mad. Of course Mariam would not be harmed, nor her husband. They aren't interested in the rebels, and they're too busy trying to keep their new shop stocked and selling to have time to be active on either side. Also, and this is important too, they're friends with quite a few people who still have political influence and will take care to protect them. My heart stops pounding quite so loudly, and I can even smile to myself as I remember how critical Bakri and I were at the party-goer our sensible daughter turned into after her marriage. How strange that their partying friends may be useful now!

Eventually, Sayed has eaten as much as he can pack in, clearing me out of bread, cheese and tomatoes while he does. I offer to make him some chips, as I was able to get a few potatoes last week and they are still in the kitchen, but he sits back, clean, tired and satiated with food.

"Mum, that was so good. It's ages since I felt so comfortable. All I need now is a good sleep and I'll be absolutely fine."

"Can't you stay for a few days? I haven't seen you since your father died. Mariam comes in the morning and she will want to see you, too. Her children must have forgotten what you look like!"

"Can we talk about it in the morning?" An enormous yawn splits his face almost in two. He covers his mouth with his hand, but it's a moment or two before he can speak again. "I think it's time for me to be in bed." I feel sure that he won't stay even to see his sister, and send him off to bed. Will he be there when I wake up? Will I sleep at all? Or will I stay awake wondering if there is going to be a hammering on the door at some dreadful hour in the night, with somebody looking for Sayed? The only thing I can do is to make sure he has clean pyjamas, then, just before he goes off to sleep I can't help but to go and kiss him goodnight as I used to when he was a little boy and the world was a safe place for all of us.

April 9th

This morning I wake up and he is gone, which doesn't surprise me, though I wish I had been able to say goodbye to him. There is a note fixed under a fridge magnet, "Sorry Mum. Had to go. Got a message. Keep safe. See you soon. Love you. Sayed." Typical! "Keep safe"! I am not the one who is deliberately running into danger, and I don't even have the satisfaction of knowing that he understands what is going on. He has picked up some crazy ideas that he half-understands, and now I may never see him again. It is too much. The tears are rolling down my face, but they are angry tears as much as sad ones. Shall I tell his sister that he has visited? She will want to know why he isn't here now, and she'll be furious with him for getting involved. She's younger than him, but she's always had more sense than him, much more like her father.

The day gets worse when my neighbour from next door comes and tells me another dreadful story about one of their workers. Before all this started they had a unit for making the local cheese, and got a very good living out of it until they couldn't get supplies of milk any more when the rebels closed the city off. They keep their workers on in hopes of better days, and because they don't want any men driven to the opposition by being desperate for money.

One of them came for his money this month very upset because he had been on the other side of Aleppo with his cousin when shooting started and his cousin was hit in the leg. A rebel ambulance drew up and he was taken away for treatment even though he wanted to be taken to a local hospital. Two weeks later his corpse was returned, with and enormous, roughly stitched cut right down the front of his body, and when his mother protested she was told to shut up and bury him. There have been a lot of rumours of organ harvesting, but perhaps they may be true. I do hope not. I hope no more evidence comes my way, then at least I won't have to think about it.

April 10th

Somebody has been using a nasty gas near Khan el Assel, a very small place to the south of the city which once was a staging post for Roman Army horses and has always been under the Syrian army. Some guards at a roadblock were rushed to our local emergency hospital just down the road from here, the Razi where Bakri worked when he first came back. And also some people who had seen them collapsing and had rushed to help them.

The opposition immediately said it was the Syrian army that did it, but the people who brought them in said the rockets came from the direction of the rebels, and some doctors were crying at what they saw. Now Mr Kerry says it was clearly the Syrian Army, and won't allow anybody to go with the army to take samples and have them examined by a neutral power. Oh well, when did the big powers ever play fair?

April 16th

I have been a widow for two months, so I'm close to halfway through my self-imposed time at home, when I wake up one morning absolutely furious. My jaw is stiff with tension, my arms are rigid at my side and my back aches almost all the way down from my neck to my hips. I'm so angry with the world that I want to jump out of bed, rush to the window and scream my anger at the passers-by.

How could my husband abandon me like this? How could he think that going to his stupid surgery was more important than staying alive for me and his family? Was this what I came to this country for? I get up and pull back the curtains, but what used to be a busy street is quiet, almost deserted, because it has been blocked off at one end to discourage car-bombers from attacking the Security

Police building on the corner. Nobody will hear if I do scream and rant.

Then suddenly all the anger is gone and I collapse onto the bed and start to cry loudly and without caring who hears me – which doesn't matter as I'm all alone so far this morning. The tears well up, dripping and splashing on the pink satin cover, and I, the perfect housekeeper, don't care. For a time I just let go and howl like a small child, mouth open and eyes streaming, until I've cried myself out. I feel empty and helpless afterwards, the anger has gone, leaving me to deal with the feeling that I've no bones left to hold me in place, and sure I've a face that my children wouldn't recognise. I wander slowly into the bathroom and looked at my swollen eyes in the mirror, then, suddenly notice that there are still 'his and hers' towels on the rail. This irritates me so much that I pull the second bath towel off the rail. 'His and hers' isn't ever going to happen again. Why have I been carefully folding the towels just the same old way when there's nobody to disarrange the second one any more? I fling the second towel into the laundry basket, and curse quite loudly when it misses on the first throw.

Tidying up my face takes some time, but plenty of cold water helps, then a few minutes poking around the back of the bathroom cabinet for a tube of concealer to cover the blotches across my forehead. It is a bit of a shock to see how thin my face is now, I have never let myself get fat, but the face looking back at me is positively haggard. I slap the concealer on with a generous hand. I shouldn't be wearing make-up if I really want to do this mourning thing properly, but so what? This morning I don't care, I want to rush round the flat, kicking things over or out of the way.

By mid-morning I've calmed down, dressed, drunk my coffee and eaten some breakfast. This is just as well as my sister-in-law will be visiting at midday, a politeness to help me get though my seclusion. Just before Rania arrives I go round the flat checking that everything is back in place, then look in the mirror, relieved that time and the concealer has brought my face back to normal. I don't feel normal, but these days what's normal anyway? Somehow the crying and the anger has changed how I feel, perhaps it has changed me. I have to get through this visit from Rania, then as soon as I can get time alone again I'll take time to think about the future and what I'm going to do with the rest of my life.

Rania comes. We drink coffee and make conversation quietly, as we always have. She is a kind, pleasant, deeply religious woman, quite a lot older than I, the oldest in her family, and we have never been close. On the other hand, she has always been helpful and didn't mind when her husband chatted to me in English which she doesn't speak much of. Now she sees me as another widow like herself and her calm, trivial conversation is soothing. When she finally leaves I feel that some of it has rubbed off on me and after lunch I settle down at my small desk in the sitting room to try and do some work.

Thank God for the internet! It is unreliable now because the electricity comes and goes, and because the main internet cable goes through a rebel area and they cut it when they feel like it, but at least, even though there is no paper post at all, people can contact each other to make sure of who is safe and where they are living now. Today I have electricity *and* the internet, so I'm catching up on my emails and trying to explain what is happening to people who have no idea at all. This time it is Margaret, someone I was in school with so many years ago. She keeps sending anxious messages and this time there are three waiting for me.

Elizabeth, I hope you are well. Let me know where you are. Margaret

Elizabeth, I'm getting worried that I haven't heard. Please contact me if you can. Margaret

Elizabeth, what is happening to you? We are all frantic about you and want to know you are safe. Margaret.

There is no ignoring this. I have to answer quickly while there is still the chance, and I had better explain as much as I can. Here goes:

Dear Margaret,

Thank you for worrying about us and I'm sorry that I didn't answer before, but we don't often have the internet AND electricity at the same time. Don't forget that 'bad news travels fast', and if you hear nothing there is probably a simple reason for it.

Love, Elizabeth

I send it off quickly while there is still the chance, but everything is still working so I carry on with another, longer, letter so she will understand a bit more. I understand how worried she is so I settle down to write again, in hopes that I can send her another email.

Dear Margaret,

I have the chance today, so I'll try to explain a bit more.

I am safe here in our side of Aleppo. Do you remember the street where we live? It is still the same as when you visited, there is no damage very close to us. The children are well. Sayed visited me after my Bakri was killed and Muna lives close by with her family, I see her every day, almost. Jamal isn't in Syria, he has a job in the Persian Gulf and seems to be happy enough. We are coping with losing Bakri in our own ways, and mine is to keep the Muslim period of mourning of four lunar months and ten days inside the house. This sounds weird, I know, but Bakri was always a good Muslim and it is the last thing I can do for him. I am so angry and sad that he was killed just doing his job, but that is nothing unusual here these days.

When my mourning time is finished I'm not sure what I'll do. Best wishes, Elizabeth

I'm glad I got that finished then, because the electricity went off a few minutes later, so now I am sitting in the dusk, trying to decide whether to use the generator now or to save it for later when it is full darkness, and watching television will be my only option.

April 17th

Mariam turned up this morning so furious that her face was quite red. I can't remember when I last saw her in such a state, but when she told me the story I could understand her feelings. Apparently a friend of theirs noticed that his son, who is about fifteen, had a wad of money in his room and didn't want to explain where it had come from. He insisted, eventually hitting the boy until he got the story (I am always upset at the way parents will hit even quite big children here).

The boy had been walking with two of his friends when a man approached them who explained that he was a sheikh and needed them to help him. He gave each of them fifteen thousand liras – enough to buy a reasonable lap-top – and told them that he would phone them when he needed them to carry a bag each to put in a place that he would tell them.

The father was horrified, having no doubt what would be in the bag, i.e. the sort of bomb which has killed and injured so many people just trying to get on with their lives, so he took his son straight to the police station to tell them all about it. I think the police are hoping to use the boys to trap the sheikh, which will save a few lives at the least. It explains to me how many bombs have gone off in peaceful areas.

Those boys only wanted cash for computers, but plenty of boys need it for their families. What a nasty place this city has become!

April 18th

My goodness, I have electricity AND water today. I've put the washing machine on quickly, on its shortest programme, and have decided to write to Margaret again as she has taken such trouble to contact me. I wish she could understand what is happening, so here goes:

Dear Margaret,

Just now, perhaps you will understand better what has happened to this lovely city if I add my own thoughts about it, and if anyone else is interested you can pass them on. Once again I hear on the BBC that the regime cannot last more than 6 months. Surely that was what everyone said last summer? If so, it is a very long 6 months. I can only give you an Aleppo view of the situation, taken from friends of all shades of opinion, and from the doctors and nurses who are still working in Bakri's old hospital, though they are mostly very pessimistic about it all.

The general opinion seems to be that anything is better than the mess we have now – comments about the pre-rebel days make it sound like a golden age of peace and security when women went to female wedding parties in all their gold and walked home in the middle of the night, whereas now they are all home soon after dark and stay there till morning. Do you remember that engagement we went to? Parties like that just don't happen anymore. Democracy may be very nice, but security is more important to people who have to get to work and don't swan round in their own cars.

The rebels seem to be too many disparate groups. There are many groups of plain bandits looting empty houses and kidnapping anyone who seems worth it, and these are feared and despised generally. They are also, I think, not trusted by the better side of the rebels. At the moment there is a lot of hostility between the Jebhet al Nisr faction, who are all very religious,I hear, and the people of the tiny town of Anadan, which is near here and has always been a rebel town since the beginning; the villagers were supposed to watch the others' backs during an attack, but when they found themselves in factories with lots of portable goods they left the scene carrying as much as they could, and the people relying on them were mostly killed.

The rebels who are actually fighting seem often to be led very badly. There have been four attacks on a small artillery unit near some friends of ours – I don't remember if you met Mustapha and Luna?. Each time, they have sent waves of fighters in who have been cut down in swathes. Last time someone was watching from his balcony and counted more than 300 bodies after the action, he had also seen a lot of injured young men being taken away. This seems more like World War 1 tactics or a horrible film than something now and real. It is certainly true that from the army's point of view, Aleppo, even though it was very poorly guarded, has not lost any army posts so far, and has suffered only minor damage to the civil airport, though some areas are really bad. Farmland and small villages fall easily, but in the city it is a different matter. What has been lost here has gone through being badly guarded, and an awful lot of people are angry about it. .

At the beginning the local people were fairly passive about who controlled an area. They waited to see who was going to win and who they would have to do business with (Very Ankh-Morpork!), however the inability of the rebels to feed the areas they hold, and the general disgust at their behaviour has swung public opinion against them. Now the army is sometimes able to rely on local groups to help defend areas (two days ago in Syriana Jedid), and then we often hear of protests against the rebels in areas they hold, though they still have plenty of of support in a lot of areas in the poor parts of town.

The most efficient rebels are those fighting for religious reasons – Al Quaida, the Salafiya and the Jebhet al Nisr – they are organized and generally honest. However they are also mostly foreign and so are deeply unpopular, together with their ideas about women, in a country where the most covered women expect to drive cars, move about freely and conduct their own business. For instance, when gold is bought for weddings, a man usually goes along to escort the women, but there is no doubt it is the women in charge.

Regime change – What do these reporters mean? The president will go in the end, but the structures will not be changed by that. The millions of Alawites, the millions of committed party members (from what I hear, I think about 3m of the latter) and the basic army, navy and air force will still be there and will still be solidly behind the party. Defections from the army were a problem before because tribal loyaties came before the army, but they are almost zero just now, and there has only been one plane lost from the air force in the last 2 years. So long as the Russians are sending gunboats to keep NATO out, I can see no real change. In fact the rebels have probably slowed down the reform process, as most people will be too anxious to get back to some sort of normality to think about anything else. Political reform is another matter, and it is where I am most hopeful as I think that it will be hard for the most hardened party members to feel they can go on as before, with corruption affecting almost everyone's lives. I can't think that they will want to put themselves in the same position again in the future.

Another thing that has made me really unhappy is the number of times I have seen things on the BBC news that were either very biased or completely untrue. This time last year I was watching fighting 'in the Aleppo area' that included clouds of dust, when I had been to a village outside town a few days before and had difficulty getting there because of the flooding. It seems that something is influencing the BBC reporters so that they are being led to great mistakes, though I cannot understand how. The result of seeing so many untruths and misleading half-truths on the BBC international news makes me disbelieve the news from everywhere. If reporters can be so wrong here, how can I accept their opinions about Libya and countries much further away? It is a disturbing thought after so many years taking the BBC as almost the only truthful channel on radio or TV. I hope I wasn't wrong to believe them before.

Love, as always, Elizabeth

April 19th

Water is very unreliable here now though it wasn't a problem in the winter. I never know when the roof-top tank will be re-filled from the mains, so I have to be careful not to use too much. If the water comes at all I have a pump attached to the meter to get it up to the tank, but that only works if there is water at the same time as electricity, though yesterday Mariam pointed out that if there is water and no electricity I should just run the little generator they brought me and it will give enough power for the pump so long as I remember to switch everything else off. Life is so complicated these days!

April 20th

There is a nasty piece of news on Syrian TV this evening, that a deeply loved and respected Sheikh in Damascus has been assassinated, I suppose because he has always opposed violent opposition to the government. I will never be Muslim, but if I were thinking of it, it would be because of him. Bakri used always to watch his Friday sermon on TV, and he always seemed to be honest, just and kind. Bakri told me, as well, that once when he was in Damascus for some business he saw this Sheikh using the local bus, although he was the personal religious adviser to the president, and the head of Religious Studies at Damascus University with a designated car and driver. I also heard from someone else that he sold his flat and sent the money to help Palestinian refugees, while he and his wife lived in a rented flat.

The attack that killed him has also killed 10 of his students so far (the number usually rises as badly injured people die). Of course, the opposition blames it all on the government, though Jala, my friend in Damascus, whose husband usually prays at the mosque where it happened, assures me that it was a man with a long beard, a stranger, who threw a hand-grenade straight at the sheikh and his group of about 40 students. I am not sure who the opposition spokesmen are talking for, because the number of people who believe them here is falling all the time. They have now announced that they will no longer use rockets to attack residential areas in Aleppo, from which we conclude that it has dawned on somebody that doing so is counter-productive. If they keep it, our nights will be strangely quiet!

I am not cheered by the official announcement from the Jebhet al Nasra that whatever the Free Army chooses to do, they are committed to going on fighting until Syria is a 'pure Islamic nation'. I suppose it makes sense of the rumours that some groups of the Free Army and the real Army have discussions for the sake of the poor civilians. A Syrian opposition leader based in France says that the Jebhet people he met from North Africa were presented before leaving with 40 perfumed handkerchiefs and two tablets of Viagra, so they will be properly equipped when they meet Houris in heaven. I like it, but am not sure what to make of it, although Bakri used to say he met people who would happily believe that sort of stuff. Hm!

A relevant story from before the troubles: when a few facing stones needed to be replaced on the side of the hospital, but three floors up, Bakri insisted that the man who did it wore a safety belt, as he would be working from a plank let down over the side of the building on two ropes. The man was furious, and accused my husband of not believing in God, who is the one to decide who dies and when. When my husband insisted, the man walked off the job, saying he couldn't work for somebody kaffar, i.e. who has abandoned his religion. The man's nephew had been killed in exactly that way two months or so before. So I sort of believe in the handkerchiefs!

April 22nd

The Patriarch of the Rome Orthodox Church and another bishop have been abducted, I knew before the TV announcement because one of his relations is a young man that Mariam studied with. I remember being puzzled that he could be 'Rome' and 'Orthodox' but someone we knew from that church explained that they are named after the 'new Rome' of Constantinople. History is always rearing its head here. I hope it isn't the Jebhet al Nisr who have taken them because Jebhet stated policy is to give Christians three choices: to convert to Islam (though Bakri would have an apoplexy at their version of Islam), to pay taxes (ransom), or to be executed (have their heads cut off).

April 24th

Someone came to visit Assia from the Kalassi district, which is occupied by the people from a small town just out of Aleppo on the north side – just after the mall we used to go to. She is horrified at the hatred these people have for anyone from Aleppo, and that some of them are so used to killing that they seem addicted to it. They also insist on the women wearing Saudi type coverings, though the people there were always covered in the Aleppo fashion even before. I suppose I've always heard city people speaking of the country people as lazy and feckless, so I expect this is the result.

The Kurdish situation seems to be a bit fluid now, and I don't have any definite information. The PKK seems to be on the side of the army, but there may be another party.

Meanwhile, the people in control of Sheikh Maqsoud announced that there had been chemical weapons used there and nobody was to go back for two days. When they were allowed back a doctor friend of Mariam's found that her house and clinic had been looted, down to the careful removal of the aluminium frames of the balcony surrounds.

Another woman, Saada, who used to work for me, tells me that she went back to her flat in a very poor part of the area and it was not damaged. She was wise enough to remove all her household goods to the cellar of her new employer near here when she first left. But she also said that she had to cross a district called Beni Zaid, and all the men there were 'foreign looking with long beards' and seemed not to understand her.

Four lunar months and ten days is the Islamic recipe for women to stay at home with no male company outside their own relations. It was designed to make sure that any children born after the husband's death were truly his – by four months it would be quite clear if a woman were or were not pregnant, so if she were the baby must be legitimate and could be counted in on any inheritance from the dead father. These days paternity is not such a problem and many women cannot possibly hide away for such a long time because they have to go to work, but the custom is still observed to an extent.

I am following it out of respect for my husband's memory, and I am finding that there are some benefits. The chief one is that I have time – time to adjust to being a widow, time to cry and also to be angry, and time to plan what I should do next. It's also convenient that I'm not expected to wear bright clothes or to bother with make-up, in fact it's very relaxing for anyone who has always spent so much time and trouble in presenting a well-groomed face to the world. I find I rather like it!

April 25th

Yesterday there was another attack on the Khaldiya. I heard the bangs because the wind was in the right direction, but Mariam told me all about it this morning. She says that six armoured cars were driven along the main road and towards the shopping centre, but the army was prepared and three of the cars were blown up and the other three escaped with injured fighters inside. I am so sorry for these young men. They are brought from all over the world believing that they are righting a great wrong and bringing sinners back to faith. Most of them die or are badly injured still believing this – such a waste of life. On the other hand it is hard to be too sympathetic when some of them are snipers shooting at anything that moves. Two children playing football and their mother who went to call them in were shot dead on the edge of the Khaldiya last week.

April 26th

Today I wake up resolute to deal with Bakri's wardrobe. I want to feel strong and capable, so I wait until I've had breakfast and my shower, then march to the right-hand closet and pull it open before I can lose courage again. As the doors open, the scent of his clothes and his aftershave waft out at me and I step back quickly, sitting down suddenly on the side of the bed. I get up and step cautiously back to the wardrobe. It's just as if he's left the house for the clinic, and will be back for lunch. Assia is due today, but I know I still have a few minutes alone in the flat before she turns up, so I push my face into the clothing and take a long sniff, and the tears start to fall yet again. I push my face in amongst the row of suits and his distinctive Bakri scent is there, and it's sad and scary. I shut the wardrobe door again. Today is definitely not the right day, but the next time it won't be so much of a shock. Tomorrow will do.

To convince myself that I'm not a complete coward, I open the doors of my own wardrobe and run my hands over the rail of my formal dresses. I used to wear such pretty clothes! Bakri always wanted me to look beautiful when we went out together so, though I did try not to be wasteful, there are eleven dresses hanging there in front of me, with their correct shoes and handbags packed below.

This last two years the parties and restaurant visits tailed off to nothing, which helped a little, but what to do with these clothes that I will surely never wear again? I pull out a dress of pale blue silk – the fabric a trophy of a romantic holiday only 3 years ago in Thailand – and push it back again quickly before I start to cry again. The dresses will have to go, though Mariam will have first choice and she may want some of them even if she only has them cut up and redesigned by her own dressmaker. Surely one day life will be pleasant again? I shut the wardrobe door carefully. Another day I'll be calm and strong and clear away the dresses, but not today.

April 27th

It must be because I looked at all our clothes yesterday, but I had a lovely dream last night. It was a coffee morning and all my English friends were here in our sitting room, chatting away. I couldn't make out what they were saying, but I knew they were happy. I woke up remembering the dream, which is very unusual for me (I read somewhere that only inhibited people forget their dreams, so that's me – defined!), and the happy feeling has stayed with me all morning.

We haven't any electricity this morning and the phones aren't working so nobody has been able to pass on any horrors. This is good. I spent the morning going through my winter clothes and preparing to put them away for the summer, and this afternoon I'm just sitting in the sunshine in a corner of the balcony where I can't be seen from the street, and reading a book I haven't read for years. It's an old Georgette Heyer story and my intellectual friends would be laughing at me if they knew, but the story carries me along and is as far away from reality as anyone could wish. What could be better than a quiet balcony, a book and a cup of tea?

May 1st

This used to be a holiday – Labour Day – and the children and I spent so many May firsts out in the sunshine with friends. It all seems unreal now.

May 3rd

The seasons change, warm weather comes so the carpets are taken up, washed and put away, all of which passes days of my isolation. Assia and I have to work hard for four days clearing them away, even though we didn't bother with too many carpets last October. I realise that when we put the carpets down Bakri was still alive so my life was completely different, which winds me for the moment and I have to sit down. However this makes Assia start fussing round me so I manage to get over it and smile at her to show her I am fine.

May 14th

Now it's almost summer and the 'time out' has nearly ended. In two days' time Mariam will invite me to lunch and I will leave the house for the first time since Bakri was killed. I've already decided that I'll carry on wearing black for the time being, though Mariam is sure that I am wrong. The time to dress the way I always used to, in pastel shades, hasn't yet arrived, though I know I can't hide behind black clothes for ever.

I'm a bit scared that it is also time to start deciding about my life. Shall I stay here or move on? Can I leave Mariam and the grandchildren and start again? Though I've always had holidays in England I only have my sister and some cousins there, I've lost touch with most of the friends I used to have. There is enough money there for me to buy somewhere small, and the years I worked, together with the years Bakri worked when he was doing his

241

specialisation, will give me a pension of sorts, but do I want to leave? On the other hand, if I stay, who will I have to talk to? I don't want to be a burden to Mariam and there is nobody left of the old group that we used to visit and go out with. It will be almost as lonely a life as starting again in England. I curl up on the settee with my cup of tea and day-dream of a rose-bowered cottage in a perfect English village, very Miss Marple, but I don't really believe that particular dream. When the tea is all gone I notice that the electricity has come back, so I stretch my arms and legs as far as they will go and try to decide how to use it before it disappears again.

May 20th

Today I have officially ended my time staying at home, I have to start 'the rest of my life'. When I wake up I know this immediately and I'm scared. I get up and there is enough water to have a really thorough shower, and even enough electricity to fix my hair reasonably well. The fates seem to be on my side today. I poke about in my wardrobe, but decide to wear my 'blacks' because I just won't feel comfortable in anything else.

It is late morning when Mariam comes and collects me from my flat, and we walk slowly down the road to her apartment building.It's strange, but nicely so, to be out on the street with the feel of the May sun hot on my back and the speckled shade if the new-leafed trees to walk under. It is so good to be out again, strolling along the street I have lived in for a lot of my life - almost all of my adult life, really - but I'm sad to see all the changes. This used to be one of the busiest streets this side of town, but now it is blocked off and pretty well silent as far as cars go, though there are quite a few people walking about and they almost all look tired and poor.

The grandchildren know I am coming and are overjoyed to see me. Sami is six now, and goes to school whenever it is safe enough, and here in this area that is most of the time. His sister is the image of her mother, and, at three, wants to tell me all about her friend at nursery school, and to show me her toys. It is a cheerful atmosphere and I feel better than I have since Bakri died, though once I realise it, guilt at being alive and happy without him takes some of it away.

Adnan comes in and kisses me briefly on the cheek before we all sit down to eat. It is so good to be in an ordinary place with family and eating a sociable meal! At home I have not much apetite, but here, eating food I haven't even seen being prepared, my apetite returns and I am able to enjoy the stuffed aubergines and green peppers which Mariam knows I love. After coffee, Mariam and Adnan both try to persuade me to stay the night and I would love to, but I know that if I do it will be even more difficult to go back to my empty apartment in the morning so I insist on going home. There is no way that they will let me walk back by myself and I'm not sure how safe that would be these days, so I submit gracefully to being driven back by the whole family, who escort me right to my front door and into the flat before leaving me.

The place feels so bleak and empty after the life going on in Mariam's home! This flat was just the same when the children were growing up, though it got a lot quieter in the last few years. I give myself a shake, mentally and physically, to try to throw off gloomy thoughts, perhaps they're just because I'm more tired than I have been for a long time. Even the fifteen minute walk to Mariam's is exhausting after more than 4 months at home and all I want to do is sleep. I'm too tired to be more than quietly sad, and bed looks so inviting that I can hardly wait long enough to change and brush my teeth. Oh! The joy of letting my head sink back on my own pillow, and my weary legs push out as far as I can stretch.

May 21st

I am awake quite early this morning, it's not quite seven o'clock yet. I slept very well, and dreamed of Bakri all night, or so it seems.Here, people don't say they dreamed about somebody, but that they saw them in their sleep. That always seemed very biblical to me before, but now I can understand because I was sure that he was there beside me, doing the ordinary things we used to do all the time. He was sitting in his armchair and reading some papers, and then we were in the mountains, where we used to take the children in the summer for picnics.It was so real that I knew I was not dreaming, even though I understood that I was asleep. Very strange – I'm not at all psychic or fey really. Anyway, in the morning it was a dreadful shock to wake up alone, I stretched out to him and he wasn't there. It was almost as bad as the first night when he wasn't there, last February. When, oh when will this feeling leave me

244

alone? How long before I stop waking and expecting him to be there?

The day swings into the routine of housework, but now I have to fit in a walk in the fresh air or I will never get back to being healthy and energetic. The city is so changed, and so many places aren't open to me any more, that walking is not a pleasure, but it is a duty to both myself and the children. I march down the steps of the building and turn along the road towards one of the few friends still here. If she's home and not too busy we can have a tea together, but even if she can't do that, her house makes a target for my walk.

Our street is dirty and full of people that I have never seen before. These last months I have heard plenty of talk, of Sheikh Maqsoud being taken with lots of horror stories, and that the Syrian rebels and foreign jehadis would be taking all of Aleppo in the next week or two, but I was cut off from the reality. The stories were just stories. Now I can see the tired faces of the parents trying to care for children when they don't have any idea how to make a living and they have to rely on charity for their daily meal and a place to sleep. The sight of so many people on crutches or in wheelchairs because they are missing one or both legs is desperately sad, so many of them are young, boys and girls, and at least the girls must just have been in the wrong place when a bomb went off. I know that a lot were killed and injured at the university when a rocket that was supposed to hit a military plane landed instead in the middle of the campus, and I suppose that some of these must have been among the injured.

During the afternoon I have to have a rest. The May sun is strong enough to be tiring after a very short walk, particularly for the feeble specimen I have become, and my friend was out so I didn't get the sit down I expected. Next time I'll try phoning, as the land lines seem to be working again, more or less. Now it's time to lie down and shut my eyes, the only question being whether or not to actually go to bed. That is too much trouble so I kick off my house shoes, stretch out on the settee, and am instantly asleep.

A noise wakens me. I am sure there was a noise, though now there is nothing. I lie on the settee thinking what to do, and am surprised at myself for being so calm. The years of sudden bangs and crashes, of threats of the fighters about what they will do to Aleppo, and finally Bakri being killed for nothing has cut me off from the earlier times when the least noise would have sent me running for help from him or the boys.

The noise is repeated and my calmness evaporates. I can hear my heart bashing away, and realise that anyone who is in the house probably knows I am here. Movement is impossible, my body feels like a dry stick, if pressed it will break in two. Then I hear whistling from the kitchen, and relax. It has to be Sayed! If he knew how near he brought his mother to a heart attack!

"Sayed, is that you?" I call, knowing that it is. Nobody else could manage to whistle Lillibolero quite so out of tune.

"Hi, Mum I hope I didn't wake you. I looked in on you, but you were sleeping so peacefully that it didn't seem right to spoil it for you."

"What are you doing?" I swing my legs down and stand up. Between waking from a deep sleep and the shock of Sayed arriving so suddenly, I have to steady myself against the arm of the settee for a moment.

"I'm fine. Don't worry." then the mothering instinct takes over and I call to him,

"Have you eaten? There's stuffed cabbage in the fridge. I can heat it up in the microwave if the electricity is on. Oh bother! It's off again. Never mind, I can do it on the cooker."

"Mum, stay there and sit down. I'm making a cup of tea. I was going to wake you up with it, it's nearly ready. Just sit down and I'll bring it in."

I lie back on the settee and wait for a minute or so until he comes in, though I can hear him whistling quietly to himself. It's a good, domestic sound and reminds me of all the happy times we've had here over the years. Then he comes in and at first I almost don't recognise him. It's a good job he didn't wake me up. The skinny, dirty, bearded man bringing my cup of tea would have frightened me into a screaming fit or a heart attack if I hadn't heard his voice first!

"Sayed, what on earth have you been doing? Why do you look like that? What's happening?"

"Mum, drink your tea and I'll tell you all about it. Everything's fine. We're winning and soon all the fighting will be over." I take my tea from him, glad that he's used a big mug because it's easier for me to get my hands right round. If it were a little tea cup I'd probably drop it at the moment. "You have to realise that the opposition is winning around Aleppo, and we'll have the whole city very soon, it might be in the next week. You'll soon see that the army can't keep control and the people want us here." I am doubtful about that, but keep quiet. "As soon as we actually drive in, the people will be out on the streets to welcome us." This time I have to say something.

"Sayed, are you sure? Most of the people I see hate the beardies more than they hate the government."

"Oh, Mum, how do you know what people are thinking? You just live in your little bubble. You have no idea..."

I am so used to being considered to have no political opinions worth listening to that again I keep silent, but inside I am aware that cleaners, hospital workers and all their relations, whose stories I have been hearing, are just the people my deluded son thinks he is saving.

"The only thing is, Mum, I think you ought to leave before it happens, because there'll be a lot of changes round here." He wags a playful finger at me (at least I hope it's playful). "No more going out in summer dresses or tight jeans. We'll have to be much more conservative at first, because the people helping us have very strict ideas. Of course, when they leave we can go back to normal."

This is truly horrifying. What has he got himself into? The 'people helping us' must be the same ones who have massacred groups of people and who have put *pictures* on the internet of themselves teaching little boys how to slice the heads off prisoners – using actual prisoners for practice. These people won't just pack up and go home when he has had enough, but I'm absolutely sure he won't believe me when I say so. Now is the time for me to really regret allowing him, his brother and (most of all) his father to believe that I am a helpless female that they must look after! I need to open his eyes. I need to protect him now his father isn't here to do it. But I can't, he won't take my ideas seriously. None of them ever has.

The best I can do is to point out that I can't leave his sister without telling her, and that I will sleep on the whole thing and discuss it with Mariam in the morning. He isn't too pleased - I think he imagined me picking up my handbag and following him - but in the end he agrees. However he doesn't leave until he has made a good meal of the leftovers in the fridge and then had a quick shower, which certainly makes him smell a lot better. I see him out of the front door with conflicting feelings. I'm quite glad he's gone and I don't have to listen to his political views which seem crazy to me, but I'm also worried sick about him and about what will happen next to us all.

May 22nd

Sayed upset me so much yesterday that I decided to take stock of what I actually have here in terms of cash and things that can be turned into cash quickly. Before I went to bed I opened the safe and counted how many dollars and Syrian lires are still there, and how much jewellery I have stashed away. I calculate that the lires will keep me for several months, even if prices carry on going up as much as they are at the moment. I did look at the safe in the first few days after the funeral, but I can't remember much about anything I did then. Now I also find a couple of wads of dollars – about thirty thousand all told (thank you, Bakri, for thinking ahead) that will be useful if I really have to leave, though how I can conceal them is a question that needs considering carefully. I know that the government won't let me take dollars out, and if I manage to evade their inspection the first rebel people I meet will take them off me.There's no way I can take more than a minimum of jewellery with me either, but I can't imagine leaving without my engagement ring and a few pieces that were for anniversaries. Mariam will have the rest, which she will be inheriting anyway in the end. I finally got into bed with so many thoughts about the children and the future and my jewellery and the dollars and how to hide them and and and … that it was early morning before I must have slept. I say "must have slept" because suddenly I was awake with a mouth as dry as the desert, so I must have been asleep on my back, with my mouth open and I expect I was snoring loudly.

May 24th

This morning everything outside looks much as usual, but the people wandering up and down the road look even more nervous than they did yesterday, so perhaps there is news I haven't heard. I phone Mariam – hurrah, our mobiles are working today – and she sounds normal, but I don't want to say anything in public that could be listened to, so I just check that she'll be coming here later and ring off. When we are face to face will be the time to give her the news and hear what she thinks, I am too well aware of my phone being listened in to. When I first came to live here all foreignors were listened to, and quite a few made a joke of it. One friend, a Syrian with a British wife with whom he used to speak French was told in the middle of a conversation with her to stop speaking 'foreign' and to use Arabic! At the moment I can't really object to the security people looking for information wherever they can, and I'm terrified that they already have my silly Sayed in their sights because he has never been able to keep his mouth shut.

Mariam arrives with the children later in the morning, and she isn't impressed by her brother's opinions.

"Oh Mum, why do you listen to him? Everyone knows the different groups fighting spend more time fighting each other than they do fighting the army."

"Well", I answer, "the army isn't doing much for us. I hear the shells going out every night but in the morning I hear that the shops in the Khaldiya have been attacked again, and I know the Damascus road is cut. Why should he be wrong? Rana called yesterday and said she and Fayez daren't go out of their house because of the rockets,and she's only just this side of town.I can walk there in twenty minutes." Mariam comes right back with,

"When did Sayed ever get it right? I just hope he doesn't get us all into trouble with the security police. Did I tell you that I'm invited to Nejwa and Ahmed's wedding? No? Well, it's going to be at midday and there will just be a lunch for their closest friends. They've actually put on the

251

invitation please not to wear too much jewellery! Poor things, it's not much of a wedding for them to remember."

I allow myself to be distracted from Sayed's warning, and we talk about recent weddings, where the whole thing has been finished before nightfall. Both my Syrian wedding party and then Mariam's wedding started at eleven at night and finished with breakfast for the guests. I'll never forget either of them. That leads me on to the dresses and I tell Mariam about clearing out the wardrobe. She is determined to stay positive with me so she calls the children and says, 'No time like the present.'

Rula wants to see in Gran's wardrobe, but Sami is more interested in the box of our children's old toys that I keep for him. I'm glad Rula is here. When the wardrobe is opened and one or two dresses are taken out she gets so excited that we both start to laugh, otherwise it could have been too sad to deal with. Mariam picks out four that will go with her colouring, because she's much darker than me, more like her father. But she wants me to keep the others, at least for now.

"Lots of people want to have dresses for weddings and engagements, but there aren't any around except at ridiculous prices that almost nobody can afford. Keep these others and if I hear of somebody who really needs a pretty dress I'll tell you. What do you think? Would you like to give them away?" That seems to me to be an ideal answer so we put the rest of the dresses back and have mugs of coffee on the balcony. We can look at her father's clothes another day.

Now it is finally night-time. I went back with Mariam for lunch and stayed until evening. I enjoyed the family atmosphere and she and Adnan never seem interested in politics – or at least they keep off the topic when I am there – which is relaxing after Sayed's visit. I've told Mariam about my money and jewellery, and we discussed it with Adnan as well, but he doesn't want me to do any thing just now, which is comforting. He's a big, kind, solid person that I want to lean on, but I mustn't. He has enough to worry about with Mariam, the children and the business, not to mention his own parents who are much older than I. And I'm also beginning to realise that I'm must start to get on with things myself without asking men to help me, however nice and reliable they are. In a way this is exciting, but it's very scary.

The streets were almost traffic-free on the way back, partly because there is nowhere to drive these days and the other reason is that there is no petrol to drive with. The crowds of people hanging around look depressed and edgy and I don't blame them. They are here because either their houses have been destroyed or taken from them by the rebels, or because they were living in areas where they don't feel safe any more because the army is shelling the rebels there. It is heart-breaking to see how families have set up home under water-proof sheeting between garden walls. The lucky ones have been given rooms in unfinished buildings, and one young man I know is spending every waking hour getting these skeleton structures joined up to the water and sewers, and supervising electricians who loop wires all over the place to give them light and a bit of usable electricity when the rebels haven't bombed something to cut it off.

Lots of them are being fed by big kitchens, one of them in a convent garden not far from here. They try to give out thousands of meals every day so that anyone on their list is getting at least a minimum of food. It is surprising how many people that I wouldn't have expected have got together to help, and the best thing about it is that they help people that they probably wouldn't have talked to before. Christians and Muslims, Arabs and Kurds.The only important thing is that a lot of people are having a really hard time and quite a few people are ready to help. I shouldn't think it will last, but you never know, there might be something good at the end of all this.

May 27th

The weather is so hot this morning that I don't know what to do with myself. The electricity came on for a couple of hours, but it's gone now so I can't use the fan. Even worse, the water is so weak that it isn't filling the reserve tank on the roof and sometimes it's too weak to get to the taps direct. I know there is still some water there so I don;'t want to waste my little store of petrol using the generator to pump up a little more. How I hate having to flush the toilet with a bucket of water! It's a good job that I am alone, because otherwise the washing would be piling up – Bakri always used to change all his clothes after his afternoon snooze in the hot weather. (I notice that I am using the past tense for Bakri, which panics me at first, but I suppose I need to start sometime.) I'm going to Mariam's for lunch, but she is taking the children to the pool near their flat for the morning and I don't think I can cope with that yet, though if this heat wave goes on and the electricity stays off I may be driven to go just to cool down and stay sane.

June 2nd

The news today is fairly horrible. Yesterday Luma, who's a school friend of Mariam's, watched a battle from her balcony! The rebels were trying yet again to take the artillery post near her building on the western edge of the city. All the people left in her building watched them assembling a few fields away for quite a few hours before they finally charged across open fields and along the high road towards the guns. They came near to the artillery post, so the guns from the post mowed them down, row after row. She said it was like those films of the First World War. Then afterwards the bodies were everywhere, and the feral dogs moved in and were mauling them until it was quiet enough for a Red Crescent truck with bright blue body bags to get near enough to pick them up. It seems such a tragedy that so many young men should die trying to do something in such a stupid way. Reform is needed here, even Bakri recognised that there was a lot wrong with the system, and a lot of the rebels are really good, honest people who want a better country, or who have suffered themselves at the hands of the security services. On the other hand, if they aren't better led I can't see them getting any reform at all. Today I'm just glad I am not able to see sights like that.

I have just talked to Adnan. He says it has been 'uncomfortable' in a lot of parts of the city today, but it's quieter now. His accountant was very surprised to find that a lot of the gunmen are fifteen or sixteen year olds who are paid fourteen thousand lires a month and given guns. This is just about a living wage for a working man so it's a fortune for kids. They attempted to attack a military post in the Medan, an Armenian part of town where they fix cars. They were beaten off and up to ten were killed – all of them very young. Another ten or so were captured, but what do you do with kids who've learnt the art of shooting rocket launchers when they should have been playing football? It's all very sad.

June 9th

The electricity came on for a few hours last night and I always leave the fan on in the bedroom, so I had a beautiful cool sleep until after seven this morning. Hip, hooray, there is a lot of pressure in the water as well, so I am using the little bit of petrol I still have to run the generator and push some water into the header tank – and it seems to be working. Wonderful! I celebrate by flushing the toilet every time I use it, and smile to myself when I realise that flushing the toilet is a great treat. What have we come to?

There is at least some good news. The rebels were chased away when they tried to get into an area not too far from us called New Aleppo. Perhaps this means that they are not going to be able to walk into the rest of the city as easily as they hoped. The areas where they are strongest are where they were able to rent small flats and slowly build up their numbers without being noticed too much – though like everyone else I wonder what on earth the security services were playing at. They were mostly the poorer areas where you just accept new neighbours because you are all poor together. Now, and in more affluent areas, people are watching out, and the security police have woken up at last, so the only way they can get in is by attacks.

June 10th

Another truly horrid happening today. How many more can I deal with? Sayed was in the house when I got back from shopping (nothing exciting, I was pleased to get some fresh fruit and vegetables, and very glad to buy some fresh bread without having to queue for hours). This time he was cleaner than last time, but surprised me by praying long and very loud. I've never thought of him as interested in religion. Bakri and Jamal used to pray in the front room, but they did so quietly and I couldn't hear them from the sitting room. When he finally stopped I asked him about it and he was very impatient with me. Apparently he has just realised what life is all about, and I had better agree with him because that is the way I will be living very soon. I was too astonished to say anything until he said that his father should have made me be a Muslim, and then I lost my temper. I absolutely screamed at him that his father was a million times better Muslim than he was and that nobody should ever tell anybody else what to believe in, at least after they are grown up. At first I thought he would stop and be my friendly son again, but then his face just went sort of cold and closed and he walked out of the house without even saying goodbye. I was shaking all over, but I managed not to cry until I heard the door slam behind him. What has happened to him?

Mariam found me still crying and I told her what had happened, though usually I try not to say anything that will set the children against each other. She is furious with Sayed, and she thinks he has joined one of the jehadi groups, Jebhet al Nisra is most likely. I can see that she's worried about him, because though she is younger she has always been more sensible than he.

"Why couldn't he join one of the Syrian opposition groups? They have a good reason to fight and it's their country. These foreigners don't know what the fight is about and they just want to take the country back hundreds of years. You know they have closed all the schools, and the girls don't even get to go to the mosque to learn to write!"

I haven't seen Mariam so angry since her brothers teased her when she was small. I absolutely agree with her that the foreigners shouldn't be here, and I'm completely confused about Sayed. When they were all growing up he was the one who only prayed twice a year on the feast days, and who used to find excuses to break his fast in Ramadan. Bakri and Jamal used to pray their five times a day and go to the mosque on Fridays, and Mariam often prayed with them, especially in Ramadan, and she fasted very carefully and always made up later in the year for any days she missed. Now Bakri is gone, Jamal and Mariam

258

are pleasant friendly people who pray and are true Muslims, and Sayed has become extreme and (though he's my son) horrible. I don't say prayers very often, but these days I pray that he won't take to 'executing' people captured by the group he seems to have joined.

June 14th

Today I am incensed by the news on the English Language programmes that picture the fighting here as 'good' Sunnis fighting 'bad' Alawis and Shias. That's crazy. Bakri, Mariam and all my neighbours, as well as all the people who drop by, are Sunni and they almost all hate the rebels far more than they hate the government. Of course change is needed, but to picture the savages who are raging through the countryside, proud of killing people who don't agree with them, as the 'good guys' means either the reporters are very naïve or they are cynical. I hope they are naïve. Anyway, I'm going back to my personal rule of not watching the news!

It is hot and the fruit is beginning to come in. I should be making the jam for next year, at least for Mariam, because her children say that mine is the best. I usually make the apricot, strawberry and plum jam in five kilo units until I hit about fifteen or twenty kilos of each, depending how conscientious I feel. I make cherry jam with the local sour cherries, too, but in much smaller quantities because the special jam cherries are quite small and I'll have to stone them by myself this year. Lots of people make a beautiful scented jam from Damask roses, but I have never mastered it. Actually, I love the smell when other people are eating it, but I don't like perfumed food myself and hate the squeaky feel of the rose petals on my teeth. I'm told you can make a delicious cordial with the rose petals as well, but I've never done it and this year doesn't seem the right one to experiment.

June 16th

Mariam came yesterday with a big box of strawberries and enough sugar so I spent the evening preparing the fruit and mixing in the sugar, fortunately I found a few lemons at the back of the fridge to put into the mixture. This morning the sugar had dissolved in the strawberry juice and I cooked the whole lot up together to make some of the best strawberry jam I can remember producing, a pleasing result. I've never got out of the habits of life here years ago when every container was precious, so I have a store of jars to put the jam into when it cools.

The grandchildren will be delighted, and if I can get the ingredients I'll make their apricot jam too, though that may be dependent on getting another cannister of gas.After that there will be the red plums, where I was actually able to teach Bakri's family something they didn't know about cooking. Nobody here made jam out of the wonderful red plums, but when I did, and sent round pots of the jam to all the family, they took to it like ducks to water and asked me for the recipe. It was the first time anybody said that they liked any sort of English food. Later they decided my Christmas dinner was worth eating, but culinary chauvinism is bred into Aleppo, they hate to admit that other people can cook.

June17th

A good surprise today. Jamal called me, as he does every few days if he can get through, and invited me to join him in Dubai now he has his papers as a resident through having a British passport. Because I too have a British passport I can go without a visa, which I knew but had forgotten. All I have to do is to get to Beirut and I can fly from there. He's invited Mariam and the children as well, but he can't invite Adnan because Syrians need visas and they are almost impossible to get. I told him as little as possible about his brother, and we had a good chat about his work and how he spends his time. He isn't one for joking, but he's very calm and comfortable to talk to these days. Mariam thinks I should go but she doesn't want to leave Adnan so she wouldn't go with me. She did point out that the road to Beirut is fairly dangerous, although I know people who travel and seem to get there.

It was only yesterday that my Armenian friend Lilli and I had a farewell cup of coffee at the cafe round the corner because she has finally persuaded her husband to leave here and start a new life in Beirut, with the idea of going on to the U.S., and she is prepared to take the risk. I'll miss her a lot, she is always so full of life and energy, but her dreams for her children don't have any chance here at the moment, and children don't wait, they keep on growing up all the time. I can see why she doesn't want to wait because her children are already almost teenagers.

June 18th

Today has been a dreadful day. Everything was going along as usual in the morning and I was thinking about the practical part of going to Dubai, for a holiday at least – I was thinking that I don't want actually to stay there for a long time. Then out of the blue Randa from the hospital called me to tell me that Lilli was dead. I couldn't believe her. Lilli is far too full of life, energy, joie de vivre and all those things to be dead, but it's true. And I've missed the funeral at the Armenian church where she worshipped. It all seems horribly impossible.

They say that she was in a bus in a convoy to travel a dangerous part of the road and the army stopped the whole lot until it was safe to go on. The other buses went on and arrived in Beirut, but the passengers on her bus voted to turn back and she couldn't persuade them not to. The bus was raked with machine gun fire and she was the first one killed, the driver was injured as well, but still able to control the bus for a short time. They got to a deserted army post to hide out, and more people were injured when the rebels shot at them while they were climbing out of the bus through the broken windows on the 'safe' side. It was deliberate murder, there is no other name for it.

How can I watch the rebels being lauded by the BBC as freedom fighters when this is happening? Do they not understand? Or are they simply using the TV channel to push a convenient point of view? I don't think I can bear to watch the news ever again. Please God Sayed wasn't with them. That would be the worst of all, and I can't guarantee that he wasn't.

June 20th

I have just come back from a condolence visit to Lilli's's home. Her husband was injured, but the bullet he took missed his jugular vein by a hairsbreadth and he is still alive to care for their children. It is so sad, and I am helpless to make it better. The children are still at school and both being brave, but they adored their mum and she was the driving force behind the family. I can only thank God that my own children were grown up before their father was killed. That's enough for today. There is nothing good to say. I'm going to bed.

June 21st

Dear Adnan woke me up this morning by ringing the doorbell, though he and Mariam have a key in case there is an emergency. The noise scared me at first, but there he was on the doorstep with a plastic sack of plums and a full cannister of gas for me, bless him! They had decided that it would cheer me up to make the jam, so he had queued for hours to get me the gas, and he won't tell me how much it cost. He stayed and made Turkish coffee for us while I went and got dressed, then sat and chatted about cheerful things before going off to the shop.

He is so kind to me that I don't like to remember what a hard time Bakri gave him when he wanted to marry Mariam. He is a few years older than her, ten years, actually, and his family is quite rich but not exactly our style, his mother especially is a bit loud. I liked him, but Bakri always wanted a knight on a white charger, preferably a doctor or the son of one of his doctor friends, for her. I tried not to take sides, but it wasn't a happy few months with Bakri and Mariam at loggerheads, each as stubborn as the other. My job was to listen to each one and try to calm them down, but it was the only time I can remember here when there was shouting almost every day.

In the end Mariam wore him down and he agreed to an engagement, and then he finally got to know Adnan a bit and to like him a little bit. If he hadn't wanted to marry Mariam, Bakri would have liked him from the start. Anyway, they did get married and it has been such a successful marriage. They are happy with each other and very contented with their life. Even Adnan's mother, who thought Mariam was far too grand to appreciate her precious son, has come round to her and seems to like her, which is a major blessing as mothers in law round here have a dreadful reputation for bad behaviour towards their daughters in law.

When I finally saw him out, I suddenly wanted a hug. How much I miss the hug from Bakri each morning before he left the house. I said nothing because Adnan would have been so shocked at the idea, but after he left I managed a private giggle at the thought even though I was sad. Now I have a job for the day so I'd better get on with it. While I am busy I can think about that trip to Dubai, because Adnan told me another bus was attacked yesterday. It would be so much simpler if the Damascus road was open, but it is in rebel hands from here to Hama so the buses have to use a route out through the desert to the east, and that is long and easily attacked because the army can't protect all of it all the time.

The trains stopped after one was derailed near Homs some time ago. It was the express from here to Damascus and the only reason there wasn't a terrible tragedy was that the people who set the charge did so expecting the train in the other direction, so instead of diving into a deep lake the train 'just' overturned and most people got out unharmed.The airport used to be the other usual way to leave, but it isn't open because it is too easy to attack approaching or leaving planes, and some people say it has been damaged, though the army is still using it. I don't really think the rebels have any chance of over-running this part of Aleppo any more, though I wouldn't have said that even a few weeks ago, but it's getting really annoying that we can't go anywhere. Bother! I'd better get on with the jam.

June 22nd

Lamia has always been a friendly acquaintance since her husband and Bakri started working at the same hospital so many years ago, and she visits me today. She arrives looking as elegant as always, hair and nails immaculate although she has walked the short distance from their flat on one of the hottest days of the year. She's fed up with the chaos, as we all are, and she sounds fed up with her husband too, because he refuses to leave though his sons are all in France with good jobs and are forever asking him to retire and join them.

Having her here, drinking coffee and smoking her ultralong cigarettes, is turning the clock back for me. We talk about various people we used to meet, mostly at restaurants and parties, and she knows all their news, and their scandals. I don't know how she remembers who married whom, and what the financial arrangements were, or why engagements were broken off or divorces happened, but she can tell me all the scandalous details. I pass a thoroughly enjoyable morning listening to her, even though I know that it isn't very nice of me. It doesn't matter because I will have forgotten most of it by the time I've had lunch, not having her memory, or her interest.

The day goes on well. After lunch when Assia goes home I finish the plum jam and have a row of beautiful jars of dark red jam to share with Mariam. There is even enough jam to give Assia some if she wants it, though usually she only likes my apricot jam, but I've already given her some of that from last year's and I haven't made any this year yet.

Perhaps I'll have a go at cherry jam when the proper cherries come in, though I don't expect I can get them ready-stoned as I used to a few years ago. It certainly makes me feel better to do these ordinary jobs and I think it's getting to be time to invite Mariam and her family here for a Friday lunch. That will be difficult because it will be the first time I use the dining room without Bakri at the head of the table, however eating in the kitchen for Friday lunch wouldn't be right either. I'll think about that and suggest it soon, but not today.

June 24th

Dr Paul and his wife, Maria, are here today, life is getting very sociable. He is another man that Bakri worked with for many years, and they've always been an easy couple to have around. They have just come back from visiting family in Beirut, and are as sorry as I am about Lilli. They had a long but mercifully uneventful trip from Beirut – a journey that used to take about five hours door-to-door took them nineeen hours, and they are not planning to try it again any time soon. It puts me off the trip to Jamal, even though I'd love to see him. They also have a grim tale about almost two years ago when the troubles were just starting.

Apparently a friend of theirs, who is Muslim and lives in Hama, was at the mosque near his house one Friday and when he came out he was approached by a man with a bunch of red roses. The man invited him to join a demonstration against the government but he said he didn't want to as he doesn't believe in violence. The man told him that only a peaceful demonstration was planned, and they would each be carrying a red rose as a sign of peaceful disaffection, and at the same time he saw one of his friends from the same street with his little son, both holding roses and joining the march. The upshot of it was that he took a rose and joined the marchers and they set off.

All was going as he expected until a man next to him pulled out a hand-gun from underneath his gellabiya and shot dead a policeman who was standing at the side of the road watching the march. Then all hell broke out, with the other policemen firing their guns and some people in the crowd as well, so a lot of people were hurt and some were killed. What made him especially angry, even more than he was already, was when he saw the event carefully filmed on Al Jezira as an attack by the police on a peaceful demonstration. He complained by email as soon as he could, but he knew it was useless.

We are all depressed at this story, and wonder what is going to happen next. There are so many countries, without even counting al Qaeda, using this poor land as a place to fight their battles that it seems impossible it will ever end. One thing that makes me angrier than many others – and there are a lot of them – is that when the Syrian army finally manages to take control, as I believe they will even if it takes years, is that there will be no real, honest opposition left and so no chance of the reform the country needs so much. My friends are Christians and Syrians, so their point of view is different. They just want to get back to the times when they could live their lives in peace, with freedom to be Christian without worrying about the future security of their children, and I am very sad for them. In some ways they have lost more than I have.

June 25th

This morning I wake up positive and decide to start clearing out Bakri's medical bits and pieces. There is a whole cupboard in his study that's full of boxes of medicine, mostly free samples from the drug companies that used to manufacture just outside the city. I'm sure that they would be useful to somebody, so I'll check out the dates on them and take them to the Red Crescent, unless Mariam or Assia know people who need them. His medical books fill his bookcase in this room, but I'll have to ask around if any other doctor or medical student wants them, they go out of date so fast. I could ask Dr Paul, too. I open the door of the study but I have to take a deep breath before I go in, it is the first time I've dared to try since he was killed – there, I've said 'killed' for the first time! Before, I could only say 'gone' or 'not here' as if he were coming back.

It's hard to be in this room, although it smells more musty than nostalgic. His desk is arranged as tidily as it always has been, but there is quite a bit of dust, which he would hate. When Assia was living here she used to come in and clean, but since she started living with her family and coming just to clean she hasn't been bothering with a room I never enter. I'll have to dust before I can do anything else. We are having a spell of electricity so I hurry to get the vacuum cleaner while there is power, it's so much easier and cleaner than brushing and dusting. I do the floor and some of the velvet chair seats before the vacuum cleaner winds down with a sad sigh and the power is off again. Never mind, there is enough done for me to finish by hand, and I'm really into the job by now so I get on with it quite cheerfully.

The medicine cupboard is always locked so it's free of dust. I take out the painkillers and one or two boxes of antibiotics for our own use, because the chemists around town hardly have any left, and fill a plastic carrier with the rest. At the back I recognise the name of strong painkillers I once took after an operation on my foot, and put one of the boxes on one side with the antibiotics before putting the rest in the carrier. I don't like them, but it would be stupid to get rid of them all and then to need the occasional one for an emergency.

Dusting and clearing the medicine cupboard has taken the whole morning so I sit down for a lunch-time sandwich with a feeling of virtuous accomplishment. The whole experience was less dreadful than I expected. Perhaps it's time I tried his wardrobe? Or maybe I'll leave that for a bit longer.

June 26th

Adnan called by late in the morning, which is not very usual because he most often comes with either Mariam or the children as escort. Before, he used to drop in, but since Bakri died he has been so careful of my reputation! I find it rather charming that he thinks there could be talk about me at my age. Anyway, today he was so incensed that he had to tell somebody and I think I was the nearest person, because Mariam is teaching at the university today.

He has heard that the factories in Sheikh Najjar, a newish industrial area, are being looted. That would not be surprising as the rebels usually include people who will take anything not bolted down. What has really upset him is the stories that the factories are being moved wholesale to Turkey, where the Customs people are not querying them at all, just letting them through to be sold there.

270

There is machinery which cost millions of liras – sometimes even millions of pounds – which is being sold off for thousands or even hundreds, if the reports are true. Like many another person here who does not support the rebels, he is broken-hearted at what the Turks are doing to Syria. The commonest comment I hear is that the Turkish government cannot live with the loss of their empire, but I think it is mixed with an idea of the Muslim Brothers who form their government that they can bring the old religious empire back. I hope I am wrong, but it is what Bakri suspected as early as last year.

Writing that brings it back like a knife to my stomach that Bakri doesn't have any opinions any more – or none that I will ever know. The loneliness wraps round me and I'm glad no one is here so I can let go and have a quiet cry. I allow myself ten minutes, then I make myself get up and make a cup of tea, but if I had the choice I would just lie down and give up. How long will it take to get used to managing on my own?

June29th

It's much cooler today, which is a blessing as some idiot has blown up the power lines again so we have only one hour of electricity all day and the water is at very low pressure. I've decided to put the new jam in the small shower room, which is usually cooler because it is the only room in the house with a north-facing window. As a shower-room it is great in the summer but hard to heat in the winter, but as a store-room it is quite reasonable. Assia helps me to heave a small bookcase there from the boys'

271

bedroom to carry the jars, and they look pretty good when I've finished.

Mariam admires the arrangement when she visits, after laughing about the new use for her dad's summer shower room. She's been to the Khaldiya, which I am cross about because it is still quite often shelled by the rebels, and has brought me lovely fresh geen beans and quite a few kilos of tomatoes. She wants me to cook the vegetarian dish called, in English, 'beans with olive oil'. About that, the names of food here are either untranslatable, like Kebbe, or highly unimaginative like beans with meat (or oil) and aubergine stew.

She has made sure that I don't sit about moping as the vegetables have to be cooked quickly in this weather, and preparing the beans and skinning the tomatoes takes ages. The good side is that she will bring the children at lunch time to eat the results, then I'll put the generator on for an hour or so to cool the fridge enough to store the leftovers, and so my lunch for tomorrow is secured as well, giving me freedom to mope then, should I want to. Result.

July 2nd

This morning is the first time in all my years here that I have been scared of the security police. Everybody knows that they have a very dark side, and I remember in the insurrection of 1980 that the building not far from us had a nasty reputation as an interrogation centre. It was said that people who went downstairs to that part of the building never came back alive, but I don't know anybody who has personal experience so I can only suspect it is true. Well, now I have to worry about it whether I want to or not.

When I was having my breakfast, I suppose it must have been about eight o'clock, there was a knock on the front door. I was still in my pyjamas, but grabbed my summer dressing gown (the beautiful pale grey silk one Bakri brought me from Malaysia years ago when he had a conference there), and I opened the door to find there were three men outside. They all looked like ruffians and they weren't wearing any uniform, and two of them were carrying machine guns so I thought they must be gangsters come to rob me or kidnap me and I was terrified.

Of course they spoke no English, but my Arabic is quite good enough for them to tell me that they were from the security police and wanted to speak to Sayed. I told them he wasn't in the house, but they asked quite politely if they could come in and check. I was well aware that they were only polite because I am a foreigner, and there is no way I could actually refuse entry to men with guns – especially dressed in my pretty silk dressing gown! I was shocked that they wanted to come into my house, because I am a woman living alone and it is really improper for them to ask. However there wasn't any point in saying that, so I had to look as if I weren't scared almost out of my wits and to 'invite' them in, hoping at least that they were who they said.

Actually they were very polite to me, but once they were in the house one of them stood by the door and the two with guns went from room to room and even took the ladder and checked the little loft space above the

273

bathroom. They were lucky that the elecricity was on, because there is no natural light up there. While they were going around I didn't know where to be. I wanted to ask the one at the door why they wanted Sayed, though I'm all too sure of the answer to that, but at the same time I didn't want strange men wandering round my house without watching that they took nothing. As it happened, the man at the door wouldn't say anything anyway so I spent the few minutes they were there in following the others round the house, especially when they checked all the wardrobes in the house, even those in my bedroom.

Before they left the told me that I should go straight to their office, which is that scary building just down the road, and tell them if Sayed turns up. I smiled, acted as if I didn't really understand what they wanted and said "Of course, of course" to everything, though they can't really believe I would tell them about my own son. The man without the gun was obviously the senior one and he did all the talking so I just agreed with him that the bad people who trapped young men like my son were hurting Syria and had to be stopped, and that the President is the only saviour of the country.

It seemed like hours and hours before they finally went, and I was wondering how long I could keep calm in front of them, but finally I was able to shut the door behind them and then my legs gave way and I slid down the wall until I was sitting on the floor behind the door and shaking so much I could almost hear my teeth rattling.

Now I have to think. I'm calmer and I've made myself a mug of strong tea so I can pull myself together again

274

before anybody else comes visiting. I definitely don't want Mariam to see me like this or she'll start again trying to persuade me to go and live with them, then what would happen to this house? There would be people moving in before I had taken my suitcase out! I'm sorry for people who have nowhere to live, but not so sorry that I'm giving up to them the place where all my married life happened. If I leave here it will be for good, because I've decided on a different life somewhere else.

What on earth can I do about Sayed? What do I want to do? That's easy. I want to take him somewhere safe and have him change back into the person I know, but at the moment I can't do anything at all to help him because I don't know where he is. At the same time I don't want to do anything that will bring the security police down onto Mariam and Adnan, especially Adnan as he doesn't even have a second nationality protect him. But if Sayed is involved in blowing up people and houses and the dreadful attacks we hear about I can't help him to do that. The realisation creeps over me that I am going to have to do what I have usually chosen to do since I first came here, I'm going to have to wait and see what happens and hope somebody else will fix it.How strange that I don't want that any more.

Shall I tell Mariam and Jamal the trouble their brother has caused? It would be a major relief to load it onto them, and perhaps I ought to tell Mariam for her own safety – Sayed seems so out of touch with reality that he just might turn up on his sister's doorstep to 'convert' her, and get her into trouble while he is there. I decide not to tell Jamal because he can do nothing except worry and I am selfish enough not to want to be bothered telling him four or five times a day that I am fine and nobody is attacking me.

The afternoon is almost no better. Around four o'clock, a polite time to visit in the winter but not now in the heat of July when most of Aleppo is asleep, there is a knock on the door. I am resting in the sitting room because there isn't any electricity and it is marginally cooler than my bedroom. I am physically incapable of moving for a moment, terrified that the security police have come back, for me this time.

The spy-hole shows me that my visitor is Im Rami from upstairs, which seems almost as bad, at least that is my first thought. She loves disaster to happen to other people, and she has always spent her time here taking sidelong looks, which I am not supposed to notice, at everything in the room, especially if it is new. I would love to ask her if I have moved anything since her last visit, but so far politeness has won out. This time she is genuinely worried about me, but I can't face having her in the flat so we talk on the doorstep.

"Was that the security police here this morning?" I reply that it was. "I knew there would be trouble when I saw that Sayed of yours coming here with his beard and dirt. I told Abu Rami that he'd bring trouble with him. What did they want?"

I find it very easy to slip back into the 'social lying' that I was always so good at.

"Oh it was nothing. They are just checking up on all the foreigners to make sure we are safe." I try to smile as if this is a perfectly normal thing to happen, but I'm sure she isn't fooled.

"Abu Rami and I both think you shouldn't be here on your own, it isn't safe for a woman to be living alone these days. We think you should be with your daughter."

"I'm sure it isn't dangerous for me. I don't take sides because this isn't my country." Then a master-stroke, I think, "After all, I have you and Abu Rami to look out for me, don"t I?"

"It's not the same. Of course we worry about you, but you should be with your own family. Are you not going to go back to your own country? They say the Beirut road is open now, though it's a long journey on the bus."

"Not at the moment. This is my home, really. If you remember, I've been in this house since before you and Abu Rami moved in, I don't want to leave if I don't have to."

"You needn't worry about the flat. I can ask our Sumaya to move in and look after it. Her house is too dangerous now and she's coming to live with me, with her three boys - that's five altogether with her husband. I don't know how we'll all get on. Abu Rami never liked children's noise and he's more cross about it now he's older." She wipes her hand over her hot forehead, pushing her scarf up and letting me see wet wisps of grey hair, but the thought of her daughter's three young boys rampaging round my beautiful flat hardens my heart.

"I'm sorry about that, but just now I'm not moving." I should invite her in for a cool drink and a gossip, but I still

277

can't face it so I mutter something about having to finish in the kitchen and watch her trail back upstairs.

Bother, bother, bother, I need peace. I suddenly long for those days when I could say goodbye to Bakri after breakfast and know that the rest of the morning was mine to do things I wanted, or to do nothing and read a book. Not having somebody to take responsibility for decisions is so tiring! I take the empty mug into the kitchen, rinse it and leave it to dry because I can't be bothered any more to keep my kitchen as beautifully ordered as it used to be and there isn't enough water or electricity to use the dishwasher. I think I'll take a sleeping pill tonight.

July 3rd

I didn't sleep very well, even with the sleeping pill. I don't think I woke up, but I can remember bad dreams of being chased and running away with the children in my arms, trying not to drop any of them. This morning I feel too weary and helpless to do anything useful. I think I'll try to have a quiet day and hope the police don't come back, especially if Assia drops by to clean up. I trail into the kitchen for my cup of tea, thankful that the tin of gas hasn't run out yet. I'll have to have powdered milk, but that is only going back to when I first came here, when milk had to be powdered or, if it was fresh, boiled for ten minutes before we could use it. We've got so used to clean milk, the 'long life' sort, that when that factory was blown up it was strange to go back to the old ways. One thing I have learned, the hard way, is that you can get used to almost anything if you really have to – though that doesn't mean you have to like it.

The enormous mug of tea that I make for myself these days revives me, and I begin to plan my day. There is still the problem of whether or not to tell Mariam about the visitors yesterday. If I tell her she will be furious (again) with Sayed, but if I keep quiet she won't be prepared if the same gentlemen turn up on her doorstep. Just for this morning I hope she is too busy to contact me, by lunchtime I may have made up my mind. Now I come to think of it, I remember she said she would be busy today with one of her friends who is going to Canada. That should give me time. Good.

Late in the morning I have a surprise visit from Juana, who used to be into all the good works of the city, as far as I could tell. It's unusual for her to visit anyone without calling first, and she's standing on the doormat looking embarrassed when I open the front door.

"Elizabeth!" she smiles, "How are you? I'm so, so sorry to come without asking. My phone has been dead for days, and you didn't answer your mobile yesterday. If it's a bad time I'll go away at once." I know she means it, but my time isn't as organised as it used to be so she's welcome to come in – much more welcome than yesterday's visitors. I show her into the front room, and realise it is slightly dusty, but to my surprise I find I don't really care. Two years ago I wouldn't have been able to talk to her properly if I could see anything not perfectly presented in the room, but, like a lot of other things, it doesn't seem to matter any more.

We sit down and I am just going to offer her the usual turkish coffee when the doorbell goes again and it is Assia, also embarrassed on my doorstep. She says that she has overslept, which must be the first time in her life, it is certainly the first time it has affected me. I usher her in and she greets Juana then rushes off to the kitchen to make the coffee for me, which is pleasant.

Juana tells me the news, and as she is in touch with far more people than I, of 'all sorts and conditions', she can tell me things I haven't heard of at all. She cheers me up when she says that the rebels are pretty well surrounded in parts of the town, and the local people are occasionally rising up against them, being fed up of being used as what they call 'human shields'. I can understand that, and they must be absolutely desperate to face all the guns the rebels have, knowing that a lot of people have been shot out of hand just for saying the wrong thing or even having the wrong surname (Assad is quite a common name, but not a very safe one at the moment!). She also tells me the real story of the enormous bang some time ago when something went off at the university.

Apparently, and she is usually right, an army plane was flying over the university campus when a missile was fired at it. The missile failed, fell to the ground and killed a lot of students. My neighbours had told me that the plane had dropped a bomb on the campus, but I always found that hard to believe because the army has been making efforts to show up as the protectors of the civilian population, and a random attack on the university campus would have been going very publicly in the opposite direction. However, you never know these days, so I ask her how she is so certain.

"My niece was driving back home and was coming over the rise by the Faculty of Engineering when it happened, so she saw it." I nod, knowing that you can see right across the campus from there. "She heard a bang and looked up in time to see the second rocket miss the plane and fall into the university area. She rushed there as fast as she could, but by the time she had parked the car there was nothing she could do. Lots of people were trying to help, they had come out of all the buildings on Fourkaan Street and they were crying while they pulled bodies and injured students out of the mess. All she could do was to ring her aunt and make sure that her cousin – you know Rula, don't you? - was safe, Thank God, she was already on her way home when it happened." I'm shocked at the story. How can these people, who want to make the country a better place, be so careless of other people's lives? On the other hand, there are so many different versions of any incident that I am now at the stage of not quite believing anyone a hundred percent.

Fortunately Assia comes in and distracts us with the coffee, and she sits down and joins us because she used to work for Juana years ago. I wouldn't have tolerated this before, but it seems natural now. Perhaps it's good? Anyway, the horror story is lost in enquiries about each and every member of their families and I wonder again how they can possibly remember all the names, ages and babies, but almost everybody here can. It's a skill I haven't acquired and I don't think I ever will. The visit ends when the coffee is finished and I have found the last remaining few chocolates to offer. What am I going to do when they are all gone? A trivial thought, but the final offering of something sweet to a visitor used to be so much a part of any visit that I can't imagine how to end a visit without it. At the same time I know it is silly to be worrying about chocolate when people I know have lost their houses, their businesses or even their lives.

July 10th

July is always the holiday month. When the children were small we used to go to the mountains, to one of the resorts, to get away from the heat. Bakri used to rent a house for us and we stayed, the children and me, with Bakri coming on Thursday afternoon and staying till Saturday evening. The children ran wild in the fields and got to know the local people. They learned to milk goats among other surprising skills, and it was a time for me to stroll in the warm fields and read or watch English programmes on Cyprus TV which we could get from across the Mediterranean. Then in August Bakri took his holiday and we travelled to England while my mother was still alive, and by the time she died the children were living different lives and didn't have time to go to England any more. Bakri and I kept on going, we visited my sister and our old friends and enjoyed the shops, but our last time was two years ago now because the road became too risky. We knew we could get out, but we were scared that we might get stuck there with no way back. Now I wish we had.

This year Mariam is taking the children to the pool almost every day. They can often hear fighting, but the pool is near her house and the risks of going aren't that great. When you are constantly at risk you seem either to live in a permanent state of being scared, which leads to heart attacks, or you start to feel that if a rocket has your name on it will get you so you might as well get on with your life. That policy didn't work for Bakri, but it appears to keep Mariam sane. I'd like to go too, but it seems inappropriate to be at the pool in a swimsuit so soon after the mourning period. I'm sure it would make people talk about me, and I wouldn't feel comfortable in myself. Perhaps in August I might think about it.

July 15th

Another blow. An acquaintance, another doctor who was returning to Aleppo because he was worried about patients having no medical help, was killed yesterday when he was on the bus back. The story seems to be that there was an attempt to kidnap people from the bus – something which has been happening – and when the kidnappers tried to stop the bus one of their shots went through the window and hit the doctor. The people who did it were very upset to have hurt him and sent the bus on its way, but it took three hours to get to Aleppo and by that time he had bled to death all over his wife.

The tribe involved in the kidnappings is supposed to have somebody in the bus company in Beirut to tell them when a good prospect is coming through, but that's only rumour. I think they are just reverting to a way of life they followed from time immemorial, as the saying is, until the president's father stopped them forty years ago. At least I know that Sayed wasn't involved because it was just one small tribe and they wouldn't want an outsider.

July 17th

Last night I had a horrible dream. I was walking into Wanis retaurant, where we used to meet for lunch quite often, and Bakri was sitting at a table waiting for me. He looked up but instead of getting up to help me to sit down, he looked straight past me, got up and walked out, leaving me standing there. The waiters didn't seem to think that was strange and I didn't know whether to follow him or to sit down myself. Then I was outside and he was walking away from me much quicker than I could go. As fast as I could run, he was faster until he disappeared in the crowd in the shopping centre in the Azizieh and I lost him. I woke up dripping with perspiration and with my heart pounding. Do dreams mean something? Doesn't he love me wherever he is now?

To forget the dream I decide to get busy and take down all the voile curtains because they are full of dust. I used to have them done every four months or so, but this is the first time since I was widowed. I don't like that word. Widow. Black clothes and a sour expression, but it's what I am. There isn't enough electricity to use the washing machine, but I know I have water in the tank. I draw a precious half a bath-full of water and put the bedroom curtains to soak. It's a way that uses masses of water, but the supply hasn't been too bad recently so I'll use it while it is here. The curtains immediately turn the water inky black, but I'll leave them for an hour or so to give all the dust time to soak up water then it will be much easier to get them fairly clean when I change the water.

That is such an energetic job that I am glad to stop for a cup of coffee (instant and not even very good instant, but at least it's coffee), and very pleased when Mariam finally drops in with the children and helps me to finish the job. I don't tell her about my dream because it seems so silly, and I'm always bored by other people's dreams myself.

July 20th

The day I have been dreading has arrived and I truly don't think I want to live any more.

The security policeman who came last time called again, but this time it was to tell me that Sayed is dead. I can't believe it, but I know it is true. In a way it is a terrible relief because if he had been captured he would be in the security centre now, which wuld be so much worse. The policeman says he was in a truck full of fighters trying to get into the prison a little to the east of here and they were all killed by the army unit defending the prison. He was quite sympathetic and said they knew it was him because he had his identity card on him, though most don't carry them. I asked him if we could have Sayed's body to bury, but he couldn't tell me. I suppose they don't want a fuss about a rebel fighter being buried, but it would be comforting if he were laid near his father.

Stupid, stupid boy. What use was his death to anybody? I am so torn between completely collapsing with grief and yet being absolutely furious with him for causing me so much upset, that I can't speak – I almost can't breath.As soon as he leaves, Im Rami creeps down the stairs and asks what is happening. I have to tell her that Sayed is dead, then I go into the house and shut the door. She knocks a few times, the electricity is off so she can't ring, and she soon gives up and leaves me in peace. I sit on the chair in the hall for a minute or two, then realise that she will be phoning the news all over town so I have to let Mariam know before she hears it from somebody else.

I finally manage to talk to Mariam, though it takes ages as her mobile network is down again and her phone line only works when it feels like. Saying the words 'Your brother is dead' is dreadfully hard. It brings back all the feelings I had when I was told about Bakri. I can hardly breathe and my stomach hurts as much as if I have been hit. Mariam understands, and comes to me as soon as she can get her mother in law round to babysit.

"The stupid idiot!" She is crying and hugging me. "Why did he get in with such horrible people?" She knows I can't answer because I am crying too, and anyway I just don't know.

"Does Jamal know?"

"Not yet. I've only just heard. I'll have to phone him when I know he won't be at work."

"Mum, I'll call him. It's not fair that you have to do everything." I'm grateful for the thought, but it's no good. It's my job and I have to do it. One part of me is surprised that I can be so definite. These last months have made me take charge without realising it. Now I know that there is only me to protect my children – and they are still my children however old they get. I made a mess of it with Sayed, but I'm going to do better now.

"No, Mariam. You have a lot to think about and it's my job so I'll do it." Mariam looks surprised, but I can see that she's relieved to avoid this particular task. She has to hurry back, and we don't know what will happen about Sayed's funeral. Will he have one? Is his body already buried somewhere? Will anybody want to come to the mourning? We don't want his crazy friends here, and the others may be nervous about attracting security police attention. We'll have to leave it until the evening when we can get Adnan's opinion.

The day drags on, but finally Adnan comes to escort me to their flat to decide what to do. They tell me that Adnan's brother has a friend in the security police, actually working at the centre near me and he spoke to him as soon as he heard about Sayed. The advice was to keep quiet for a day or two until he finds out what Sayed had been up to before we decide. Adnan says he will have prayers said for Sayed in the mosque, but not a proper funeral service. For one thing we don't have a body, and for another it would be unwise to make too much noise and bring attention to ourselves. Either the security police might start bothering us, or the Shebiha could, just conceivably, start thinking of us (and me as a foreigner) as opposition. We agree about all this and Adnan takes me home, quiet and sad. Now I truly know the meaning of the phrase 'heavy hearted'.

July 21st

No news today about burying Sayed, but we expect to hear tomorrow. Something else happens, though, that amuses me for a bit and breaks the sadness for a short time.

There is a ring at the doorbell and when I look through the spyhole I see Im Rami there, all dressed up and with a handbag. Our usual way of meeting is when one or other of us is on the stairs, and her usual clothes inside the building are the plastic work flipflops we all wear for housework, a long sleeved galabiya and a large scarf – she tends to shades of purple which are not a good idea with her red face. I open the door and greet her correctly, but she is unusually shy and asks to come in. This is interesting. I would prefer to be alone today, but she's here so I have to be polite.

After she has offered the correct condolences about Sayed we go into the formal sitting room and sit, then exchange the standard questions about each other's health, families and very distant relations, a process that has to be completed at any meeting, and which drives foreign businessmen crazy, I'm told. When we've run out of gossip I excuse myself and go to make the coffee, as Assia isn't here today. I am now completely mystified by her visit, I can't imagine what it's about.

The coffee takes a few minutes, and when I return to Im Rami with everything set out correctly on one of the kitchen trays – for Im Rami I am NOT going to get out and polish the big silver tray. She has obviously been poking about the room, and rushed back to her seat when she heard me coming, but I pretend not to notice her flushed face and nervous hands. We arrange ourselves again, and while she sips at her coffee she suggests that it must be very lonely for me on my own, and I agree that sometimes it is. Then I choke on my coffee when she tells me that her brother – Doctor Munir – has been widowed for six months and is looking for a new wife.

I can't believe my ears. Doctor Munir is somebody that I remember laughing about with Bakri. He has always been a little, dry stick of a man, a cigarette usually in his mouth and the smell of smoke around him like an invisible cloud. His wife was a big fat woman with an enormous personality and a vast collection of rude jokes. She wouldn't tell these in mixed company, but when she was with a group of women she took her scarf off and really let her hair down in both senses! Often I couldn't quite follow the jokes, and asked Bakri to explain later. He usually did, but once or twice he just went very red, told me he couldn't translate that one and changed the subject super-quickly.

The thought of being connected to Doctor Munir, even as a friend, let alone marrying him, leaves me speechless and with my mouth hanging open for a moment, then I pull myself together and manage to tell her to thank him for his suggestion, but I am not planning on marrying again. She then points out that this is just a preliminary talk and he doesn't actually know she is here. She is going round the 'possibles', as a good sister should, to make up a short list for him to choose from.

Of course, once she tells me I am back 'in the loop', remembering all the women who came to see Mariam when she was single. I am stabbed with sadness again when I remember that I won't ever get to do this for Sayed, but I struggle to stay polite and we finish the visit with chitchat about the old neighbours and where they have got to now. I am surprised and relieved that she is tactful enough not to ask about Sayed's funeral, I would have expected her to go on about the problems, but she keeps away from the subject altogether.

It is odd that this building, which used to echo with noise from the children, one family on each floor, is now silent. We are older, of course, but so many people have left that neither of us have very many friends close at hand any more. There is a displaced family on the ground floor, I think they rent from the owners and they may be some sort of relation, but I don't know them though I hear the children, lots of them, playing in the little garden sometimes in the afternoon. I suppose there will be plenty of noise again when Im Rami's daughter finally moves here. Im Rami is right. My life is quite lonely now. I am going to have to start planning or I'll end up a burden to Mariam, which is the last thing I want.

I wash up the coffee cups and put them away, thinking about the choices I'll have to make sometime soon. I can stay here and hope that friends will drift back as the fighting stops, but who knows when that will be? By that time most of them will be settled in their own countries and won't want to up-root and start yet again. When the internet is on I get emails from a few of them, but that will stop in time because we will be living such different lives that we won't have much to say any more. I would probably end up like an old English woman I knew here

290

who lost her group of friends when one of the wars started, then lived almost as a recluse until she died a year or two ago. I used to visit her sometimes and listen to her stories of a very grand social circle, but I wouldn't want to end my days living on memories like that.

The other choice is to move back to England and buy a house there. I don't know much about prices, but I'm sure there is enough between the cash here, this flat and the investments Bakri made in England over the years to buy me somewhere small, perhaps near my sister and her children. The worst part about that would be leaving Mariam and the children, and I don't know if I can face that.

There's one thing to be said for Im Rami and all the ideas she's provoked, it is lunchtime and I haven't had time to cry for Sayed, though the sad, flat feeling never really went away even when she was proposing me as a 'short list candidate' for her brother. I make myself a boring cheese sandwich and retreat to Bakri's big armchair in the bedroom with a book I haven't read for years, then wake up in the late afternoon to the sound of Mariam arriving with the children for a 'cheer up Granny' visit. I decided not to tell her the story, but while the children are playing on the balcony and we are drinking my lemon squash it all comes out and we have a giggle about it, though we both feel guilty at laughing about anything just now.

July 23rd

There has been a horrible chemical attack that seems to have killed a lot of families in Damascus. The rebels say the army did it, but the army says it was the rebels. It doesn't seem likely to me that the army would do something like that so close to all the foreign correspondents in Damascus, after all, if they want to make a chemical attack there are plenty of places away from the cameras. It seems to me like a rebel way of dragging the outside world into Syria, whatever it takes.

July 26th

The news gets worse. Now the Americans want to bomb the army and my own country seems to want it too. People are gathering in worried groups in the street outside the building, wondering when the rockets will start and how many of us will be killed. The atmosphere is grimmer than I have ever seen it, we have nowhere to go and everyone remembers the stories of all the Iraqis who were killed in the course of being liberated, though that word has a nasty taste these days. The nun, Sr Agnes I think, who keeps wandering around Syria looking for evidence when there has been something horrid, says she thinks that it is surprising to find so many people, especially so many children, in an industrial zone of Damascus, and one that has seen so much fighting. She also says that some of the people whose children were kidnapped by the rebels near Lattakia are sure they have seen them among the dead bodies shown on TV. Why can't my own countrymen see that their good name is being used by people who care absolutely nothing about people's lives, but only about money?

July 28th

It is a strange day. For the first time in my days here I can see people sitting on the pavement around little radios, listening to what is happening in Parliament in London. The debate about whether to support the American attacks is going on, and nobody can believe that the British parliament will not do what the Prime Minister wants. When the result of the vote is announced, and we hear that the idea has been rejected, there is a slight cheer from the men on the street below this flat. Later in the afternoon I go for my walk and feel the difference in the air. I even see a few people smiling, and they are all so happy that some Members of Parliament in England are worried about them. Just for once these days, I am proud of my country and it's a good feeling!

August 1st

Horrible news today. Something turned up Syrian TV. It was a boy of about 13 who had been on youtube having a lesson about how to cut off a man's head, and had shown he could do it on a prisoner. He was recognised by someone at a roadblock near Deir Ezzor and taken to the police. What can they do with a child who has learned that sort of thing? Mr Hague, why are you helping these people?

August 2nd

Mariam came this morning with the children. She was as upset as me about that child yesterday. I know she is worried about her own children's safety – she takes them to school and brings them home although the little school they have found is literally next door to their building. They know it isn't very good, but keeping the children safe is more important than anything else these days. The internet is off again, but we just curse the idiots with the bombs and keep on going these days. I'd love to hear what Bakri would have said about them!

August 5th

There seems to be more evidence that some of the bodies of children in the chemical attack in Damascus were really children abducted from Lattakia during the horrible attacks there. It seems almost impossible to believe, but then most Germans in World War two didn't believe there were concentration camps either.

August 10th

The phone was working today but I didn't realise until it rang and it was my sister on the line! She is very worried and wants us all to come and live with her. Their children are long grown up and gone, and there is plenty of room for us all – she says this and I know it's true. I don't know. Until Sayed was killed I'd have said that my family is here so I'm staying, but things have changed now. All I can say is that I am thinking about what to do, and she rings off. I know she is worried and it makes her cross with me, but there are so many things to think about, and if I go there I think I would have to live away from her, at least in my own home. I don't think I could stay for very long anywhere that I wasn't responsible for. These last months have made me happy to be alone some of the time, and I think I am capable of managing life by myself – but I don't know.

August 13th

Last night Shadi Helwi was on the TV when I had nothing better to do than watch the news. He is a local boy who has cheered people throughout the last year with his gung-ho attitude and his belief that the army is good and will win in the end. This time he was talking to various people in the street or standing in bread queues (it takes at least an hour to get bread these days, though the bakeries in this area are working all day and night). They wanted to know when there would be food, water, electricity, petrol, heating diesel, and cooking gas, and he took those questions to the governor, the head of the Chamber of Industry and the police chief.

The answers were reasonable – that the gas, diesel and petrol are brought in by drivers who risk their lives to do it, and they can only be asked when the road is believed to be safe. That the electricity, which has been much better recently, I must say, should improve as more parts are repaired, and that the water is back in the system after the last lot of pipes were blown up, but it will take time to reach everyone. I'm not too high up in town, so I've already got some trickling through.

There was also a nasty report of as many as eight thousand children being under arms, mostly abducted from their families. Those who are not given guns seem to be kept for the 'entertainment' of the foreign fighters. Thank

God that Ahmed's nephew cannot have been pretty enough for that, at least he died a clean death! The news had a lot about the trouble the Muslim brothers are causing in Egypt now they have been removed. The BBC isn't interested, but a lot of the rest of the world is when we see raging mobs shouting 'Allah akbar' and burning down churches (eight so far, I believe).

August 14th

There are two villages between Aleppo and the Turkish border which have always been Shia rather than Sunni, though as most people in the villages here don't marry out of their own tribes this was not a particular problem before. The foreign fighters however regard any Shia as wicked and have been laying siege to them for at least eight months, though the BBC seems to agree that as they are not anti-government it doesn't matter. They have wells, I suppose, and every now and again the army sends a helicopter in to deliver basic foods.

A few days ago there were rumours of two young boys, aged about 12 or 13, who had strayed to the edge of the village called Zahraa and been captured and murdered by the fighters, but 'rumour is a lying jade' and we didn't particularly believe it. Today their murders were put on Syriatube for the world to see. They were knelt down and shot, one after the other. What is happening to this pleasant country? They all managed to live together before!

August 19th

Mariam was here this morning and left the children with me while she did some food shopping, so I have put a bowl of water on the balcony and given the children some plastic jugs to play with. I can hear them shouting and laughing and I don't think I want to go and see what they're doing, but I suspect it involves throwing water over the balcony at people on the street! Nothing changes. I can remember our boys being in trouble for the same thing.

When Mariam comes back she sits with me and tells me that she and Adnan are thinking of leaving. They are not earning enough to live comfortably (who is, these days?) and Adnan's UK visa will run out at the end of this year, so if they don't move soon they will have all the hassle of getting a new one. I know they have some money outside the country – part of what her father left is hers, too, and she says they'd like to open a business somewhere near my sister, who as it happens lives not far from one of Adnan's cousins in Kent. I don't know what to think. This is my home, we chose everything in it together, Bakri and me, and part of it is having family near. If Mariam goes I'll be really on my own. She notices my face and says quickly,

"Of course we won't go without you. We couldn't leave you behind."

"Thank you, dear, but I'm not sure...." I need time to get used to yet another bombshell, although this explosion is only in my head. Now I can't wait for her to go so I can sit down and be calm by myself. If I go, how can I start to organise the flat, our clothes, all the things I wouldn't want to leave behind?

August 20th

I am beginning to think that I may have no future here. I m furious that my own country is supporting the people ho are doing such awful things. Of course the security services are really bad, but if you didn't get into politics they left you alone, and anyway they were being reined in slowly and steadily by the president – we all noticed the difference in the two or three years before the trouble started. Now it seems that the fighters are getting information about movements of the army from US spy planes (drones or whatever they are), and using that information to track anything moving. It explains how they know each time there is a bus travelling from Aleppo so they can attack it. How can we leave if the road is so dangerous? Perhaps we have all left it too late and we'll just have to get on with it here and hope to be alive at the end.

I spend the late afternoon at Mariam's flat, discussing what to do, with her and Adnan. They have been planning this for some time, and have been managing to send money to England for a few months, probably since Bakri died, though they don't say so. I know it's illegal and I don't want to know how they did it, but it is a relief that they won't be destitute when they first arrive. I will have to choose just a few pieces of jewellery, as it isn't safe to travel with a lot, and we'll leave the rest with Adnan's mother, telling her that it all belongs to Mariam - which it

298

will when I die. I tell them how much money I still have, and we decide that what can't be sent out, or won't be used for the journey, will have to stay here, so I think I'll give it to the Red Crescent to be used for relief. Adnan sees me home before it is too late, but I can't settle to sleep. I wander round the house trying to decide what is important enough to keep and what I can just walk away from.

The next days are secretly hectic. We need to find somebody reliable to live here if possible, because an empty flat will soon be taken over by strangers who will break the door down and move in. I ask Assia to move back in with me, on the pretext that I'm a bit nervous, and the day we go I'll suggest she brings some of her relations here as well. They aren't family, and they won't care for the place very well, but it's the best I can do. We are going to travel to Beirut by bus, which will be tedious because the journey takes so long now and the weather is still very hot. Adnan assures me that the buses are the best ones from before the troubles, but he also says Mariam, Rula and I all have to wear scarves from here until we pass Hama and get back on to the main road again. That will be a trial for all three of us!

August 30th

Each time Mariam comes here or I go there I take something I don't want to lose, and she puts it with her own possessions to go to her mother in law. I have decided that when I go I'll tell Assia to take any clothes she wants and to give the rest away. In a way it's a relief that the decisions about Bakri's clothes will be out of my hands, but it's a strange feeling to be growing so uncaring about possessions that I have spent years collecting and worrying over.

I asked them how much I can take, but the answer isn't cheering. I have to take only what I will be able to carry on the flight to London, that is, a twenty kilo suitcase and a carry-on bag. How on earth can I take enough clothes for a new life in England? I start poking about in my drawers and wardrobe, but I can't decide. What is better? A lot of light clothes or a lower number of heavy clothes for the winter? I'll certainly take as many pairs of shoes as I can fit in, and a heavy coat. It's time for bed and I refuse to think about it any more.

September 1st

I really have to start organising my luggage today! I get out the blue suitcase I bought two years ago but never used. I've always found that suitcases don't last for more than four return trips by air – I don't know what they do to them once they disappear behind the check-in desk, but they certainly don't look after them. This one was bought locally and is Chinese made, but it's very light and will do for this journey. I start to drop in things I know I'll need – underwear, a couple of nighties, practical shoes, but put the pretty high-heeled ones to one side to give away. It isn't very nice, but it has to be done. I start to put in my cosmetics and skin creams, but decide to go through them first and take only the most expensive, which I probably won't be able to afford to replace. That's enough for this morning. It's time for breakfast, and I have to put the suitcase away in the wardrobe before anyone sees it and knows we're leaving.

Mariam comes in the afternoon. She is trying to pack for the children and it isn't easy. The clothes aren't really a problem, children grow out of them so fast. The problem is in persuading the children to take just one small bag full of their personal treasures. This means choosing some cuddly toys and leaving others and isn't going down well. I can see that she's very stressed, and it breaks my heart that I can't make anything easier for her, except by not making problems myself. When she leaves I go back to my own case and make a more determined effort to pack. By bedtime I pretty well know what I've decided. Tomorrow may bring different ideas, but I'm tired and sad. I'm going to bed.

September 3rd

My big suitcase is packed now. I woke up early and finished it before Assia stirred, because she came yesterday to stay. I hope I've made the right choices, but I still have the cabin bag to fill so if I remember something important I won't have to start all over again. The suitcase just fits into Bakri's wardrobe, though I am red in the face by the time I manoevre it in, and I shut the door on it in relief. Later in the morning I go through my paperwork, money and jewellery to make finally sure that I have everything I need, then in the afternoon Adnan stops by to tell me, quietly while Assia is out of the room, that our tickets are booked for the Beirut bus for three days' time.

The news takes my breath away. The time has finally come and I am so shocked that my hands are trembling. Assia comes back with the turkish coffee and looks daggers at Adnan because she assumes he has upset me. She has never liked him much, she is very conservative in her ideas – sometimes it's like having a Victorian in the house – and doesn't like his family because they aren't 'people like us' (meaning Bakri's family). She has refused to work for people that I recommended because their families weren't up to her standard, so it was impossible for her to understand our letting Mariam marry Adnan. She has got used to him, but now she is sure that she was right all the time, I can see it in her face.

I tell her quickly that I was asking after people we knew, but as she thinks I should be protected from bad news that doesn't help very much – he should have lied rather than upset me. She serves the coffee to him, puts my cup on the table nearest me and stomps back to the kitchen to drink her own in peace. Adnan is used to her, and now finds her quite funny, but he knows how upset I am and tries to chat about trivial doings of the children while I calm down. What a nice person he is.

This evening after Assia goes to Mariam's old room to bed I shut myself in our bedroom for almost the last time. It seems like saying goodbye to Bakri all over again and I can't stop crying for a long time. But why should I? We lived a life that was supposed to be stable and to end in our own flat with our children around us. This is what happened to Bakri's parents even though they saw the end of the Ottoman Empire, French occupation and fighting against it, invasion during the second World War, the Israeli wars and the turbulent years of independence. Somehow society managed to keep on going despite it all, but it has caught up with us at last.

I know I'm crying for everyone I have lost. Of course Sayed and Bakri are top of the list, but the others I knew who are dead, or have left and are struggling to make a life in other countries, also come into my head and force more tears out of me. I have to cry quietly because I don't want Assia to hear, so I have a towel pushed against my face and carry on until I don't have any crying left.

The pain is still there. I can feel a heavy lump in my chest, just above my stomach. I suppose it could be something to do with my heart, but I don't believe it is. It is just sadness, such sadness that it has actual weight. I have to drag myself to the bathroom, quietly so as not to disturb Assia, to get ready for bed, and tonight I say a few prayers – something I haven't done much since I was a child – asking for peace for us all. It seems to be what I need. I begin to feel calmer, and sink into my pillow to drop to sleep almost immediately.

September 4th

Knowing I'm leaving in two days time but unable to tell anyone, I'm finding it hard to concentrate on anything today. Have I got the right things into my suitcase? I try to remember what I put in, and go through my wardrobe again to check what's left. My small case has to be packed today, or tonight at the latest, so that I can help Mariam with the children and her packing tomorrow. I send Assia out for a few groceries so I can work in peace, and spread the jewellery I'm taking between my makeup purse and my toilet bag. I debate pushing earings down into the tube of toothpaste, but they won't fit so that won't work. Then I have the bright idea of pushing them into a bar of the lovely local olive-oil soap, which takes some time but works very well. At least they'll be clean when I get them out! I'll wear two of the rings I'm taking, and trust to luck and my generous makeup purse to protect the others. I've always liked makeup and perfume, so I have quite a big bag for travelling and now it is coming into its own. One extra necklace which I can't bear to leave behind, and my toilet bag is full as well.

Finally, this case, too, is finished and squashed into Bakri's wardrobe on top of the big one. For the rest of the day I have to try to act as if it's just another day with nothing special happening.

Fortunately for me, Assia comes back with news of fighting in the Kalassi, where she has family, and of the problems of getting bread this morning because there is a shortage of diesel oil to fire the bakery ovens, so we have plenty to keep us occupied. I decide that Mariam and her family should come here for lunch tomorrow so she will have time to pack, but when I call her to say so, she counters with an invitation from Adnan's parents to lunch for us all at their house, and it would be very unkind to refuse.

When I think about it, they are losing so much more than I am. Adnan has looked after them since his father became unwell – I'm not sure what it is, as they are quite quiet about it, which is really unusual here – and now they will have to rely on their daughters for everything, which is not the local way of doing things.

Shadi Helwi is on TV again, though he was injured in an attack on him and his film crew. He is still as cheery as ever, and manages to make people feel that this is just a nasty time that will be over one day due to the heroic efforts of the army. Certainly the army is the safest force around at the moment, and a lot of them are being killed in trying to keep the rebels out. Good luck to them, I say.

September 5th

Heavens, what will I do? We have a rather sad lunch with Adnan's parents and some of his sisters, then an hour or so after I get home there is a call from Mariam to say that the Beirut road is closed again so we are leaving early in the morning through Turkey, and somebody will be at my house in half an hour to pick up my bags! Thank God I packed them before! Poor Mariam must be going crazy trying to finish hers, but she doesn't want me to come and help. She says I'll hear all about the arrangements when they pick me up at half past seven tomorrow morning.

Now I have to tell Assia what is going on, and to swear her to secrecy. I tell her that she can bring anyone she wants to live here, but I prefer it if she stays here herself, and she bursts into tears and wants to kiss my hand. Very embarrassing! I must go round the house telling her what she can have, but almost straight away Adnan arrives with a man I've never seen before and they take my suitcase and my small case. Adnan says all the luggage is going to be taken across the line between the two sides tonight, so that we won't attract attention tomorrow by moving with bags. Apparently one of his brothers in law has arranged everthing but I mustn't speak a word of English as the driver taking us to the border mustn't know I'm a foreigner. I can see the sense of this, as foreigners are seen as perfect kidnapping material by quite a lot of the groups. He leaves me with a head covering and a black galabiya to wear, so I will look like a local woman going shopping.

They go with my cases, and I take Assia around the flat pointing out what I want her to have, which is pretty much everything, really. She cries when I open Bakri's wardrobe and show her all the clothes I want her to give away, and I know she's crying mostly because our organised, predictable life is over and she has to get used to a new, unsafe reality. I feel the same, and we end up hugging each other and crying together, until she pulls away, wipes her eyes and tells me we need a cup of tea and she is going to make it.

She is so strong and sensible that I'm sure she'll survive unless she is unlucky enough to get in the way of a random bullet or shell. I follow her to the kitchen and we drink the tea, but we have nothing more to say to each other, and soon we go to our separate bedrooms even though it is barely eight oclock. In my room I wrestle with the two pieces of the head cover, which is black knitted cotton and very soft, though extremely hot in August even though the sun went down a while ago, then pull the galabiya over my head and down for the skirt to reach the floor. I look at myself in the mirror, but hardly know who I'm looking at, I could be any elderly woman off the street. It's a bit scary, but I have to share it with Assia and make her laugh.I go and knock at her room and when she answers I put my head round her door. She screams, then recognises me and collapses onto her knees on the floor.

"What is that? Where did you get it? Oh, Madame, how can you wear such a dirty old thing?" I suppose she is right. The galabiya does have a musty smell to it, though I was trying to ignore it. She helps me pull it off over my head and takes it away to the kitchen, muttering to herself. I follow her, alarmed that she is taking the disguise that I have to wear in less that twelve hours time, but she pushes me aside, tutting that she can have it washed, dried and ironed in a few hours, God willing, because the weather is still so hot it will dry at once. I stop arguing and hand her the washing powder so she can get on with it, and before we finally go to bed the offending galabiya has been washed out of weeks of its life and is hanging on the line, already only damp in the hot September night.

My last night here, perhaps my last night ever in Aleppo, and I'm in such a state of nerves about everything that I lie tossing and turning on my hot, sweaty bed. Needless to say, today when I need the fan to sleep there is no electricity. I get up twice in the night to stand under the shower to cool down. The water is warm, but I don't dry myself much and leave my hair wet, which is cooling enough to let me sleep until the effect wears off.

The background noise of shells and bombs that I've learned not to hear is ominous again, as it was when it first started. Then it was because it was new and we didn't know what was happening. Now it's because I know too well what is happening and I'm scared almost out of my wits at the thought of going out into it tomorrow. It's a long time since I prayed so much, except when Bakri died, but tonight seems like a good time to be doing so.

September 6th

It's evening now and I can hardly remember all the details of today in order. I have travelled quite a bit, both with Bakri and before we met, but never before like this and, I hope, never again!

Adnan and Mariam picked me up in their car, and I squashed into the back with Mariam and the children because another of Adnan's brothers in law was driving the car back after dropping us at the bridge across the almost dry river bed which is the front line of the fighting. When we got out of the car, Adnan took Mariam and the children and I found my hand in the firm grasp of the brother in law who was going with us. We walked quickly but calmly across the bridge, among quite a lot of people going either way, to work or to their businesses, until I suddenly heard 'ping ... ping' and saw everyone was bending down and running. Ahmed, the brother in law, pulled me along much faster than before and I tried to keep up and not to fall, because the road was very rough and broken. I remember being surprised that bullets do sound like the cartoon noise, they really do go 'ping' as they hit the road or a building.

Then the shooting stopped and we walked a little more slowly until we reached the other side. The men took Sami and walked on a little more quickly to find the bus that should be waiting for us, while Mariam stayed with Rula and me as we walked more slowly, though as fast as we could.We were picking our way among vegetables being sold on the street when I was pulled over be a tiny woman grasping my arm and saying,

'Come here with me.' She was wearing some sort of uniform and had a pistol in her hand so I wasn't in a position to argue, and as soon as she saw what was happening Mariam followed me with Rula. We were pulled into a narrow doorway, and the woman started feeling me to see if I was carrying anything. I took out the little bag I once got from an airline, which was hanging round my neck, and showed her I only had my passport, a small necklace and a few twenty pound notes. I was very worried that she would search me properly and discover I had more than a thousand dollars in my tights, which would have got me into serious trouble, and would have endangered Mariam, too. She gave me the impression that she was rather a nasty female, though it was difficult to judge too well as she was wearing a black yashmak over her nose and jaw.

Fortunately, she was distracted by the sterling I had given her. She didn't know what it was and I was not going to open my mouth and give myself away as a foreigner to tell her. Mariam told her it was English money, but she carried on shouting at me. Then she went over to a young man who must have been her superior, and they both examined the money, giving us time for the miracle to happen.

Rula started to cry at the shouting and the tension. The young man obviously saw that the money didn't amount to enough to be illegal, and was very sympathetic about Rula, so he told the woman to let us go! She was definitely not pleased, but he insisted, so we were off as fast as we could walk, to find the men searching frantically for us and Sami looking scared. We went on a little further to where there was a ruined half-house with a man they called 'the Somali' guarding it, and he let us go through the house so we would be protected from any more shots.

The next step was a short trip in a rickety old minibus to the shop of some relation or other, and we had to wait there for more than an hour to be picked up again. Rula was very distressed, but managed to smile when she was reunited with her brother, and all we females got the chance to take off the headgear for a time while we were safe in the store room above the shop. Adnan sat on the balcony, but we couldn't as it would have attracted notice. He said that a lot of the armed men he saw seemed to be very blond and European, though they were mostly dressed in Afghan clothing. Some were probably Arabs, and a few sounded like Syrians, but there were also a fair number of Africans, probably Somalis, strolling along the street as if they owned it – as in fact they do, now.

There was a tap there with clean water, which was a great relief with the day getting hotter and we females wearing about three times as much clothing as we were used to! We drank cool water and took photos of ourselves with our phones to pass the time and to amuse the children, but the almost two hours we spent there were hot, uncomfortable and unnerving because we knew that if anyone happened to decide to search the building, or to loot the shop, we would be in 'serious trouble', in fact we might be simply taken out and shot.

I was beginning to think something had gone wrong, and even Adnan was looking worried, when our contact returned and we covered ourselves again (how do women wear all this every day in the summer?) and followed him to a decidedly battered, grubby taxi, which we all squashed into. Then we were taken to another place to meet our driver, who was enjoying a relaxed glass of tea before setting off, and our luggage appeared on the back of a pick-up truck, ready to follow us to the Turkish border.

From this point on I had been warned not to say a word, whatever happened, so as to cover up my foreign identity, but that didn't stop me listening, and I heard that our driver was delayed by having to execute some prisoners who had been found guilty – but I don't know what of. It seemed strange that he would help us if that was what he had been doing, however, by now there was no way but forward so I sat back, squashed against the door and with Rula on my knee, and hoped for the best.

The driver eventually finished his tea and put on a sleeveless jacket over his shirt. It had the sort of collection of large pockets to be seen in American war films, and they bulged in an alarming way, but he was very friendly and cheerful while he stashed his submachine gun between himself and Adnan's relation in the front seat. There were affectionate goodbyes with the friends he was leaving behind – but then there always are in this country - then we were off through the ruined industrial and poorer residential areas which were still being fought over. It was a dreadful sight, but by now we were so involved in our own journey that we hadn't much sympathy to spare for the lives and livelihoods lost.

We already knew that, because of me, we could not use the most direct road to the border, one which I travelled so many times in taking friends to see the Roman, Hittite and Byzantine ruins that are all over the area. This time we drove through miles of farms and saw that some were still functioning with harvests to gather while others were just black, burned land, and nobody was indiscreet enough to ask why. We were hotter and more squashed with each kilometre, but it wasn't the time to complain. There were a lot of checkpoints, mostly managed by boys who should have been in middle school but were carrying guns as big as themselves. After we arrived in Turkey I was told that if we had been stopped our driver was equipped to blow us all up rather than have us taken prisoner. The lumps in his pockets were all hand grenades. I'm glad I didn't know that at the time!

Meanwhile, Mariam and Adnan were asking the driver about his opinions, and he was quite open in telling us about the Chechen and Chinese fighters who were also fighting the government, and how they fought between themselves – the Chechens had won the last battle and were now governing the border area. He explained why he was a rebel, how his brother had been tortured and killed by the security police for belonging to an opposition group, and his honesty and firmness were very convincing.

However when he was asked what would happen to the foreigners when his side won we were all much less convinced.

"Oh, they will just go home," he told us, waving his left hand towards the distance while steering on the bumpy road with his right.

"But what if they don't want to?"

"Then we'll force them to leave. We're much stronger and it's our country."

There was no answer to this although none of us believed it would be so easy, so Adnan and Mariam dropped the subject and concentrated on their over-heated children who were beginning to wriggle and complain. I thought Rula was beginning to run a temperature, however it turned out later that she was just hot and tired. Fortunately we had a short stop at some farmhouse for water and toilets, which calmed all of us, before there was yet another long, hot hour's drive to the Turkish border and the hope of stripping off these dreadful headcoverings.

The border was occupied by yet another set of different rebel groups, each with its own flag and set of followers, and most of them looked about fourteen years old! We were waved through, though there was some discussion that our bags would be 'searched' (read 'looted'), and while the discussions were going on Mariam and I moved the children away to the side. This was better for the discussions, but where we stood we could see the rows of small tents full of displaced families on the other side of a heavy wire fence. It was dreadfully sad to see them all squashed together and yet managing to find some sort of stability in their new place. However bad their housing had been, and there were some dreadful slums in Aleppo, this was much worse.

We were called back a few minutes later when our driver, whose name I never learned, prevailed and we were through the border and in a place where a British passport was a help rather than a danger. The first thing that Mariam, Rula and I did was to strip off the hot, sticky coverings from our heads, and to remove our galabiyas. The relief was tremendous. Then Mariam, her children and I were all given Turkish visas on our UK passports, and Adnan got one on his Syrian passport reasonably quickly, our luggage was processed smoothly and we were off to Gaziantep in a clean, well cared for taxi by mid afternoon.

Travelling so suddenly through countryside that looked and was so normal and peaceful was strange and disturbing after what we had seen only a few kilometres before, and entering Gaziantep felt positively weird. It's a small, clean prosperous looking place, absolutely full of Syrians who cannot get any further, and Adnan soon found the hotel they had booked from Aleppo so we could wash off the dust and sweat of the road. Not a day I want to repeat!

September 19th

The next day we travelled to Ankara through mile upon mile of peaceful farmland on a cool, clean bus. We stopped at clean, well-stocked cafes for rests, because the journey takes nine hours, and all we adults were depressed to see the difference between the two countries – especially since we all really blame the Turks for making the problems in Syria so much worse than they need to be. The children were pleased to be in a cool bus, after a good night's sleep induced by an endless children's programme on the TV in their hotel room. They got fairly bored, but I decided before we started that they were not my responsibility, so I had one or the other every now and again, then handed them back to their parents when they got grizzly. Sometimes it's good to be Nana!

We have been in Ankara for nearly two weeks while Adnan sorts out some business with Syrians there. I'm not sure of the details, but he's been exploring ideas for opening up a business in England. We are staying with old friends of Adnan and Mariam's who have lived here for a very long time, and it's strange but good not to hear bangs and thumps all night. During the day Mariam and I wander round a shopping mall with the children, trying not to spend money from our reserve, or take them to a local park, where they stroke their first dog and feel very brave.

Our major problem is trying politely not to eat all the food which their friends keep setting in front of us with true Syrian hospitality, but it is so kindly done that it's comforting instead of irritating.There isn't much to do there in the way of sightseeing, but we all needed the peace and kindness to find our balance again before setting off on our travels for the last time (I hope) and flying to Istanbul and then London.

Here in Ankara it is extraordinary staying in a place which is so peaceful. We are all relaxing, though a car door slamming makes us jump, and the children asked me if the

315

house would be safe when the bombs come back, which almost broke my heart. They are so young to be worrying about things like that, but at least they are not to be counted among the children even younger who have seen parents, brothers and sisters killed in the most horrible ways. I wonder how those poor children will ever be able to grow up to be normal adults.

September 25th

At last. We have our tickets and we are going. We start off before daylight to fly from Ankara to Istanbul, then move across Istanbul airport to the International side and we are, really and truly, on a flight to London. Considering all the problems that the Turkish government has caused us when we were in Syria by encouraging anyone and everyone to cross the border and fight, wherever they came from, I would have preferred another airline, However beggars can't be choosers and it's good enough to be leaving and going home.

We arrive at Heathrow at lunchtime, and there in the arrivals hall is my sister, waving like mad and then almost crying as she hugs me first and then everybody else. The children are bemused but polite. Being from Syria they are used to being told to kiss hello and goodbye to their parents' friends and the training stands them in good stead now.

Bless her. My sister has arranged for a people carrier–taxi to take us the two hour-long drive to her home in Kent, and when we finally arrive my brother-in-law has the table laid and lunch ready. It is so gratefully normal.

We eat and the children rush into the garden to explore, but all I can do is fall into bed and catch up on some sleep. Time enough tomorrow to decide about the rest of my life.

POSTSCRIPT

Now Bakri has been dead for two years and I'm nearly getting adjusted to this strange new life. Sayed and Bakri are always in my thoughts in the pretty, calm Tunbridge, where I am hoping to settle, they would have loved it here. It's not quite real yet and I still jump at sudden noises, I can't ever imagine being comfortable on bonfire night or when the occasional helicopters pass overhead. The news is a constant sadness.

The lovely old city I knew seems to have been mostly destroyed. Before Bakri died we knew that the covering of the old soukh – the biggest in the world – was partly down and that the oils and herbs in the perfume soukh had burned so ferociously that there is nothing of that part left. Then we heard about the churches in the Jedaida, where Christians built a new suburb outside the city walls in the time of the Crusaders because they were seen as a potential fifth column. The oldest of the churches, the Armenian church of the Forty Martyrs, was looted and I think they all were before they were blown up.

The Great Mosque has been looted and damaged, though the best of the decoration seems to have been taken to Turkey, like the things looted from Kasseb, where my friend saw the Turkish cars carrying away goods from the oldest church. The news about the ISIL people and the dreadful things they do has made me sure I will never be able to go back, though I'd love to visit and collect a few more of my belongings – if they are still there for me.

It's a mad world, and but for Mariam and her family I wouldn't want to live any more. My sister and her family do their best to make life good, and I am grateful, but I suppose it takes time to adjust to such big changes and my seventieth birthday is getting closer all the time. On the other hand, I am not wearing black any more, and have found a pleasant group of bridge players who are helping me to remember how to play well, the way I used to before marrying Bakri.

Mariam and Adnan have bought a small shop, a 'convenience store' and are making a living, though they work all the hours in the day to do so. The children are both in school now and seem happy and positive so the only thing left for me to do is to count my blessings and look forward to seeing Jamal when I go to visit him in the New Year.

If you enjoyed this book you may want to read the next one about Aleppo. Called 'Two's Company', it is a fairly light-hearted look at weddings and marriage from the local point of view. You can read about Captain Samir's entry onto the marriage market, among others.

For details of the publication date, contact:

angelamformby@yahoo.co.uk